ROMANCED TO DEATH

A Selection of Recent Titles by Susan Rogers Cooper

The E J Pugh Mysteries

ONE TWO WHAT DID DADDY DO?
HICKORY DICKORY STALK
HOME AGAIN, HOME AGAIN
THERE WAS A LITTLE GIRL
A CROOKED LITTLE HOUSE
NOT IN MY BACK YARD
DON'T DRINK THE WATER
ROMANCED TO DEATH

The Milt Kovak Series

THE MAN IN THE GREEN CHEVY
HOUSTON IN THE REARVIEW MIRROR
OTHER PEOPLE'S HOUSES
CHASING AWAY THE DEVIL
DEAD MOON ON THE RISE
DOCTORS AND LAWYERS AND SUCH
LYING WONDERS
VEGAS NERVE

The Kimmey Kruse Series

FUNNY AS A DEAD COMIC
FUNNY AS A DEAD RELATIVE

ROMANCED TO DEATH

An E.J. Pugh Mystery

Susan Rogers Cooper

This first world edition published 2008
in Great Britain and the USA by
SEVERN HOUSE PUBLISHERS LTD of
9–15 High Street, Sutton, Surrey, England, SM1 1DF.

British Library Cataloguing in Publication Data

Cooper, Susan Rogers
  Romanced to death
  1. Pugh, E. J. (Fictitious character) - Fiction 2. Women
  novelists - United States - Fiction 3. Women private
  investigators - United States - Fiction 4. Detective and
  mystery stories
  I. Title
  813.5'4[F]

ISBN-13: 978-0-7278-6632-5   (cased)
ISBN-13: 978-1-84751-071-6   (trade paper)

All Severn House titles are printed on acid-free paper.

Typeset by Palimpsest Book Production Ltd.,
Grangemouth, Stirlingshire, Scotland.
Printed and bound in Great Britain by
MPG Books Ltd., Bodmin, Cornwall.

In loving memory of my husband, Don Cooper, who created E.J. and will always be my Willis

I would like to thank the best readers around, Nancy Bell, Jan Grape, and Evin Cooper for reading, rereading, and re-rereading this manuscript. I would also like to thank Vicky Bijur, my agent, for all her hard work on my behalf.

Prologue

Black Cat Ridge, Texas
1999

It was my week to drive the car pool. After a long, wet weekend I was more than happy to bundle up my kids and get them to their respective schools. Rainy days and small children don't go well together. I got my two – Graham, six years old, and Megan, four years old – into the station wagon, got them buckled up and honked the horn for my next-door neighbor, Terry Lester. Her two younger children – Aldon, ten, and Bessie, four – were to ride with me. Her oldest, Monique, sixteen, was driven to school by her father. It was bad enough that I had to take my troops to two different schools – the expensive private pre-Kindergarten for the two four-year-olds, and the public elementary for my Graham and Terry's Aldon.

There was no response from the house next door. Cursing under my breath, I told my kids to stay put and ran to the Lester's back door. The door was unlocked as we usually didn't lock up much out here in suburbia. Stepping inside Terry's kitchen, I noted no signs of activity and figured they'd overslept again. I called out Terry's name, then headed for the staircase leading to the bedrooms. This wouldn't be the first time I'd had to wake up the Lester family.

I had only taken one step up the staircase when I saw the stains on the walls. Then I smelled it. I stepped back, my mind gone suddenly blank. Without much thought I ran out of the house, got my kids out of the station wagon and into our own home.

'Take your sister upstairs!' I yelled at Graham.

'Why?' he yelled back.

'Because I said so!' I said, grabbing the phone in the entry hall. I dialed 911 and told the operator to get someone out to the Lester's address. While I was still on the phone with 911, I felt a presence on the stairs. I turned and saw my daughter Megan standing on the stairs, tears in her eyes, her pretty face scrunched up in her mad look.

'Megan, go back to your—'

'I'm not playing with Bessie no more—'

'Anymore,' I automatically corrected. 'Honey, I'm on the phone—'

'She won't even wave at me!' Megan wailed.

'Megan, I don't know what you're talking about—'

'She's just standing there at the window being mean!' Megan said.

The implications of what my daughter was saying finally dawned on me. I dropped the phone and ran up the stairs. In Megan's room, her window overlooked the connecting driveways of our house and the Lester's. Straight across from Megan's window on the second floor was Bessie's. And Megan was right: Bessie was standing there, her face and clothes matted with rusty red.

I grabbed Megan and took her into her brother's room. 'Graham, watch Megan.'

'Mom!'

'Do it!' I said. There must have been something in my voice. For once, my six-year-old son actually obeyed.

I ran out of the house to the Lester's back door. It was still open, just the way I'd left it. And somewhere upstairs, beyond the blood I'd seen on the stairway, Bessie stood, obviously hurt but alive. I knew I couldn't wait for the police, or an ambulance, or anyone else. I was there. And so was Bessie.

I've never thought to ask myself if I'm brave. That's not one of those characteristics women think a lot about. That's a man's bailiwick. In retrospect, I don't think going after Bessie was all that brave, not if bravery is a conscious decision. I was running on instinct; there was nothing conscious about going into that house at all.

Once inside, I headed for the stairway and turned on the light. The marks on the walls were reddish brown and the smell was distinctive. I hurried up the stairs to the landing and, turning, started to head up the second half of the flight but tripped, falling face first. I landed on ten-year-old Aldon, lying on his back, his eyes opened, the formerly feisty blue eyes now almost opaque in death. The top of his pajamas was covered in blood. I scrambled off him, throwing myself backwards against the wall. I felt the bile rise in my throat, and jumping to my feet, ran back down the stairs for the clear air outside.

I gulped in lungfuls of warm spring air. My body was shaking all over and I knew I had to get home, back to my own babies and away from whatever had happened at the Lester house. After two steps in the direction of my own home, I remembered Bessie. Standing at the window, staring into space – covered with blood and gore. But alive. I couldn't leave four-year-old Bessie in that house. I couldn't.

I hugged the wall as I gingerly stepped around little Aldon, trying not to touch or disturb him in any way. At the head of the stairs I turned right again, starting toward the end of the hall where Bessie's room was. Terry and Roy's room was the first on the left. My eyes seemed to have a mind of their own and swiveled to the open doorway of the parents' room.

Sitting on the floor, his back against the open door, was Roy – or what was left of him. I only recognized him from the pajamas I'd helped Terry pick out last Christmas. Royal blue Chinese silk. They'd cost $150. Between the legs of royal blue silk rested a shotgun, Roy's finger still on the trigger guard, although the muzzle had dropped across his left arm. His face was gone.

I gripped the doorjamb to steady myself. When I moved my hand to continue on down the hallway, I saw the bloody handprint – my own. I looked down at my hands and the front of my shirt, all covered with blood. Aldon's blood, no doubt. At some point I heard a high keening sound. It took just a moment before I realized it was coming from me.

I forced myself to go on. The first room to the left was Monique's, my babysitter, the girl who trusted me with her heart's secrets. The door was open. Monique was in a sitting position against the back wall, her eyes squinched shut, her mouth in a grimace. Blood from her body had spattered the wall behind her, leaving a red Rorschach pattern on the colorful posters hanging on the wall. Terry lay across Monique's bed, the back of her nightgown covered in blood.

I moved to Terry's body and gingerly picked up her hand, feeling for a pulse I knew wasn't there. I sobbed out loud.

One eye was hidden by the blanket, the other stared dully at me. I touched the lid softly, pulling it down to close over the big, cocker spaniel brown eye. I wanted to stay there forever, just hold her in my arms and cry. But I didn't. Turning, I quickly moved across the hall to Bessie's room.

She still stood where I had seen her from Megan's window. Staring ahead of her into space, her little arms by her sides, her back to me. She looked so angelic standing there, her pretty little pink nightgown, her long dark-brown hair falling in tresses down her back.

I gulped in air, steadied myself against the doorjamb and said, 'Bessie, honey, it's me, Auntie E.J.'

There was no movement from the window. 'Bessie, honey, we're going to go to my house and play with Megan, OK? You want to do that?'

I moved cautiously towards her and gently turned her to face me. Her eyes, carbon copies of her mother's, didn't track. They moved where her body moved, but they weren't seeing anything. From the back she had seemed angelically aloof from all the mess around her, but turning her I saw the front: the blood-matted nightgown, clumps of something foul on her face and in her hair. I picked her up in my arms. 'We're going to go play with Megan now,' I cooed. 'Just you and me. How does that sound?'

I pressed her face against my breast as I made my way out of that house of death.

Black Cat Ridge, Texas
Thursday, April 11, 2006
He sat in his car, on the other side of the park from the junior high, and watched. His last visit to the Spy Store had netted him a nifty pair of thick sunglasses that were binoculars in disguise. His car was parked in a vertical space, so to any casual observer, such as a cop, he was just a guy sitting in a car, staring at nothing in particular. He even turned his head to the left on occasion, as if waiting for another car.

But mainly his eyes and his binoculars were trained on the circular entrance to the school. Finally, it came. It wasn't what he'd been waiting for, not what he usually saw when he sat here watching. It wasn't the Volvo this time, but the dad's

SUV. Where's the mom? he thought. Why is the dad bringing them to school? Maybe she's sick, he thought. Or gone.

That thought made him smile. Maybe she wasn't home this weekend. Maybe she got called to her parents' home in Houston on some emergency. Maybe she had business out of town. Smutty business. He laughed at his own wit.

Then there was his girl. So much smaller than her pretend brother and sister. They were both big, the girl tall and gangly, the boy just tall. But the sister ran ahead of her, and the older one, the boy, got back into the SUV. The sister always did that, he thought, getting mad. She always left her behind. But then the redheaded girl turned, grabbed his girl's hand, and pulled her along. He would bet a million dollars his girl didn't like that one bit. But what could she do? She was defenseless against these people. All of them. But he was going to save her.

One

Austin, Texas
E.J., Thursday

I parked the Volvo next to a fire hydrant, about half a block from the Sam, and just sat there, motor running, and stared at the hotel, the oldest and grandest in downtown Austin. Over one hundred years old, the Sam Houston Hotel took up an entire city block. No Austin native or anyone who had stayed there for more than an hour called it anything but the Sam. Until about twenty years ago, there was a city ordinance that no building could be built taller than the State Capitol; the Sam had always been the second tallest building in Austin. Not any more, of course.

Its five-story height shaded that stretch of Sixth Street like a favorite uncle spreading his arms for a hug. My husband and I had had drinks there when we were dating in college, and had met friends there for dinner a couple of years ago, but it was not a place I frequented. Although there was family history here. My grandfather, a traveling salesman for DeSoto Auto Parts, was headquartered in Dallas, but Austin was part of his territory. He would leave Dallas at night, taking a Pullman car on the train to Austin (expense account, even then), take the bus to the Sam, where he'd walk in like he owned the place, going straight to the men's room to shave and change for his meetings. Of course, he never actually stayed there, claiming the ten-dollar-a-night room rental was too rare for his blood. And here I was, spending four whole days in this beautiful hotel. I was seriously getting a Cinderella vibe. And Grandpa, wherever you are, eat your heart out!

Let me introduce myself, or re-introduce myself, as the case may be. My name is E.J. Pugh, and it doesn't really matter what the E.J. stands for. I know it's been six years since we last spoke, but it's been a quiet six years in my hometown of

Black Cat Ridge, Texas. No murders, no unexplained deaths, no stumbling over dead bodies. Instead I've been able to concentrate on who I really am, in order of desire, nurture, want and need: a romance writer, wife and mother. Yes, I know, I can hear you now. You didn't say mother first? No, I didn't, and there's a reason for that. I'm the mother of three teenagers. Need I say more?

It was a Thursday morning in April, and we were having a spring like the rest of the country: blue skies, flowers, moderate temperatures. Something was obviously wrong, but only a meteorologist would question it. In South Central Texas there were basically two Aprils: the one where the temperature reached ninety degrees and the flowers that were beginning to bloom a month earlier were wilting on the vine, and the one where flood waters were reaching epic proportions. I'm not saying we don't get the occasional beautiful spring day. We do. Once, maybe twice a year. But so far we'd had a week of this and nerves were on edge.

I was at the Sam this beautiful Thursday morning because I'd been nominated for a Lady, which is the coveted Association of American Romance Writers' top award, and since the convention was being held in Austin this year, just a little over an hour's drive from Black Cat Ridge, I was attending. My roommate for the convention was going to be Maybella LaRue, aka, to her friends and family, Jane Dawson. We'd never actually met but had been writing emails to one another and talking on the phone for the past three years, and I felt I knew her well. She was a rowdy lady and I was looking forward to our four-day play date. By the picture on the jacket of her books, she was a slender yet well-endowed woman, about my age, with jet black hair, what my husband calls 'smoldering' eyes and a mouth my husband calls something else that I won't go into here. I knew the picture was fairly old, as Jane had grown children and grandchildren now, but I doubt she'd changed all that much. It would be a little daunting rooming with a woman who looked like that, but maybe I could pick up some make-up pointers.

I almost hadn't made it here. First, there was the dress drama: I'd saved money from my last royalty check and planned on buying an evening gown for the awards banquet. Romance writers tend to like to play dress-up, and I was going to do my best to fit in. I'd even been on a diet and was down to a size fourteen, so I was very excited. Knowing me I'd be up to a sixteen or an eighteen two weeks after the event and never be able to wear the gown again, but as far as I'm concerned, that's what eBay is for.

However, I've discovered in my forty-something years on this earth that nothing is ever easy, at least not for me. First there wasn't a size fourteen formal gown to be had in the towns of Black Cat Ridge or Codderville, which is the town next to which our subdivision of Black Cat Ridge is located. I finally drove to LaGrange and found two size fourteen evening gowns: one would have looked good on a chubby sixteen-year-old going to the prom; the other would have been perfect for a grandmother-of-the-bride. I knew my only salvation would be driving into Austin. I went straight to the Neiman Marcus discount store, where outrageously priced clothes go to die. And that's when I found it. It was a full-skirted, formal length, summer-green, satin dress with a sleeveless, scoop-necked bodice studded with gold beads. The color looked fantastic with my still mostly red hair (if I fix it just right, I can still hide the gray) and green eyes. The dress was marked down from $1,200 to $400. What a bargain. I didn't give myself time to think about it; I just stuck out my Visa card and closed my eyes. The piece de résistance was that I had in the back of my closet (unworn by me) gold ballet slippers and a gold clutch bag passed on to me by my mother, which would go perfectly with the green dress. At this point I thought the gods were smiling.

Never, ever think that. It's Murphy's Law: the minute you think things are going your way, all hell breaks loose. I went home. Not my smartest move, but I had nowhere else to go. Megan, one of my two thirteen-year-old daughters, had a temperature of 103 degrees and was projectile vomiting. By Wednesday morning Bessie (sorry, she goes by Elizabeth now), my other thirteen-year-old daughter, had it and I put both girls in one room to keep the running around to a bare minimum. I thought about calling Jane, my would-be convention roommate, and telling her I wouldn't be able to make it, but something kept me from doing that. That something being that I just didn't want to! I wanted to go to the convention. I fixed Jell-O, bought bottle after bottle of ginger ale, and cleaned the bathroom on an hourly basis. By nine Wednesday night, both girls were in front of the TV in the family room, eating ice cream. I decided I was glad I hadn't called Jane.

This morning, however, as I was getting ready to leave, Willis, my husband, had his doubts.

'You're not leaving me with two sick children, are you? I mean, not really?'

'They're not sick any more,' I said.

'What if they relapse?' he queried.

'They won't,' I said.

'Yeah, but what if they do?' he insisted.

'Then buy more ginger ale,' I said, slamming shut one of my suitcases.

'What if Graham comes down with it? Or, God forbid, what if I come down with it?' he asked, getting very nervous at the thought of his own potential illness.

Willis is a big bear of a man, but he has this thing about vomit – his own more than other's, although he's not that crazy about either. When Graham was little more than a year old, he got a stomach bug and woke up in the middle of the night vomiting. Willis was the first in the room upon hearing the sounds emanating from his son's room. When I got there, only seconds behind him, there was a puke duet going on, both guys going full blast.

'You won't get sick,' I told him, shoving my suitcases toward the hallway. I noticed he wasn't offering to help with them.

'At the first sign of anything I'm calling you!' he threatened.

'You do that,' I said, hauling my belongings toward the staircase.

'You *know* somebody's going to get sick!' he said.

'No, I don't know that,' I said, sliding a suitcase down the staircase.

'It's inevitable,' he predicted, a smug look on his face. 'You go away, somebody's going to get sick.'

'Even if you have to stick your finger down your throat, huh, Willis?' I said, sliding the rest of my luggage down the stairs.

'Don't be disgusting,' he said, then glanced at the pile on the floor at the bottom of the stairs. 'Why did you do that?'

he asked, a surprised look on his face. 'I would have taken that stuff down for you.'

I didn't kill him, I didn't even hurt him. I just left.

Now here I was at barely eleven in the morning, staring at the granite and gingerbread trim of the Sam. I pulled the Volvo back on to Sixth Street and went in search of the hotel entrance.

OK, so I'm not a world traveler. How was I supposed to know check in is at three p.m.? No one told me. You'd think, when I called to make my reservation, they might have mentioned it. They were, however, gracious enough to store my luggage – I don't think three medium-sized suitcases, a duffle bag and a briefcase are excessive for a four-day stay, do you? Well, by the bellman's eye roll I gather he did. They can be such snobs – in a storeroom behind the counter, which gave me several hours to kill.

I spent a good ten minutes of that time staring at the grandeur that was the Sam's lobby. Pink granite floors that rivaled those in the capitol building only a few blocks away, mahogany front desk that was older than the great-grandparents of those now working behind it, six huge crystal chandeliers lighting every nook and cranny of the vast lobby, crystal sconces on the walls holding fresh flowers, brass elevator doors – all original to the grand opening of the Sam back in 1899. The only changes had been in fabrics: the drapes and upholstery. The overly large, round settee in the middle of the lobby had been there since the grand opening. A small alcove featured a pictorial history of the settee's life, from the original tufted dark-green velvet, through the twenties' gold satin, the fifties' plaid taffeta, the seventies' crushed red velvet, the eighties' gold lamé, to its present tufted dark-green velvet, bringing it back full circle.

I decided to have lunch in the hotel. The Sam had a fine dining restaurant, where prices started at thirty dollars for appetizers, and a cafe. I opted for the cafe, which is something I'll probably not do again. I had to pay twelve dollars for a grilled cheese sandwich and a glass of iced tea (fifteen total with tip). I realize ten dollars of that was for ambiance (or paying for the new decor, most likely). The cafe was Dick Clark chic, with black-and-white checkered tile floors, pink bar stools and pink booths with black-and-white checked

Formica table tops held up by chrome legs. A little jukebox was at each booth and, wonders of wonders, you could get three plays for a quarter. The only pricing in the place that reflected the fifties ambiance.

I left the hotel and wandered down Sixth Street. When I was at college in Austin, Sixth Street was the Mecca of good music and good food, and good drugs, if that was your thing. Four years before I got to Austin, for my freshman year at UT, Sixth Street was a desolate wasteland; then Clifford Antone came to town. He opened his club, Antone's, and changed the history of Sixth Street forever. My husband, Willis, who had been at UT for two years by the time I got there, saw a lot more of the scene than I did. Things were changing by the late seventies. But in its heyday, Sixth Street was *the* place for rock and roll, outlaw country and the then new punk sound.

These days Sixth Street is one of the big tourist draws in Austin, but it is definitely for the younger crowd – the UT students and high school students, the under thirty urban professionals. Since Austin is the self-proclaimed live music capital of the world, every other establishment was a bar with a sign out front saying who was playing live and when. I'd only heard of a few of them, which I think was more a sign of my age than any particular band's popularity. Of the establishments that weren't bars, most were restaurants, with signs out front saying who was playing live and when. Then there were the record stores, with posters saying who was playing live and when, and the shops: outrageously expensive clothing stores for people who wanted to look like they were manual laborers; card shops with greeting cards Hallmark would gag over – with pictures of bare-breasted women and men with elephantine penises; and a lingerie shop that seemed to specialize in crotchless panties. The highlight of Sixth Street since 1977 was, is and hopefully always shall be, Esther's Follies. It's a burlesque-type club specializing in skit comedy that has a window looking out over Sixth Street at the back of the stage, often making the passers-by on the street part of the act. I'll never forget one of the skits I saw there, a take-off on a TV craft show where a woman made crafty items out of maxi-pads. It was a memorable show, to say the least.

I made my way by a side street over to Fourth Street, the adult hangout. And by that I don't mean it was nearly as

X-rated as Sixth. I mean that this was the place to go for a good martini, a faux-Cuban cigar, killer tapas and entertaining conversation. And, of course, live music. I walked the few blocks of Fourth, trying to decide where I'd take Jane to show off the city.

Finally it was three o'clock and I could check in. I went to the desk and gave the clerk my name.

'Oh, Ms Pugh. Your roommate, Ms LaRue, has already checked in.' He did something with his computer, had me sign a few hundred documents, and finally handed me a key card. He smiled a professional smile and said, 'Welcome to the Sam. If you'd like to go up to your room, I'll have a bellman bring your luggage in just a few minutes.'

I thanked him and headed to the elevator. The brass doors opened on to white and gold marble floors, mahogany paneling and a small crystal chandelier that would necessitate my six-foot four-inch husband ducking his head.

I'd never been upstairs at the Sam and was giddy with delight. I felt like a kid sneaking into an adult hangout. This was *the Sam*, and *I* was going to hang out here just like a real person. OK, I'm forty-five years old, I should be beyond that kind of silliness, but the Sam had always been, to me, the height of Texas chic and old oil money. And here I was, little old E.J. Pugh, youngest daughter of Holiday Inn traveling parents, and wife of a Motel 6 kind of guy, actually staying in the Sam! Giddy hardly described the sensation.

The brass doors opened on the fifth floor and, admittedly, I was disappointed. The carpet was that 'tread on me all you want' kind of commercial stuff with designs you don't care to even notice. The walls were just plain white sheetrock. But the sconces on the walls were crystal, some maybe original, and the tables with the large vases of fresh flowers at least looked old.

When I finally found our room, to be polite I knocked on the door, not wanting to use my key card and barge in on Jane. The door opened. I'm five feet eleven inches tall. The woman who opened it was at least a foot shorter than me. I had to look way down to see her. She appeared to be in her late sixties, was as round as a ball, had snow-white hair and large brown eyes made even larger by glasses with heavy lenses.

'Well, hell's bells!' she shouted and grabbed me somewhere around the middle. 'You must be E.J.!'

I had my hands up in the air, afraid to touch back as she greeted me with a bear hug. I was speechless and I'm sure my mouth was hanging open. When she released me and looked up, she covered her mouth with both hands. 'Oh, Lord,' she said. 'You weren't expecting the babe on the book jacket, were you?'

I mutely nodded my head and Jane Dawson burst into peals of laughter. Grabbing my hand she pulled me into the room. 'Good God, I thought you knew! That's my daughter-in-law Sarah Anne, about fifteen years ago. She's fat as a cow now, after the four babies, and that hair's blonde this month, I think. She changes it a lot. She gets a real kick out of having her picture on my book jackets, though. Sells more books than a picture of this old face would!'

She jumped up to sit on one of the two queen-sized beds, her feet dangling several inches above the floor. 'Now, E.J., sit down and open your mouth. I know you're not the shy, retiring type, so get over it.'

I grinned. 'Hi, Jane,' I said.

She giggled. 'Hi, E.J.'

I laughed and sank down on the bed opposite her. 'I've got to say, I did expect the lady on the book jacket,' I said. 'This has thrown me for a loop.'

'Hell, I thought everybody in the biz knew!'

I shook my head. 'This is my first convention, like I told you. And I don't really know anybody but you.'

She jumped down from the bed and grabbed her purse. 'Well, we're gonna fix that!' she said. 'Let's head downstairs and register you, and then start meeting all the movers and shakers. Hell, girl, you're a nominee for the biggest booby prize in romance! You gotta make yourself known!'

'OK,' I said, and got up, glancing at myself in the mirror. Make-up still OK, but the hair had decided to rebel and was frizzing like usual. I sighed and followed my pint-sized room-mate out the door.

My cellphone rang as I got on the elevator. One glance at the screen told me it was home, so probably one of my kids. Gingerly I hit the on button, hoping it wouldn't be a replay of this morning's debacle, which had gone something like this:

Megan, the drama queen: 'Mo-other!' At the top of her voice.

Me: 'Wha-at?' Sarcastically.

Megan: 'Elizabeth stole my top!' Screeched.

Elizabeth: 'It's my top.' In an irritatingly calm and rational voice.

Megan: 'Is not!'

Elizabeth: 'Is too.'

At which point Megan grabbed said top, which Elizabeth was holding in her hand, and pulled. Elizabeth pulled back, buttons flew, spandex ripped. Both girls screamed recriminations.

I grabbed both pieces of the top and threw them in the trash.

'Now, it's nobody's top,' I said.

'Mo-other!' Megan wailed. With hands on hips she said, 'If you were a *real* mother you'd fix it!'

'*Real* mother?' I said.

'*Real* mothers sew!' Megan informed me.

'Janelle's mother sews,' Elizabeth stated flatly.

I picked up the two pieces of spandex and threw them in the direction of my daughters. 'Then get Janelle's *real* mother to fix it,' I said.

Megan rolled her eyes and Elizabeth dropped her half of the top. 'That is too rude for words,' she said. 'I won't lower myself to even comment on that!'

'You just did,' I stated, at which point both girls looked at each other, rolled their eyes and walked off, having found a common enemy to bond them. I felt I'd done my job.

But that was this morning, hours ago. Lord only knew what new injustices had conspired to tear my daughters' worlds apart. With quiet desperation, I said, 'Hello?' into my cell-phone.

'Hey, Mom.' It was my son Graham.

'Hi, honey,' I said, holding my breath for what was to come.

'Where's my NASCAR T-shirt?'

'Which one?' I asked.

'The black one!' he said, his voice indicating just how dumb I was not to know instinctively which of his three NASCAR T-shirts he wanted. My son is fifteen; it'll be a good ten years before I'm smart enough to converse with him on a semi-equal basis.

'Probably in the dirty clothes,' I said.

'You didn't wash before you left?' he demanded.

I sighed. 'Lift the lid of the washing machine,' I said. 'There are instructions on how to run the machine written right there. In English. If you can't figure it out, go out on the sidewalk and see if you can find a ten-year-old to help you.'

'You're not funny,' he said. 'I know you think you are, but you're wrong.' With that the phone went dead in my ear. We were going to have to have a talk about polite telephone etiquette. Again.

I put the phone back in my purse.

'I take it that was one of your kids,' Jane said.

'How'd you figure that one out?' I asked, grinning.

'Had to be a kid or a husband, and it's too early for a husband to want to wash clothes. That call usually comes around three in the morning,' Jane said.

'I'm proud to say my husband knows how to wash clothes. He can also cook, make a bed and wipe himself.'

Jane patted me on the back. 'You are a truly liberated woman,' she said.

'Hear me roar,' I said as the elevator doors opened on to the mezzanine level.

Black Cat Ridge, Texas
Graham, Thursday

On the banks of the Colorado River in South Central Texas, there exists a town called Codderville. Codderville came into existence in the late 1800s when a man named Jasper Codder, and several of his cohorts from Tennessee, drove out a small band of Tonkawas that had been living there for possibly a thousand years. This is a fact not celebrated in the town's yearly founder's day festival.

Although it began its existence as one cattle ranch and a saloon, with the advent of the railroad there came farmers, families, churches and developers. In the 1930s, paved roads led others to the town, and in the 1950s a highway was put through, cutting Codderville, if not in half, then maybe three quarters on one side and one quarter on the other. The smaller portion, of course, became the African American community, and land prices dropped to an all time low.

All was going well in the township of Codderville until 1975 when an enterprising young man from Trenton, New Jersey, Gavin Mickleberry, left his state for the wilds of Texas, where land was still cheap and there was a lot to be had. He found seven hundred acres on the opposite side of the Colorado River from Codderville. The only obstacle to his claim to riches and fame was a small enclave of shacks and singlewide trailers on the banks of the river. They claimed status as an artist's colony and called the small area Black Cat Ridge. Unfortunately none of these artists actually owned their shacks or singlewide trailers, or the land they sat upon. These things were owned by a man named Lester Truman who saw the advantage of a large sum of money in hand from the newcomer over a dribble of small sums of money promised over a long period from the artists. Thus, the artists of Black Cat Ridge were, like the Tonkawas on the other side of the river before them, driven out, their shacks and trailers torn down, and in their place was begun Gavin Mickleberry's dream.

By the year 2006, Black Cat Ridge was more than a mere subdivision of middle- to upper middle-class refugees from Houston and Austin. It was a town, complete with its own school system, fire department, police department, shopping centers, gyms, country club, public and private pools and utility system.

Thus began the demise of Codderville, as even its own inhabitants found refuge from old houses with bad plumbing and faulty wiring in the brand new wall-to-wall carpets, tile kitchens with granite countertops, garden tubs and fully sodded lawns of Black Cat Ridge.

In one such house, already remodeled to house an expanding family, lived a young man named Graham Pugh. At fifteen, he lived in the home of his parents and his two younger sisters. He was not a bad young man, maybe reckless, possibly bored, definitely horny, but not a *bad* young man. His adventure this weekend would take him over the river, into the jungles of Codderville and, hopefully, back again to hearth and home.

We begin our story on the sidewalk leaving the Black Cat Ridge High School on a Thursday afternoon.

'So, then, maybe I'll see you tomorrow night?' Graham said, with the nonchalance only a teenage boy can muster while talking to a member of the opposite sex with whom he is totally smitten.

'Maybe,' Ashley said, 'if I'm there.'

'Yeah, me, too. If I'm there, I mean,' Graham said.

'So you might not be there?' she said, a frown on her pretty face.

'Oh, yeah, well, probably,' Graham said.

'Yeah, me too, maybe,' she said.

'So, then, OK,' Graham said. 'I'll see you if I see you.'

'Yeah, I guess so,' she said.

The girl turned and walked back to her pack, with Graham unable to take his eyes off her. This wasn't just any girl, this was Ashley Davis, indisputably the hottest girl at Black Cat Ridge High School. She wasn't one of the movers and shakers, not a cheerleader or a beauty queen, she was just Hot, with a capital 'H'. Blonde hair, blue eyes, pouty lips, big tits and a killer ass. She walked the school like she knew exactly who she was and how hot she was. And she had been talking to Graham now for three whole days. Three whole days leading up to this: a date. Sort of.

Graham walked back over to his boys.

'Well?' demanded Leon, Graham's best friend, a geek with glasses, zits and a keyboard for a brain.

Graham smiled. 'Oh, yeah!' he said.

'Score!' Leon said, hand up for a high five.

'She bringin' her posse?' Tad asked. Tad was white but wished he were black.

'Yeah, might be,' Graham answered.

'Smooth,' Tad said and knocked knuckles with Graham. At sixteen, Tad rounded off at five foot five and weighed, in wet sweats, about 125 pounds.

'Maybe she'll do a Clinton on ya,' said Hollister, the last of Graham's current pack, a large young man with curly blond hair and a laugh like a snake hissing.

'A gentleman never tells,' Graham said.

'Yeah, well, if we ever see one a' them, we'll beat the shit outta him 'til he talks!' Hollister said and hissed his laugh.

'So who's got wheels tomorrow night?' Leon asked.

The four boys looked at each other. 'My mom's outta town,' Graham said.

'My old man said hell'd freeze over 'fore I get his car again,' Tad said, lowering his head in shame as they all remembered Tad losing control of his father's minivan and plowing into a hay bale out on County Road 17. All would have been fine if any of them had thought to look at the undercarriage and discovered the half bale of hay stuck there before Tad's father found it.

Leon stayed quiet. Leon had failed his driver's license test three times and couldn't take it again until the summer after graduation. Finally Hollister said, 'If my old man passes out in time, I can probably get the truck.'

'There aren't enough seatbelts in that old truck,' Leon said.

'Ooo, listen at Leon, afraid he's gonna get his hair ruffled without a seatbelt holding him in!' Tad laughed.

'Yeah, well, if we weren't wearing seatbelts when you hit that hay bale, one of us'd still be in the hospital,' Leon shot back.

'Man, if you don't wanna come,' Graham said, 'then don't come.' To Hollister, he said, 'So when's your old man likely to pass out?'

Hollister shrugged. 'Depends on how much beer we got in the house. He drank a lot last night, so I'm not sure how much is left.'

Tad rifled in his pockets. 'I got a twenty,' he said. 'Y'all got any money?'

They all dug in their pockets, coming up with a total of forty-four dollars and some change. Now all they had to do was figure out how to buy the beer.

Austin, Texas
E.J., Thursday

I hardly got a chance to take in the mezzanine level of the Sam, its incredibly intricate dark wood paneling, its grand-as-the-lobby chandeliers, the conversation nooks of dark leather love seats and chairs, before all hell broke loose.

'Oh, my God, it's Maybella LaRue!' someone shouted as we walked into the registration area. And that's when it started. The mobs. It must have been at least fifty women who converged on Jane and me. It was overwhelming for me, and

I stood a head higher than most of those surrounding us. I could only imagine how it must have seemed to Jane, a foot shorter, stuck in the middle of the mob. But she held her own, I'll say that for her. She deftly autographed program books, scraps of paper and even one woman's stomach, while simultaneously introducing me, and gently removing us from the throngs of her admirers. We made it to the registration table pretty much intact.

'Jane, I need to talk to you!' a large woman behind the registration table said. 'See me in my room in ten minutes!'

'I don't think I can make it in ten, Angela. How about eleven? Angela, have you met E.J. Pugh? She writes that wonderful eighteenth century series—'

'Well, of course! God knows that's no pseudonym. Why don't you use one? Everybody else does! Personally, *when* I get published – you'll notice I didn't say *if*,' she said, laughing a deep, barking laugh, 'I plan on using Beatrix Coty. Isn't that a lovely name?'

'Why, yes—' I started.

'In honor of Beatrix Potter and the first make-up brand I ever used!' she said, cracking herself up.

'It's very nice meeting—' I tried again.

'Jane didn't really introduce us, dear. I'm Angela Barber, and I'm running this little shindig. Anything goes wrong you just come to me! Anything goes right, well, you can come to me about that, too!' Another barking laugh.

I noticed the smile on Jane's face looked strained; I felt the one on mine must look the same way.

'I need to get register—'

'Rosalie!' Angela shouted at the woman sitting next to her. 'Don't just sit there! This –' she said, pointing at me – 'is a real writer! How many books do you have, dear?'

'My eleventh is—'

'At least eleven or twelve!' she said to poor Rosalie. 'So be quick about it! We don't want our *real* writers just standing around twiddling their thumbs!'

In a quiet voice, the timid Rosalie began to register me. Behind me I could hear (everybody could hear) Angela Barber still going strong. 'Jane, do come up to my room as quickly as you can. I'm having a few people in for drinks and I want to talk to you privately before they get there!'

'I'm not sure if I can make—' Jane started.

'See you then!' Angela roared, then said, 'Alice Cleaver! I need to talk to you!' And she stormed off after another unwilling conversational victim.

When I'd finished registering and had gotten my book bag and all the free goodies therein (nobody had told me about free goodies – if so, I'd have come to one of these things a lot sooner!), I asked Jane, 'Dare I ask who was that woman?'

Jane shuddered. 'We call her The Beast, at least behind her back. She's involved in every one of these events, but this one is going to be the worst, because she actually lives in Austin and is running the entire show. God only knows how bad this thing is going to get!'

'She seems a little . . .' I hesitated, trying for a diplomatic approach. 'Aggressive,' I finally said.

Jane laughed. 'Shall I translate that as obnoxious, insidious, boorish, manipulative and just pure-dee old bitch?'

I couldn't help but laugh. 'That works,' I said. I knew Jane lived in Ohio, but I had to ask. 'Where are you from originally?'

'Meridian, Mississippi. The pure-dee gave me away, didn't it?'

'Just a little bit. But I'll keep it to myself.'

Jane patted my arm. 'You're a good girl, E.J.'

'E.J.?' a male voice said. Jane and I looked up to see a man standing in front of us. I'd never laid eyes on him before. 'Are you E.J. Pugh?' he asked.

'Yes,' I said.

He was several inches shorter than me, had a very bad comb over, appeared to be in his mid-fifties, carried about thirty pounds too much weight (I know, who am I to talk, but I *am* down to a fourteen, you know), and was dressed head to foot in 1980s polyester. Even his shoes had that plastic sheen to them.

He stuck out his hand and I felt the only polite thing to do was to take it. I should have been rude. The hand was wet and clammy and the clasp was that of a dead fish. 'DeWitt Perry,' the man said. 'I'm your biggest fan! I knew you had to be a woman, not a man! On the board it's about fifty fifty whether E.J. stands for a man's name or a woman's!'

'The board?' I asked, quickly releasing his hand.

'On the Internet. Your fan site.'

'Oh,' I said, trying to appear as if I knew I had a fan site. This was something I was going to look up just as soon as I got home. Jeez, a fan site! I'm a star!

'This is Maybella LaRue,' I said, indicating Jane.

DeWitt Perry barely looked at Jane, curtly nodding his head toward her. To me, he said, 'I just knew a man couldn't write the love scenes in your wonderful books!'

'Ah, thank you,' I said, wondering if that was an appropriate response.

He moved into my space, reaching for my hand and grabbing it before I had a chance to get it out of his way. 'You bring me so many hours of pleasure!' he said, his stale breath making me want to gag as a little sprinkle of spit sprayed me with the 'p' of 'pleasure'.

I again removed my hand from his and backed away. Jane came to my rescue. 'Mr Perry, it's so nice of you to introduce yourself. E.J. will be signing in the book room later, why don't you come by then?' she said, deftly taking his arm and escorting him toward the hall. 'It was wonderful meeting you!' she said, gracing him with a brilliant smile as she turned and headed back to me. 'Let's go to the bar!' she said, grabbing my arm.

Personally I was thinking tequila shooters straight up.

Black Cat Ridge, Texas.
Elizabeth, Thursday
Elizabeth Lester Pugh was of two minds when it came to what she wanted to be when she grew up: a Nobel Prize-winning quantum physicist or the Poet Laureate of the United States. Maybe both. She had no concerns whatsoever about make-up, clothes, shaving her legs, all those things girls her age seemed to fixate on. She believed highly in personal hygiene, would never go outside without washing her face and combing her hair, and was always careful not to have a booger hanging out of her nose. But that was about it. Except, and this was a big exception, when it came to her sister Megan.

Megan was a total girly-girl. Her existence was tied up in her make-up, her clothes and what boy said what about what girl. Megan's goal in life was to be a wife, mother and fashion consultant, not necessarily in that order. So Elizabeth, who was smaller than Megan, was very careful to buy the clothes that Megan wanted but couldn't wear, borrow things from Megan's closet when Megan could never borrow anything from hers, and generally make Megan's life as miserable as possible. It was her duty: they were sisters.

On the other hand, nobody, and I mean nobody, said a bad word about Megan in front of Elizabeth, and visa versa. And that went double for their brother Graham. On the Graham front, the two girls were totally bonded.

On this beautiful Thursday in April, the two girls got out of the minivan that was their carpool vehicle of the week, and raced to the front door, Megan of the longer legs winning as usual. They knew that today they were latchkey kids, as Dad was still at work and Mom was off to her romance convention in Austin, so they dug the extra key out of the flowerbed and used it to get in the house.

Megan, heading for the kitchen, said, 'I'm hungry.'

Elizabeth answered with: 'You'll never lose weight that way. I'm going upstairs.'

Megan wasn't really overweight but Elizabeth never missed an opportunity to point out that she *could* be. She bounded up the stairs and into her room, throwing her backpack on the bed and heading straight to the computer. She turned it on and checked her email. And there it was: an email from Tommy.

Elizabeth wasn't really into boys, but Tommy was different. He was smart and funny and he understood her. She had to admit, to herself at least, that she was beginning to have a bit of a crush on him. The email was simple:

TO: Skywatcher75
FROM: T_Tom37
Home yet? IM me when you get there. T

So she did. They'd met in a chat room several weeks ago, one dedicated to astronomy nuts, which they both were. They were the only non-college aged kids in there and had gravitated to each other. Now neither visited the astronomy site much, but talked to each other by email and Instant Messenger as often as possible. Elizabeth sent out an IM:

Skywatcher75:   T, u there?
T_Tom37:   Hey, E, been waiting for u
Skywatcher75:   Just got home
T_Tom37:   Missed u
Skywatcher75:   How was school?
T_Tom37:   Usual – u?
Skywatcher75:   Same
T_Tom37:   Gotta talk bout something
Skywatcher75:   What?
T_Tom37:   This is serious, E

Elizabeth felt a stab of panic laced with joy. Was he going to profess his undying love for her? Was he going to say he couldn't talk to her anymore? What?

Skywatcher75:   What?
T_Tom37:   I haven't been telling u the whole truth
Skywatcher75:   About what?
T_Tom37:   Me

Oh, God, Elizabeth thought, he's not a boy in the ninth grade like he said, he's some thirty-year-old freak . . .

Skywatcher75:   Go ahead
T_Tom37:   U have to be brave and hear me out
Skywatcher75:   T, stop. Just tell me
T_Tom37:   My name's not Tommy

This was it, Elizabeth thought. His name is Herman and he's in his fifties. Oh, gross.

Skywatcher75:   What is it?

There was a long silence from the other end, so long that Elizabeth thought for a moment that Tommy, or whatever his name was, had gone away. Then her computer pinged and words she'd never expected to see popped up:

T_Tom37:   My name is Aldon

Elizabeth stared at the letters, not sure she was reading them right. Finally, she wrote:

Skywatcher75:   I don't understand
T_Tom37:   I'm your brother, Bessie

Two

Austin, Texas
E.J., Thursday

T he main bar of the Sam was all dark wood and dark fabric, with discreet lighting in Frank Lloyd Wright-style shades. The bar itself was long and as old as the hotel – or so a little plaque in the center stated. The wood gleamed from over one hundred years of hand rubbing – by bartenders and patrons alike. It wasn't the kind of place made for four deep at the bar and extra chairs shoved up to the heavy, dark-wood tables. But that's what we found when we got there. Jane followed voices to get where she wanted to go, as identifying people in the gloom of the bar was nearly impossible.

You wouldn't believe the people I met in the bar. There were, of course, lots of other writers, as well as agents and editors and publicists and editors' assistants, and a whole parcel of wannabe writers. The bar was crowded, which Jane said it always was at these things.

'You're lucky if you go to a panel discussion and only *half* the participants are drunk,' she said. 'The bars usually open at eight in the morning when there's a convention of writers around, and they're full by eight fifteen.'

I shook my head. 'I feel like an idiot that I've been missing out on this for so many years!' I said, laughing.

Jane shrugged. 'It gets old, believe me.' Then she grinned. 'After ten or twelve years.'

We joined a table with Mary Sparrow and Lydia Michaels, two of the top names in romance. They were old friends of Jane's, but I was in awe. They both were women in their early fifties, Lydia slightly overweight with champagne blonde hair and a lot of make-up, Mary very thin, with a dark-brown helmet of hair and a lot of make-up. After about fifteen minutes of discussing who was doing what panel and when they were reading and signing, Angela Barber's name came up.

'I can't believe the powers that be are letting her run this entire thing!' Lydia Michaels said. 'Remember last year when she was just in charge of programs? She used a picture of me from five books ago, and misspelled somebody's name—'

'That was me, darling,' Mary Sparrow said. 'She had me down as M-e-r-r-y Sparrow! Which translates to "happy bird", I think!'

We were joined at that moment by two more people, a young woman in her late twenties or early thirties, with what looked like natural blonde hair, big blue eyes and just a touch of make-up, and a much older gentleman. He was a tall, thin, dapper man, with a full head of snow-white hair and a mouthful of snow-white teeth. I think the hair was natural, but I doubted the teeth were. The three women already sitting at the table jumped up to hug the older man, then the two joined us.

'Ladies,' he said, 'I want you to meet Candace Macy,' he said, introducing the young blonde. 'My competition for the Lady.'

At that moment I realized the dapper old man speaking was Jerome MacIntyre, aka Jasmine West, another nominee for the Lady.

Jane laid her hand on my shoulder. 'She's not your only competition, Jerry. This is E.J. Pugh, another Lady nominee.'

Jerome MacIntyre sighed heavily. 'I'm just surrounded by beauty, brains and talent. I'll never win!' He put his head in his hands and we all laughed.

'What *were* you four talking about so earnestly when we walked up?' Jerome asked.

The three voices of Jane, Mary and Lydia spoke up in unison: 'Angela Barber.'

'Oh, Lord. I hear she's in total charge of this thing!' he said.

'If you thought it was bad before . . .' Jane started.

'You ain't seen nothing yet!' Lydia finished for her.

'You guys don't have to room with her,' Candace Macy said in a quiet voice.

'What?' Lydia said loudly. 'You're kidding!'

Candace shook her head. 'I don't know how it happened. I told the woman in charge of rooms that I needed a room-mate, and that I was up for the Lady. I thought I'd get another writer, but I ended up with Angela.'

Everyone was speechless for a moment, then Jerome burst out laughing. 'Oh, sweetie,' he said, 'if you decide to kill her I'll give you an alibi.'

Three hands went into the air, with choruses of 'me, too' echoing around the table. With the experiences I've had over the past ten years or so, I'm not one to take that kind of humor lightly; I knew they were kidding, but mine was not one of the hands raised.

Jerome patted Candace's hand. 'I'm rooming by myself; you're welcome to stay with me.' With a gleam in his eye, he added, 'Of course, I only have the one bed, but it's a king size.'

Candace laughed and said, 'Mr MacIntyre, if my daddy found out I was rooming with you, you'd be in big trouble.'

'Lay off, Jerry,' Jane Dawson said with a laugh. 'She's young enough to be your granddaughter!'

'I'm just trying to help!' he said, the twinkle still visible in his eye.

'Your kind of help she doesn't need,' Mary said.

'I heard that,' said a man standing behind Jerome MacIntyre. He was introduced to Candace and me as Hal Burleson, aka Sara Swan, the Susan Lucci of romance. He'd been nominated for every award there is over the past ten years, but had yet to win anything. He was somewhere in his mid-fifties, round of belly and flat of chest, with skinny shoulders and an egg-shaped head. A fringe of pale, reddish hair circled his head from ear to ear. He took a chair on the other side of Candace. 'Hell, Jerry, if I said that to a woman she'd have me up on charges!'

Jerome MacIntyre patted Hal on the shoulder. 'I'm so sorry, Hal. We can't all be as fascinating as I am.'

'Fascinating?' Hal repeated, laughing.

Jerome sighed. 'I was trying to be kind. Shall I add hand-some, charming, debonair and just downright sexy?'

'No!' Lydia Michaels said with a laugh. 'Please don't, you old goat!'

Again, Jerome sighed. 'Darlin' Lydia,' he said, 'I didn't mean to hurt you so much when I turned down your sexual advances last year.'

Lydia laughed. 'You wish, old man. You know I could kill you with one romp in the hay.'

'What a way to go,' Hal Burleson said with a sigh.

'Did you find a roommate, Hal?' Jerome asked. To the rest of us he said, 'Hal wanted me to room with him, but I always like to leave room in case, well, someone of the fairer sex needs accommodations.' He wiggled his eyebrows at Candace who just shook her head and laughed.

'Oh, yeah,' Hal said, 'but you're not gonna like it.' He grinned at Jerome.

'This sounds ominous,' said the older man. 'Who, pray tell?'

'Cyrus Sullivan,' Hal said.

Jerome actually turned pale, placing his hand on his heart. 'Are you trying to give me a coronary?'

'Hey, I told you I needed to share expenses,' Hal said, grinning and shrugging. 'He's all I could find.'

'Obviously you didn't look very hard! There are many rocks right out there on the patio,' he said, pointing to said patio, 'and I know you could find a better roommate by just picking one up and looking under it!'

'Oh, Jerome,' Mary said, 'Cyrus isn't that bad.'

'Cyrus is a festering wound,' Jerome said.

'You only say that because he loves you so,' Lydia said.

Candace and I just sat back and enjoyed the show. I certainly didn't know who Cyrus Sullivan was and I doubt Candace did either.

'That man has been stalking me for twenty-five years!' Jerome said. 'I've had to have my phone changed twice because of him. And I really would like to know who gave him my number that last time!' he said, staring daggers at the group.

All denied culpability.

To me, Jane said, 'Cyrus wrote a book back in, what was it, Jerome, 1973?'

'At least that long ago,' Jerome said, still rather huffy.

'He's never been published since, but having that one book seems to be an open door for him. He comes to all these events. And,' she smiled, 'he does dote on Jerome.'

'I have nothing against gays,' Jerome said, directing his words to Candace and myself. 'I have a nephew who's gay and I adore him. He has incredible taste. It's not that Cyrus is gay, or even that he considers himself in *love* with me, it's that he's a royal pain in the ass!'

'So, don't come to my room,' Hal suggested.

'Who's not coming to our room?' asked a voice behind Jerome, his small hands resting on the back of Jerome's chair.

'Well, speak of the devil,' Hal said, grinning.

'Were you speaking of me?' the little man asked, a big smile showing pearly white, incredibly straight teeth that didn't quite fit. 'Hello, Jerome,' he said, leaning down almost to Jerome's ear.

He was taller than Jane, but that was about it. He was very thin, except for a round little belly, and he looked to be about Jerome's age, maybe a tad bit younger. He was dressed in a plaid sports jacket from what I would guess had been the Penney's boy's department, circa 1955. His faded blue jeans were bell bottomed, and he wore two-tone loafers. His head sported the worst toupee I've ever seen. What was left of his real hair was salt and pepper, heavy on the salt, and the toupee was auburn.

'Mary,' Cyrus said, bowing his head toward her. The back of the toupee stood up a little as his head lowered. 'Lydia, darling, how are you? And Jane, so good to see you.'

'Let me introduce you,' Jane said, and proceeded to introduce Candace and myself.

With each of us, as he shook our hands, he declared, 'Cyrus Sullivan, seventy-three years young!'

When he shook my hand he held it entirely too long, and squeezed it as if milking a cow. I was beginning to understand Jerome MacIntyre's dismay at being the object of this person's affections.

'Mary Sparrow!' came a loud voice, and we all looked up to see Angela Barber looming above us. Cyrus quickly scooted off toward the bar.

When I said Angela Barber was a large woman, I wasn't

trying to be unkind. She was just that. Well over six feet tall, she had to run to 300 pounds, and little of it appeared to be flab. She had broad shoulders, narrow hips, and looked like a lineman for the Green Bay Packers. Her bottle red hair had an orange tint to it and was permed into a tight Afro around her head. The bright blue eye shadow and circle of red on each cheek gave her face a clownish appearance. However, the scowl she was wearing didn't fit the clown image.

'Yes, Angela?' Mary Sparrow said with a sigh.

'I need to talk with you!' Angela demanded.

'Can it wait?' Mary asked.

'No! It's dreadfully important!' Angela said.

Again Mary sighed. Looking at the table and its occupants, she said, 'If you'll excuse me.' We all nodded and she got up and left the table, following the aggressive walk of the Beast.

Jane stood up. 'Well, I'm leaving while the getting is good,' she said. 'I think I'll hide in my room until I know Angela is otherwise occupied.'

Lydia Michaels stood too. 'You're all invited to my suite, especially you, Candace,' she said. 'I mean, God forbid you try to hide out in your room and the Beast comes back!' Lydia shuddered at the thought.

'Thank you!' Candace said with what appeared to be great relief.

'I'm up for room service,' Hal Burleson said, 'unless you brought a bottle of Johnny Walker with you?' he said, wiggling his eyebrows at Lydia.

'And when have you known me to come to one of these things without Johnny in tow?'

'That's my girl,' Hal said, following the two women out.

Jerome MacIntyre stood and held out his hand to me. 'It was my great pleasure to meet you, Ms Pugh,' he said. 'I hope we haven't scandalized you with what we pass off as wit. And I do apologize for . . .' He looked toward the bar where Cyrus Sullivan was deep in conversation with a woman in stretch pants and a button on her blouse that said, 'Ask me about my grandbaby.'

I laughed. 'Actually, Mr MacIntyre, I haven't enjoyed myself so much in ages. Thank you for letting me sit in.'

He kissed my hand. 'There's always room for a beautiful redhead,' he said.

Jane rolled her eyes. 'Watch him,' she said. 'We never know if he's serious or not!'

'Only about you, my love,' he said, winking at Jane. With one last look to see where Cyrus was, and that he wasn't watching him, Jerome walked off in the other direction.

Jane and I headed to our room, but only Jane made it to the elevator. As I started to step inside the car, I felt a tentative tap on my shoulder. Turning, I saw a very young woman, the youngest I'd seen yet at this convention, with very dark curly hair, skin so pale the veins showed through, a sprinkling of freckles on her cheeks and turned-up nose, and a lush body that, without hard work, would blossom to unfortunate proportions by the time she was thirty.

'Mrs Pugh?' she said.

I waved Jane and the elevator on and said, 'Yes?'

She giggled nervously and said, 'My name is Lisbet Carson?'

By the inflection in her speech I wanted to answer, 'Yes, dear, I'm sure you are.' But I just said. 'Yes?'

'I'm a reporter with the *Mullet*? That's the school newspaper at Concordia University?'

'The *Mullet*? As in Billy Ray Cyrus's old do?' I asked, incredulous.

'Oh, no, of course not. Who's that?' she asked, perky head turned sideways as she tried to figure out what I was talking about.

I knew Concordia was a private Lutheran university, and one of many colleges and universities in the Austin area. You could see it as you drove down the main highway from Oklahoma to the coast, Interstate 35, right in the middle of Austin.

Deciding to ignore the humor-tempting name of the school newspaper, I just said, 'What can I do for you, Ms Carson?'

She giggled again. 'Please, call me Lisbet!' She took a deep breath and rushed into what could only have been a prepared speech. 'You're my favorite author in the whole world and I begged my sponsor at the paper to let me cover this convention and I told him I could get an interview with you. I sorta

lied and said we were related, so if you would please grant
me an interview you'd save my life really!'

I put my hand gently on her arm. 'Take a breath,' I said,
smiling. She did. 'I'd be happy to do an interview.' I glanced
around the Sam and saw that the giant round settee in the
middle of the lobby was empty. 'How about if we sit there?'
I said, pointing toward the tufted green velvet.

'Oh, gawd, yes! That would be great! Thank you so much!
You don't know how much this means—'

'Over here,' I said, ushering her toward the settee and
trying to shut her up. I had to wonder what kind of interview this was going to be and if I'd actually be doing any
of the talking.

We settled down and she pulled out a small tape recorder.
'So I can get your quotes right,' she said.

I smiled. 'Good idea,' I said.

Turning it on, she said, 'Interview with romance writer E.J.
Pugh, April 11, 2006 5:03 p.m.

'Mrs Pugh,' she said, moving in close, and whispering, 'do
you and your husband try out all the sex stuff in your books
before you write it?'

Black Cat Ridge, Texas
Graham, Thursday

Many Black Cat Ridgers had Coddervillian relatives, such as
Graham's grandmother, who had raised her children in the
same home in which her husband had been raised. The same
could be said for Graham's friend Leon, who had not only
one grandmother but two, and a grandfather as well, living in
Codderville. Then there were also the aunts and uncles and
cousins all living there. If truth be known, most felt that Leon's
parents were acting pretty damned uppity when they moved
their family to Black Cat Ridge. But being true to their Texas
values, none felt a need to take this out on the children, and
usually treated them kindly.

'So when's he supposed to be back?' Graham whispered to
Leon as they sat in his cousin's living room, talking to Leon's
aunt.

Leon shrugged, turning to his aunt. 'Aunt Sue, when's Les
supposed to be home?'

'Well, honey, I don't rightly know,' she said, folding towels as she talked. 'He was going over to LaGrange to pick up some parts for his truck, but he shoulda been back ages ago.'

It was then that they heard Les's truck pulling into the driveway. It wasn't a subtle sound as Les hadn't had a muffler on the truck since 1999.

'There he is now!' Leon said, jumping up. 'Thanks, Aunt Sue.'

He ran through the kitchen to the back door of the old house and out to the garage, with Graham hot on his heels. Les was already out of the truck, motor turned off, standing at the back with his arms resting on the rim of the bed, staring into it. He was a tall drink of water, close to six feet six or seven. He wasn't sure since it didn't really matter to him. He weighed the same as he had in junior high, when he'd only been five foot ten. He wore a John Deer gimme cap over his sandy blond hair, oil stained blue jeans and a western shirt that had seen better days.

'Hey, Les,' Leon said.

Les turned his head slowly and focused on Leon. 'Yeah, hey, Leon. Hey, Graham.'

'Hey, Les,' Graham said.

'Les, we gotta talk,' Leon said, his hands working each other like worry beads.

'Yeah?' Les asked, his attention once more back to the item in the bed of his truck. 'Got me a roll bar for the truck,' he said.

Leon and Graham moved to the truck and leaned on the rim, staring into the bed.

'Sweet,' Leon said.

'Yeah, man,' Graham said. 'Cool.' Although a phrase of his grandmother's came back to him: 'A ten dollar saddle on a five dollar horse.' He hadn't really thought about what that meant until he saw the shiny chrome roll bar Les was going to put on his ancient blue and rust Chevy truck.

Les turned and looked at the two boys. 'Whatya want?' he asked.

'OK, so here's the deal,' Leon said. 'See, Graham's got a date tomorrow night with this really hot chick—'

'Well, not really a date—' Graham cut in.

'And she's bringing her girlfriends,' Leon said, elbowing Les in the ribs, 'know what I mean?'

Les frowned. 'I think I can follow,' he said in his slow drawl.

Leon cleared his throat. 'Well, anyway, we don't have wheels—'

Les turned back to the cab of his truck, opening the door. 'No,' he said.

'What? No what?' Leon demanded.

'You ain't borrowing my truck,' Les said.

'Oh no, man, that's not it at all,' Graham said.

Leaning on the cab door, Les turned to the younger boys. 'Then what?'

'We need some beer,' Leon said.

And thus began the adventure.

Austin, Texas
E.J., Thursday

This wasn't the Barbara Walters' interview of my dreams, to say the least.

To answer Lisbet's first question, I simply said, 'I have no intention of answering that.'

So she asked, 'What kind of underwear do you wear while writing?'

'Excuse me?' I said. I'd never been asked *that* before.

'You know. Do you wear like a thong, or something to make you feel sexier? Or maybe no underwear at all?'

'Pass,' I said.

'Pardon?' she asked.

'I'm not going to answer that,' I said, thinking that the true answer, my high-waisted granny undies, would probably set this young woman's sexual fantasies back centuries.

She sighed. Two for two. She wasn't doing well. The next question was: 'Is there a particular diet you're on to help you come up with juicy sex scenes?'

I was beginning to feel sorry for her. I had to answer something, and so far this seemed the least obnoxious question. 'Yes,' I said, making it up as I went along. 'For breakfast I have strawberries and chocolate, for lunch oysters, and for dinner liver and spinach.'

Lisbet Collins nodded her head, a slight smile on her face. 'That makes perfect sense!' she said. 'Strawberries and chocolate for sensuality, oysters for stamina, and the liver and spinach for fortification!'

'Exactly!' I said, beaming back at her.

'Do you ever pretend your husband is one of your fictional heroes while making love?' she asked, leaning forward eagerly for the answer.

Thinking quickly, I said, 'My husband *is* one of my fictional heroes,' I said. Her eyes were like saucers in her head. 'Actually, one of my books is really autobiographical, the story of how I met my husband, placed in another time and place, of course.'

'Which one?' she demanded.

I laughed and shook my head. 'I'm not going to tell you that!' I said. I patted her cheek with my hand. 'You're going to have to figure it out.'

With that I excused myself and headed to the bank of elevators, thinking, that was fun!

When I got to our room, Jane and I sprawled on our respective beds and talked. After an hour's discussion of who slept with whom at which convention, whose husband found out about it, and the repercussions of said event, Jane and I changed into clothes fit for the evening's opening event. Jane was giving the keynote address at tonight's affair, followed by what Jane called 'your usual dead chicken dinner', and a performance by the Dixie Chickens, a group of aging romance writers who – Jane's words – 'thought they could sing'.

'But most of it's tongue-in-cheek and the lyrics of the songs – when you can understand them – are usually quite funny.'

This was cocktail attire, so I put on my standard black dress from four years ago, when I was a size fourteen for a short period of time, pulled on black pantyhose, donned my grandmother's pearls and two-inch black patent heels, and followed Jane downstairs. Her dress was pink chiffon and would have been knee-length on anyone else – on her it reached the tops of her ankles. Her three-inch strappy silver sandals added some much needed height, as did the white hair piled high on her head.

The first person we saw when we got off the elevator was the Beast, dressed for the opening ceremonies in a brown shirt, brown pants and sensible brown shoes.

'Jane, you didn't come to my room!' Angela Barber accused.

'I'm so sorry, Angela,' Jane said, attempting a maneuver around the larger woman. 'It's just been so hectic today.'

Angela blocked her. 'We have to talk!' she screeched.

I took Jane's arm and said, 'Oh, look, there's Mr Johnson! We're late meeting him!'

'Oh, dear,' Jane said, shrugging. She smiled at Angela. 'I'm so sorry. Later?' she said as I hauled her off to find the non-existent Mr Johnson. She squeezed my arm. 'Very good, E.J.! You're learning!'

We giggled as we headed into the conference room where the opening event was being held. It was a breathtaking room: with glass chandeliers and walls 'papered' in white silk shantung and, for this event, draped in rose-colored satin; the tablecloths were a matching rose satin with white china edged in gold, gold tableware, and a huge centerpiece of multi-colored rosebuds in the center of each table – all different shades of pink and ivory. The dais was draped with the same rose satin and each place setting had its own bouquet of roses in front of it.

I sat at a table with my earlier companions: Jerome MacIntyre (Jasmine West, fellow Lady nominee), Mary Sparrow, Hal Burleson (Sara Swan), Candace Macy, another fellow Lady nominee and Lydia Michaels. My roommate Jane (Maybella LaRue) was up on the dais, being the keynote speaker of the evening.

Mary and Lydia obviously had a heads up on the room's color scheme for the evening because they'd coordinated their outfits: Lydia was wearing a pale rose satin suit with a double strand of graduated pearls that made my grandmother's pearls look like plastic, while Mary had on an ivory slip dress with rhinestone encrusted spaghetti straps and a row of rhinestones at the bodice. The diamond at her throat would have choked a horse. I felt terribly underdressed in my old black knit.

To Candace and me, Lydia Michaels said, 'Don't expect much from tonight, ladies. The food will be awful, the speeches long and the humor non-existent. Except for possibly Jane. She does get off a good one every now and then.'

'I can't believe she even came to this,' Mary Sparrow said. 'I mean, after losing her contr—'

Lydia gave her a hard stare and Mary quickly shut up. Hal and Jerome exchanged a look, then began to fidget with their tableware. Candace and I glanced at each other but quickly glanced away. It was none of our business, was the obvious answer to that. Strangely enough, Angela Barber saved the awkwardness. She picked that moment to barge up to the table.

'Jerome MacIntyre! You promised you'd speak to my writer's club while you were in town! We're having a special meeting here tomorrow morning at seven.'

'How unfortunate,' Jerome said, taking a sip from his wine glass and looking dapper as ever in a three-piece suit with a striped tie and matching pocket-handkerchief. 'I'll be very much asleep at seven tomorrow morning.'

'You promised!' Angela screeched.

'No, Angela, actually I didn't. I told you to get a hold of my publicist and see if she could fit it into my schedule. That's the last word I heard on the subject. Did you speak with my publicist? Lovely young lady by the name of Deirdre. I believe I gave you her email address.' I noticed Jerome didn't look at Angela during any of this, but fiddled with some rolls and butter already on the table.

'I emailed her and told her you'd be speaking to us and she never emailed back saying you wouldn't!' Angela said, hands on hips.

Finally, Jerome looked up. 'Angela, my darling Angela, the lack of a negative does not necessarily translate into a positive.'

Angela, for once since I'd been forced to meet her, was silent.

'That means, my dear, that you did not book me for tomorrow. I will be asleep. I will not be at your writer's club meeting. I'm terribly sorry if you'll be inconvenienced or embarrassed, but there it is.'

'You'll pay for this!' Angela said through clenched teeth.

Reaching into his pocket, Jerome brought out a twenty-dollar bill. 'Will this handle it?' he asked.

She twirled around on her sensible low-heeled shoes and stormed away.

'Oh, man, you've done it now,' Hal said. 'She's going to sabotage your reading or your panel or something.'

'She'll do it, too,' Lydia said. 'Remember the time Anne Bradford told her off about something? The next day the room Anne was supposed to read in had a contamination sign on it and no fans would even go in there!'

'And what about Suzie Nguyn? Remember when she told the Beast no about something, and not one of her microphones worked all convention?' Mary Sparrow said.

'Does she really have that kind of power?' Candace asked.

The rest of us could have been wearing sackcloth and ashes in comparison to Candace. It was a simple silk coral colored dress with a draping neckline. The dress fell from her breasts in a straight line to just above her knee. Well, it would have been a straight line if it weren't for the swell of her nicely shaped breasts and the curve of her enviable little butt. The coral looked great with her peaches-and-cream complexion, and I felt it was really a shame she seemed to be so nice; I'm sure I was the third woman at the table who wanted to see her dead.

'She usually doesn't officially have the power,' Hal said, who hadn't bothered to dress for the occasion and was still wearing his white, button-down collar shirt and stay-press slacks that he'd worn earlier in the day. 'She just takes it. None of those things should have been allowed, but everybody's afraid of her. But this convention, with her running it, she could probably get away with anything.'

'Well, I'm happy to say my fans will follow me anywhere,' Jerome MacIntyre said. 'Even into a supposedly contaminated room.'

Lydia laughed. 'I'm afraid he's right about that. His fans would definitely drink the Kool-Aid.'

'Charisma can be a terrible thing,' Jerome said, then wiggled his eyebrows. 'Thank God I'm on the side of good not evil!'

'I've always said that about you, Jerome,' said Cyrus Sullivan as he sauntered up to our table, leaning heavily on the back of Jerome's chair, which made Jerome lean forward, almost landing in his dinner plate.

Cyrus was wearing a tuxedo, obviously from a boys' department somewhere a very long time ago. The material was so old it was shiny, actually reflecting light. His bow tie was crooked, which I understand from watching movies means it was a real bow tie and not a clip on; unfortunately it was a lemon yellow, as was his matching cummerbund. His tuxedo shirt was pale blue with ruffles, and the cuffs, shot out from his jacket sleeves, were frayed.

'Oh, Cyrus,' Mary said, a smile on her face, 'I'd ask you

to join us, but we only have the one chair left, and it's for Jane when she gets down from the dais.'

'Oh, no bother, Mary, dear, I'm sitting with my editor,' he said. 'We're talking about a new deal!' he said brightly. 'I just wanted to drop by and say hello.' Leaning forward he said softly, 'Hello, Jerome.'

Not turning around nor leaning back, Jerome said, 'Hello, Cyrus.'

Rubbing Jerome's shoulder, Cyrus said, 'I'm off now. Wish me luck!'

There were a few weak good luck's bandied about, then Cyrus was gone.

'Well,' I said, 'looks like he's back in business.'

Several headshakes met my statement.

'He buttonholes some poor editor every year and always says "there's a new deal in the works!".' Jerome shook his head. 'I'd feel sorry for him if he didn't give me the shivers.'

At that point, Angela Barber tapped harder than necessary on the microphone at the podium on the dais. 'Good evening, ladies and gentlemen,' she said. And thus began the evening.

Black Cat Ridge, Texas
Elizabeth, Thursday
Dad wasn't much of a cook, but he gave it his best effort, Elizabeth thought to herself. Wieners chopped up in macaroni and cheese and salad out of a bag. She played with her food, not seeing her brother and sister scarfing down Dad's efforts like they were good. Normally she'd take a shot at Megan's eating habits and style, but tonight she didn't even think about it. She had too much on her mind.

Aldon, he'd said. Her brother. Her dead brother. The brother who'd died when she lost the rest of her birth family, nearly a decade earlier. Elizabeth didn't understand what game Tommy was playing, or why he would do this. Aldon was dead, she knew that; she went to his grave at least twice a year.

After Tommy had written those words, Elizabeth had blackened the monitor, too numb with fright and bewilderment to even think about responding. It had taken her so long to lay her family to rest in her mind, and here was this guy bringing it all back up again. What was he doing? Aldon was dead. Just like her sister Monique and her real mom and dad. She knew who had killed them and why. Mama E.J. had told her the whole story when she was eleven. She didn't have all the details – she didn't want them – but she knew enough to know that her brother Aldon was definitely dead.

Elizabeth nibbled on a slice of wiener. What was Tommy up to? she wondered. Why in the world would he say such a thing? And how did he find out about her brother Aldon?

The taste of the wiener made her sick to her stomach. She sat at the table hoping she wouldn't puke into her plate – one of those personal hygiene things she was so fond of.

'What's wrong with you?' Megan asked from across the table. 'You're acting weirder than usual.'

'Nothing,' Elizabeth answered.

Graham and Megan looked at each other. No come back. No shot at Megan having cleaned her plate. Something was definitely wrong. Megan looked at her father who sat oblivious at the end of the table, going for his second helping of wieners and macaroni and cheese. Best not bring anything up now, Megan thought. Not in front of Dad.

So they left her alone. Elizabeth didn't notice; she was too wrapped up in the 'what if's' and 'maybes' Tommy's message had aroused in her. What if Aldon wasn't really dead? What if he had somehow survived that awful night? Then why wouldn't Mama E.J. know that? And if Aldon had survived, who was buried in his grave? Elizabeth shook herself internally and told herself to stop it. No way had Aldon survived that massacre. No way had he been wandering the world from the age of ten until now. Tommy was playing some horrible joke on her, but she would refuse to be anybody's punchline. She just wouldn't talk to him again. That's all there was to it.

Austin, Texas
E.J., Thursday
Actually the dinner wasn't all that bad. I cleaned my plate. I could have cleaned Candace's and Mary's too, if I hadn't had on my company manners. Angela's introduction of Jane

was more of a speech and, predictably, was entirely too long, mostly boring, and a little bit mean. She left the podium without lowering the microphone, which necessitated Jane having to reach far over her head to lower it to her level. When she began to talk, though, the evening got a lot livelier.

As Mary had explained to Cyrus Sullivan, our table wasn't completely full, one chair next to me having been left empty for Jane. After Jane's speech, while the dessert was being served, I felt a presence in the seat next to me. I was turned to my right, talking with Candace who sat on that side. When her eyes left mine and traveled behind me, I turned to see who it was. To my chagrin, it was DeWitt Perry, the noxious little man from earlier in the day.

'E.J.,' he said, smiling at me. 'I hope you don't mind if I join you!'

All conversation at the table stopped.

I said, 'Ah . . .' I'm quick-witted that way.

Jerome came to my rescue. 'Oh, we're so sorry, but that seat's being saved for Maybella LaRue. She'll be coming down from the dais shortly.'

'Oh,' said DeWitt Perry, the smile vanishing from his face. 'Well, could I speak with you for just a moment, E.J.?' he asked.

Mary Sparrow made a show of looking at her watch. 'Oh E.J., I don't think you have time before your meeting with Mr Davis,' she said.

I had a feeling Mr Davis was a close associate of Mr Johnson, the non-existent man Jane had a meeting with earlier in the day.

'You're right, Mary,' I said. I looked apologetically at DeWitt Perry. 'I'm so sorry, Mr Perry,' I said. 'I have to be in a meeting in just a few seconds!'

'How long will it last?' he asked.

I looked at Mary whose shrug indicated I was on my own. 'I have no idea,' I said. 'You know how these business things go!'

'What's your room number?' he asked, moving into my space. 'I'll come by your room later.'

'Oh, E.J., there's Mr Davis now!' Mary said. 'You'd better scoot!'

I jumped up. 'Bye!' I said to everyone at the table and hurried off to the ladies' room.

I leaned against the counter of the elegantly appointed bathroom and remembered I hadn't called Willis, my husband, since I'd gotten to Austin at eleven a.m. It was now nine thirty in the evening and, although I knew he wasn't worried, I did know he was probably not particularly happy with me. I pulled out my cellphone and dialed home.

'Hello?' said a deep male voice that didn't belong to my husband.

'Hi, honey,' I said to Graham. 'How's it going?'

'Who is this?' he asked suspiciously.

I sighed. 'It's your mother,' I said.

'Oh. You wanna talk to Dad?'

'Sure,' I said, knowing those were the most words I would get out of my son. I wanted to ask about his NASCAR T-shirt just to keep the conversation going, but was afraid of where that might lead.

I heard the phone hit something – a counter, the floor, my husband's head, whatever. Finally Willis's voice came on the line. 'Thanks for letting me know you got there safely,' he said by way of greeting.

'If you were worried you could have called *me*,' I said. 'The phones work both ways.'

'I asked you to call me as soon as you got there!' he accused.

'Yes, you did, and I forgot. Can we get over that now?'

There was a sigh. 'Having fun?' he finally said.

I said, 'I'm having a blast! There's infighting, backbiting, gossip aplenty, and I have my very own stalker!'

'Hey,' my husband said, 'congratulations! I hope he's not too good looking?'

I sighed. 'No, not at all, more's the pity.'

'All this and it's just the first day?'

'I know! I can't wait to see what happens tomorrow!'

'So, are you bringing your roommate home for a visit?' he asked.

'Down, boy,' I said, then explained about Jane's daughter-in-law and the picture taken four pregnancies ago.

'Oh, man!' he whined. 'I was really looking forward to meeting her!'

'Well, the real Jane is great! I really think you'd like her.

And besides, you have plenty to look at when *I'm* around!' I reminded him.

'Yes, dear,' he said dutifully. 'My eyes would never stray to another woman.'

'So long as it's only your eyes, buster, I don't really care.'

'So, tell me about the stalker. Is he a problem? You need me to come over there and rough him up for you? I take it it is a "he"?'

'Yes, it's a "he" and, believe me, I can handle him. He'd probably run home to Mama if I messed up his comb over. So,' I said, changing the subject, 'any new vomiting going on?'

'Hush your mouth and knock on wood, woman!' my husband said. 'So far so good.'

Before I got a chance to respond, I heard, 'Megan! Stop it! Graham!' as Willis shouted, his mouth barely away from the phone.

'What are they up to now?' I asked.

'The girls want to watch *Gray's Anatomy,* Graham wants to watch *CSI.* They're having remote wars.'

'I told you two remotes would never work in our house.'

'In theory they should.'

'Tell one of them to Tivo it,' I suggested.

'Naw, I'm just gonna put it on C-Span and let 'em all scream.'

'God, I love a mean man!' I said, grinning.

Pitching his voice low and sexy, Willis said, 'And, baby, I'm the meanest!'

I laughed. 'Talk to you tomorrow.'

'Right. I'll hold my breath waiting.'

'I like you in blue,' I said. 'Bye.'

I hung up and instantly missed my family. That lasted about fifteen seconds, then I used the facilities and headed back out to dinner to see who was being dissed now.

Three

After the opening festivities, Jane and I listened for about fifteen minutes to the Dixie Chickens (Jane was right – they really couldn't sing), then left the ballroom to take a walk around the book room, a vast room filled with umpteen booksellers, all displaying the opuses of those writers present, as well as a few best-sellers who rarely came to these things. There were also a few merchants selling jewelry, some selling T-shirts and various and sundry other items they hoped would be of interest to a captive audience. I was happy to see that all the booksellers had at least some of my books, and most had my newest, which is the one I was here pitching in the first place. Last year's book was the one nominated for the Lady, and all the booksellers had that on display. Seeing my picture and my book cover everywhere was both exhilarating and embarrassing. Go figure.

I bought a copy of Mary Sparrow's latest and Candace Macy's book that was my competition for the Lady. I hadn't read it and thought it would be the politically correct thing to do. I'd already read the competition written by Jerome MacIntyre and figured he would be the definite winner. Tomorrow morning the panels and readings started. I had an eight a.m. panel entitled 'Location, Location, Location' and a one p.m. panel entitled 'Time is of the Essence'. The first one I assume is fairly obvious; the second was a panel of writers who wrote anything other than modern or regency-period romances. Since some of mine were set in the 1700s, I was included in this one. On Saturday I had two readings, and on Sunday I had another panel on 'Keeping the Heroine Fresh', a subject on which I had absolutely no comment. Saturday night was the awards banquet, so I'd probably be a blithering idiot during my Saturday readings, and a disappointed idiot at my Sunday panel.

As we were headed toward the door of the book room, I spotted Lisbet Carson cruising the sellers, tape recorder in hand. 'There she is!' I stage whispered to Jane. I'd already told her about the college girl and her inappropriate interview questions.

Jane giggled. 'We should do a double interview with her and really give her some dirt! Stuff there's no way her teacher would let her publish!'

'About you and I being secret lovers?' I said, giggling.

'And about the foursomes with our husbands!' she offered.

'And the Wesson oil and the hot air balloon,' I added.

Jane stopped for a moment. Looking at me, she said, 'OK, I get the Wesson oil. Explain the hot air balloon.'

I shoved her toward the door. 'Not even if I could.'

Lydia Michaels and Hal Burleson caught us as we were leaving the book room. 'We're on our way to Mary's room,' Lydia said. 'You guys need to come. Angela's on the warpath and I heard her asking where you were, Jane.'

Jane shuddered. 'Oh, Lord, get me out of here!'

The three of them shoved their way on to an already crowded elevator. There wasn't room for me. 'What's Mary's room number?' I asked. 'I'll take the next elevator and meet you up there.'

Lydia whispered the number in my ear and barely got her head back inside the car before the doors closed. I pushed the button and waited patiently for the next car. It didn't take long and was thankfully empty. I got on and just as the doors began to close, an arm snaked its way between the doors, causing them to open again. DeWitt Perry stepped inside and the doors closed.

He smiled at me. 'I knew we'd get a chance to talk!' he said. 'Are you on your way to your room?'

'No,' I said, trying not to make eye contact, instead studying the numbers flashing by on the electronic readout. I'd noticed he had not pushed a floor button. 'I'm going to meet some friends.'

'Well, I'm glad we have this little time together,' he said, reaching out and pushing the button to stop the elevator.

That did it! I slapped his hand and pulled the button out.

'Do not do that, Mr Perry!' I said, shaking my finger in his face like I did to my kids when they were being particularly themselves. 'You are being rudely aggressive and making me very nervous! If you don't leave me alone I'm going to report you to hotel security!'

He pouted. 'Well,' he said, crossing his arms over his chest. 'I'm just trying to be friendly!'

'There's friendly, Mr Perry, and there's stalking! I think you've just moved into stalking!'

'Oh, for heaven's sake!' he said. 'Can't a man even approach a woman nowadays without you people crying rape?' He'd moved into the corner of the elevator car. Yes, I can be intimidating when I want to be.

The elevator reached Mary Sparrow's floor. I got off, holding the door open with my hand. 'Mr Perry, I suggest you leave me alone. I also suggest you don't pull this kind of stunt with any other writers at this convention. I'm going to tell the convention authorities what has happened here and you can answer to them.'

Hands on hips, DeWitt Perry glared at me. 'Why, you're just a big old bitch, aren't you?'

I smiled. 'Damn straight,' I said, and let go of the door.

Black Cat Ridge, Texas
Graham, Thursday
Like most teenaged boys, Graham Pugh had no appreciation of the home his parents had lovingly acquired for him. He really saw no difference between his relatively palatial two-story home with the formals and the family room and a bedroom for each child and an office for his mother, and the two-bedroom shotgun house of Leon's Aunt Sue and Cousin Les that he'd been in earlier in the day. If asked, he probably would have been able to admit that Leon's relatives' house was smaller than his own, but that would be his only concession. If it didn't involve Graham directly, he really saw no need in observing those things around him. He was fed, clothed, had a roof over his head and occasional spending money. And for all of this he was required to mow the lawn and take out the garbage. He thought the price was fairly high, but he didn't know where he'd find a better bargain.

When the phone rang and he heard a female voice, Graham's

heart leapt. Unfortunately, it was just his mother. Leave it to her to call when he could be getting a phone call from Ashley. Not that she said she'd call. Not that he'd asked her to call. Not that she even had his number, to his knowledge. But she *could* call. It was possible.

He dropped the phone and yelled for his dad, heading for the stairs to his room, after a quick stop at the refrigerator. With two slices of cold, leftover pizza in one hand and the carton of milk in the other, he sat down at his computer and IM'd Leon.

Gandolf147:	Leon, you there?
Studleyman:	Yo!
Gandolf147:	Get beer?
Studleyman:	Stashed in mom's oleanders
Gandolf147:	Hollister?
Studleyman:	Pick it up tomorrow
Gandolf147:	Cool
Studleyman:	Out

Graham had nothing left to do but study for his history test the next day. He sighed and opened his book. The price of freedom was good grades. Again, a high price to pay but there appeared to be no alternatives.

Austin, Texas
E.J., Thursday
When I got to Mary Sparrow's room, the conversation stopped dead while I told them what had happened in the elevator. Which led to advice:

Mary: 'Turn him in to hotel security.'

Hal, laughing: 'Oh, no! Sic Angela on him!'

Lydia, who'd been imbibing liberally from the second bottle of Johnny Walker: 'No, no! Let's find his room number and we'll sneak in and short-sheet his bed! Ooh, ooh, no, shaving cream on his privates!'

Jane: 'Cut his comb-over hairs!'

When they ran out of revenge ideas against DeWitt Perry, they started the crazy fan stories.

'Remember that one woman who followed Joan into the bathroom and shoved a book under the stall door, demanding an autograph?' said Mary.

'What about that one who followed Liz out of the hotel and actually tried to get in a taxi with her?' Hal said.

'I had a woman follow me into the men's room once,' Jerome said.

'Oh Lord, Jerry,' Lydia said, 'they *will* follow you anywhere, won't they?'

He inclined his head in a mock bow.

'Now, come on, guys,' Jane said. 'You know those are the exceptions. Most of the people who come to these things are just here to get books signed in the normal way, go to panels to learn something, just normal, well-behaved people.'

'Thank God for the crazies, though,' Mary said. 'What would we have to talk about without them?'

'Angela!' said four voices in unison.

Lydia patted Jane's leg. 'Oh, you poor dear! I would have died if I'd been up there on the dais, waiting for her to shut up so you could speak! My God, she's awful.'

Jane shook her head. 'She's certainly not subtle.'

'Subtle like a hand grenade,' Hal said.

There was a small silence, then Mary turned to Candace. 'So, dear, are you married?'

Candace smiled and said, 'Haven't found Mr Right yet.'

To me, Mary asked, 'You, E.J.?'

'Oh, I found Mr Right, or a reasonable facsimile,' I said. 'And we have three kids – two girls and a boy. You?'

'I have two grown daughters, both married and one about to make me a grandmother! As for a husband, I lost mine to cancer about twelve years ago,' she said.

'Oh, I'm so sorry,' I said, Candace joining me in condolences.

'The only good thing about it,' Lydia chimed in, 'is that all the guys at these conventions know she's single now, and they follow her around like puppy dogs. And since she doesn't want any of them, I can usually catch me a slow one.'

'Quite like a hungry coyote cutting a calf out of the herd,' Jerome said.

'No, darling,' Lydia said, 'more like a horny coyote.'

'Then I take it you're single?' I said to Lydia.

'Oh, God, don't get me started!' she said.

'Yeah, please don't,' Hal said.

'I'm in the midst of divorce number three. Michael!' She fairly spat out the name. 'I thought he was sensitive,' she said. 'Please spell that w-i-m-p. When God was handing out balls, Michael thought He was talking about tennis. Now I've done them all – the macho jock, the playboy and the wimp. I'm three for three.'

I was sitting next to Mary and she whispered, 'Don't *even* ask her about the playboy—'

'I heard that, Mary!' Lydia said, liberally pouring more Johnny Walker Black into a paper cup. 'I'm still paying that bastard one quarter of all earnings on five of my books! Unfortunately that was a very lucrative six years I was married to that gigolo.'

'And the jock?' I asked, trying to curb the anger I could see building up in Lydia.

'Ho! The jock! My college sweetheart. A football player. We were married eight months when he *tried* to hit me.'

I was more than willing to play Lydia's straight woman. 'Tried?' I said.

'I blocked him with a chair.' She grinned. 'And not one of those break-away Hollywood chairs, either. This was a heavy oak dining chair. During the divorce he tried to get me to pay alimony – on an assistant editor's salary, no less! He said I ruined his professional football aspirations. The judge, bless him, laughed at him.' She grinned. 'To this day he walks with a slight limp.'

'What about you guys?' Candace asked.

Hal shifted in his seat and said quietly, 'I was married once, a long time ago. It didn't take.'

Jerome said, 'My darling Martha passed away three years ago. Spitfire of a woman.'

'That she was!' Jane said, holding up her glass. 'To Martha!'

We all toasted Jerome's late wife.

'Children?' I asked.

Jerome shook his head. 'Unfortunately we were not so blessed. But after seeing how some of my nieces and nephews turned out, I wonder if the blessing wasn't *not* having children.'

I held up my hand. 'Please, no horror stories. I have a sixteen year old and two thirteen year olds. I have enough worries as is.'

'The thirteen year olds?' Mary asked. 'Girls or boys?'

'Both girls,' I said.

Mary crossed herself. 'I'll pray for you,' she said. 'You'll need it.'

'Twin girls!' Candace said. 'That must be a joy!'

'They're not twins,' I corrected. 'They're actually six months apart.' When all eyes bugged out at that, I said, 'No, I'm not a medical miracle, one's adopted.'

'Oh,' they all said in virtual unison.

'You had me worried for a moment,' Lydia said. 'I had this image of the longest pregnancy in history.'

Not being much of a drinker, it only took two Diet Cokes and bourbon for me to feel the need to find my room.

'Come on,' Jane said, a little arm reaching up to hug my waist. 'Let's pour you into bed.'

'We'll let you off this time,' Lydia said, 'but from now on there's a four-drink minimum in my room!'

I gagged at the thought.

We got back to our room a little after midnight and Jane helped me get my clothes off and my sleeping T-shirt on. I laid down in my bed, keeping my eyes open to help the room spin a little less. Jane did her nightly toilet then came to her bed, rubbing lotion into her hands. 'How're you feeling?' she asked.

'Like I'd have to get better to die,' I replied.

'Those girls do like their bourbon, don't they?'

'That's an interesting robe,' I said, not being able to take my eyes off the huge, hot pink cabbage roses larger than Jane's head.

She laughed. 'Awful, isn't it? But my granddaughter helped me pack, and she bought this for me last Christmas, all by herself, and with her own money. What was I to do?'

'Wear it,' I said.

'Exactly. Now, you try to close your eyes, OK?' She reached for a book on the bedside table between us. 'Oh! Is this Candace's book?'

I dutifully nodded my head, then wished I hadn't.

'I'm going to read for a little bit then turn off the light,' Jane said. 'Will it bother you?'

'No. The only thing bothering me is too much bourbon.'

'Next time mix your own like I do. I pass the bourbon

bottle over it without really putting anything in there. I always drink straight Diet Coke.'

'Now you tell me,' I said and burped loudly.

Jane laughed. 'Close your eyes, E.J. Try to get some sleep.'

I did and I did.

Black Cat Ridge, Texas
Elizabeth, Friday

By her digital clock on the bedside table it was three a.m. when Elizabeth woke up. Her computer was pinging. It took her a moment to figure out what it was, then she remembered Tommy and the horrible things he'd said. She stared at her computer like it was a cobra about to strike her heart.

The pinging continued and she finally got up and moved to her desk, lest the noise wake up the rest of the family. She turned on her monitor and saw the instant message.

T_Tom37:	E, u there?
Skywatcher75:	What do u want?
T_Tom37:	Sorry if I scared u
Skywatcher75:	U didn't scare me – just pissed me off!
T_Tom37:	Didn't want 2 do that either
Skywatcher75:	I don't want 2 talk 2 u n-e-more, Tommy, or whatever ur name is
T_Tom37:	Bessie, ur n danger

The only danger Elizabeth felt she was in at the moment was from flying glass when she punched in her computer monitor. God, what was he up to?

T_Tom37:	Do u want me to prove I'm Aldon?
Skywatcher75:	Yeah, u do that
T_Tom37:	Our parents were Roy and Terry Lester and our older sister's name was Monique

Elizabeth felt her stomach turn over, but wrote:

Skywatcher75:	U could find that out n-e-place. Big deal

T_Tom37:   U have a mole on ur R hip, shaped
                      like a star

Elizabeth felt the bile rise. Not many people knew that. Her
mom, Megan . . . Oh yeah, and anybody in any gym class
she'd ever taken! Again, big deal.

Skywatcher75:   So u no some-1 I took gym w/, huh?
T_Tom37:   What do I have 2 do 2 prove I'm
                      Aldon?
Skywatcher75:   B dead

Elizabeth wrote those words, then turned off the monitor and
the computer at the box. No more pinging in the middle of
the night, thank you very much.

Austin, Texas
E.J., Friday
I'm not sure what woke me up. The bedside clock said four
sixteen a.m. The bed next to mine was empty. I sat up and
looked at the closed door of the bathroom. There was no light
shining from underneath. I turned on the light and got up,
checking the bathroom. It was empty. That's when I noticed
the deadbolt latch on the hotel room door was sticking out,
keeping the door from shutting all the way. Jane must have
gone to the vending machines or the ice machines, I thought,
and left the door as it was. I went back into the bathroom,
used the facilities, washing my face and brushing my teeth,
something I'd neglected to do in my drunken stupor of the
night before, and came back into the bedroom. Jane still had
not returned.

I opened the hotel room door and looked down the hall in
both directions. To the right I could see the outline of the
alcove that housed the vending machines and ice machine.
No sounds of activity were coming from there. To the left
were the elevators and the stairwell. The elevators were quiet,
as they should be at four in the morning. However, something
was sticking out of the door to the stairwell. After a quick
debate, I left the deadbolt latch sticking out of the door to
keep it open, and gingerly headed down the hall in my panties
and T-shirt. The closer I got to the door, the sicker my stomach

felt. The object stuck in the door was fabric – fabric printed with large, hot pink cabbage roses.

I opened the stairwell door, stepping over Jane's robe, and walked out to the landing, calling Jane's name. There was no answer. The hotel, as I mentioned, was very old. The stairwell was one of the old fashioned kind that spiraled down. You could look over the railing and up, and see the stairs of the floors above you; you could look over the railing and down and see to the bottom floor. I did both. Unfortunately the bottom floor wasn't empty. The tiny round figure of Jane Dawson lay in a broken heap, blood pooled around her head.

As you know, nine years ago, when my daughter Bessie – Elizabeth – was four years old, she lived in the house next door to ours with her birth parents, Roy and Terry Lester, and her big brother Aldon and big sister Monique. Monique was sixteen and our babysitter; Aldon, at ten, was older than my son Graham but still his favorite playmate, someone he looked up to and idolized. Terry and I were best friends, as only women could be: we knew all there was to know about each other, up to and including our sex lives, both before and after our husbands. Willis and Roy were best friends as only men could be: they fished together and discussed sports and lawn care. One night someone broke into their home, for reasons so unfathomable as to be unspeakable, and killed almost the entire family. Only Terry, falling on her youngest child as she died, kept Bessie from being killed along with the rest of her family.

I found them. It was an experience forever engraved on my psyche. Something, even after nine years, that will wake me up in the middle of the night in a cold sweat. The only thing good to come out of that is my daughter Elizabeth. She's the spitting image of Terry. Sometimes when I look at Elizabeth now, at her mass of curly, dark-brown hair, her big cocker spaniel brown eyes, the freckles across the bridge of her nose, it breaks my heart.

I kept a lot of Terry's things in storage for Elizabeth, and last summer when we moved the girls to separate bedrooms, Bes— sorry, Elizabeth and I went to the storage unit where I keep Terry's stuff, to pick out anything she wanted for her new room. She is definitely her mother's daughter. She saw the silk and bejeweled material Terry had used for drapes and they became swags for her mother's four-poster bed. Shortly after they married, Roy went to work for an oil company stationed in the Middle East. The vases and rugs and other things Terry picked up there were right up Elizabeth's alley. Now, when I walk in her room, sometimes I see her lounging on her bed, books and papers spread around her, surrounded by all Terry's things, wire-rim glasses perched on the end of her nose, and my heart breaks and soars at the same time. Funny thing, that old heart.

I'd only met Jane Dawson in person that day, but seeing her at the bottom of that staircase, her life's blood spilling out of her on to the concrete floor, I felt a lot like I did when I found Terry's bloody, broken body all those years ago: profound horror, sadness and anger. There was no way little Jane Dawson had fallen over the banister to her death: her center of gravity was too low for that. She had been pushed. There was no doubt in my mind. Someone had snuffed out the life of this endearing, funny, loving, spitfire of a woman, and no one, no one, had the right to do that.

I rushed back to my room on finding her, grabbed my cellphone and returned to the stairwell. I called the front desk and the police as I rushed down the five flights of stairs to where Jane's body lay. That had been several hours ago. I'd been allowed to go back to my room, once the authorities got there, to put on pants, but I was back now, sitting on the second-floor landing, watching the professionals do their job. I didn't want to think how many times I'd seen this take place. Too many. Way, way too many times.

'Mrs Pugh?' a male voice asked.

I looked up from where I'd been studying the tiles of the stairs to see a large African American man with a shaved head, wearing blue jeans, a coral Polo shirt and a navy blue APD windbreaker. He held out his shield and badge. It said 'Eric Washington, Detective Second Grade.'

I nodded my head. 'Detective Washington,' I said.

He sat down beside me on the landing. 'Sorry about your friend,' he said.

'Thank you,' I said, still on autopilot.

'Wanna tell me what happened?'

So I did; starting with drinks in Mary's room, and ending with the deadbolt lock and finding the cabbage rose bathrobe stuck in the stairwell door.

'Why do you think she left the room?' he asked.

I shook my head. 'I have no idea.'

'You didn't hear anything? Like a knock on your door, something like that?' Again I shook my head. 'No. Nothing. Like I said, I had a little too much to drink.'

'Enough to follow her out the door and down the hall, maybe bump into her as she stood by the railing?'

When his words got through my numb head, I just stared at him for a full minute, then said, 'You think I killed her?' He didn't say anything, just sat there staring at me. 'Why would I?'

'I don't know,' he said. 'Why would you?'

I almost wanted to laugh, but knew that would be inappropriate. Instead I stood up. 'Look, I told you all I know about this. As far as me being a suspect, I suggest you call Elena Luna at the Codderville P.D. She can vouch for me.'

Luna was a detective on the Codderville force and we had met when Elizabeth's birth family had been murdered. We took an instant dislike to each other – she thought I was a meddlesome bitch and I thought she was just a little stupider than a bag of rocks. We were both wrong. Now, after having been involved together in several murder cases, and with Luna having lived next door in Terry and Roy's old house for the past eight years, we have a grudging respect for each other and an on-again off-again friendship.

I started to walk off when Detective Washington said, 'Eddie Luna's wife?'

I swung around. 'You know Eddie?'

'Hell, I served with him in the Gulf War. I was with him the night he got in trouble. How's he doing? How's Elena and their kid?'

I grinned at him. 'Two kids now. She was pregnant when he got sent away. But actually, he gets out next year. Their oldest is graduating from college next year and the youngest is finishing his sophomore year, but he's talking about joining the service.'

'Yeah, well I heard she went to work as a cop for some small town. Didn't know which one. How's she doing?'

'She's a detective like you. She and the boys take two weeks off every year and go to Leavenworth for vacation.'

'Hell, Eddie was a hothead but a good guy. Always felt he got the shaft. That asshole officer hit him first. Wasn't Eddie's fault the guy fell wrong and broke his neck.' Washington shook his head. 'I was his sergeant. I was gonna testify for him at the court martial, but they shipped me out before I had a chance to. Always thought that was a little fishy. That's why I didn't re-up. Felt it was time to get the hell out.'

'He's kept his nose clean in Leavenworth. All he thinks about now is getting out and coming home to Elena and the boys.'

'Man, I'm glad to hear that. What's Elena's number? I'm gonna give her a call.' He grinned at me. 'Gotta check you out, Mrs Pugh.'

I gave him the number and made my way up the stairs to my room, reality slamming hard on my shoulders with each step. I needed to make some phone calls. In-house calls this time.

She's the second person I call, right after Willis. 'Hello?' she says upon answering her phone.

'Jane? It's E.J. . . .'

'Well, hey, girl—'

'Sit down!' I say as I myself sit down. Then jump back up. I'm too excited to figure out what to do with myself.

'What's wrong?' Jane asks, concern in her voice.

'I've been nominated for a Lady!' I practically shout.

A high screeching noise comes over the wire. Then: 'Oh my God! Oh my God! E.J.! Well, it's about damn time! Best best?' she asks.

'Yep,' I answer. The categories are Best First Novel, Best Short Story and Best Novel of the Year. I was up for Best Novel of the Year – or, simply, best best.

'So I guess this has made the decision for you! You are coming to the convention!' she says.

'If it harelips Texas!' I say.

'Oh, my God! I'm so excited! You have to dress up, E.J.! Something fancy. Romance writers like to look the part, you know.'

'I don't have anything fancy,' I say.
Jane sighs. 'Then go buy something!'
I think about it. 'Yes. Yes, I can do that.'
'I'll get us a room, we'll be roommates!' Jane says. 'We are going to have so much fun, it's going to be illegal!'

Mary and Lydia sat on Jane's bed, Mary bent at the waist, sobbing quietly. Lydia had her arm around Mary's shoulder and whispered soothing things in her ear. Jerome sat in one of the two chairs at the small table by the window, looking all of his eighty-something years, his shoulders slumped, his eyes downcast. Candace sat next to me on my bed, hands clasped in her lap, eyes on the floor, while Hal paced the room, mumbling to himself.

It had not been an easy thing, telling these people that Jane had been killed. Most of them had known her for years, had loved her for years. Candace and I were the odd ones out, having just met her, but I for one felt I'd known her, if not long, at least well.

'She probably just fell?' Lydia said, looking up at me with a tear-streaked face.

I shook my head. 'I don't see how,' I said softly.

'But no one in their right mind would want to kill Jane!' Mary wailed, looking up for the first time since I'd told them the news.

'Anyone who would kill another human being is obviously *not* in their right mind,' Jerome said from his seat by the window.

Mary stood up abruptly, her whole body shaking. 'It had to be Angela!' she said. 'She was looking for her all day and all night! Said she had to talk to her about something important . . .'

'She says that to everybody, Mary,' Lydia said, reaching for Mary's arm.

Mary pulled her arm away from Lydia. 'You heard the snide remarks she made about Jane at the dinner last night! She was out to get her!'

I stood up and approached Mary. 'We have to let the police sort this out,' I said. I touched her tentatively on the arm. 'When they interview us, you can tell them what you think about Angela.'

'You bet your ass I will!' Mary said, then burst into a new bout of sobbing. Lydia pulled her down to the bed and took her in her arms, Mary's head resting against Lydia's ample bosom as she sobbed.

All I wanted at the moment was to get these people out of my room. I needed time to think and, yes, time to go through Jane's things before the police did. I wanted to know if there was anything in this room that could tell me a reason why, or point a finger in the right direction. But most of all I wanted to call Willis. I wanted to talk to someone I loved.

As if reading my mind, Lydia Michaels stood up, propping Mary up with an arm around her waist. 'I think I'll take Mary to her room,' she said, and quietly led the sobbing woman out the door.

Jerome stood up from his seat by the window. 'I think I'll take my leave as well,' he said.

Hal put his arm around the older man's shoulders. 'Buy you a drink, buddy,' he said.

'Make it a double,' Jerome said as they walked out the door.

That left just Candace and myself. We still sat side by side on my bed. She gingerly touched my hand. 'I'm so sorry you had to find her that way, E.J.,' she said.

I nodded my head, not trusting myself to speak at the moment. Mary's sobbing seemed to be contagious and I was having a hard time controlling the tears pooling behind my eyes.

She stood up. 'Look, if there's anything I can do . . .' Her voice trailed off and she looked at the floor. 'I can't think what, but if you need anything . . .'

I stood and hugged her and she hugged me back. 'Thanks,' I managed to get out.

She smiled wanly and left the room, leaving me alone in a hotel room filled to the brim with a tiny, round ghost.

Four

Her cellphone rang as she was leaving fourth period English, heading for her geology class. She didn't recognize the number. Flipping it open she said, 'Hello?'

'Bessie, it's me, Aldon.'

Elizabeth stopped dead in the hall. The girl behind her bumped into her, said, 'Retard!' and kept going. Elizabeth barely noticed her.

'How did you get this number?' she asked.

'That's not important,' he said. 'What's important is that you're in danger. I need you to meet me—'

'This stopped being funny a long time ago, Tommy, or whoever you are. Don't call me, don't email me, don't IM me. If I hear from you again, I'm calling the po—'

'Bessie, whatever you do, don't call the police! They're in on it. At least that friend of E.J.'s is – that Elena Luna. She and E.J. were both in on this from the beginning—'

'In on what?' Elizabeth said, stopping traffic around her. She'd spoken louder than she intended. Seeing kids staring at her, she moved closer to the lockers that lined the hallways and spoke more softly into the phone. 'What are you talking about?'

'You didn't buy all that bullshit about the preacher and his family, did you? This goes high, Bessie. Way high. You know Dad worked for the gaming commission, right? At the beginning, when they were setting it up. Who do you think was the gaming commissioner back then? J. Patrick Reynolds, that's who. You know who he is now? Railroad commissioner, Bessie! Do you know what that means? That makes this guy the most powerful man in Texas, next to the governor. Do you know what the railroad commissioner does, Bessie? He's in charge of transportation, sure, but he's also in charge of oil and gas. What's the biggest cash crop in Texas, Bessie? Oil and gas. And where do you think he'd be right now if Dad had been able to get the information he had to the right people? In prison, that's where. No railroad commission, no millions of dollars to control – and take. Like he took from the gaming commission. And none of this came out back then, did it? No, it was all swept under the rug. By who? By your precious E.J., that's who. Along with her pal the police detective. I've been in hiding for nine years, but it's time I came out. I want to see you! I want what's left of my family back, Bessie! You're all I have! But once E.J. and Willis and that Luna woman find out I'm back, we're both in danger. Do you think they'd let you live now that you know what's really going on?'

'Go away!' Elizabeth hissed into the phone. 'You're insane!'

'No, Bessie, I've finally come to my senses. I've been hiding too long—'

'OK, if you're Aldon, then who did we bury nine years ago?' Elizabeth demanded.

'I hate to think who it might have been,' Aldon said in a hushed voice. 'Some poor kid, a runaway maybe. They killed him and put him in my place.'

'My God, you sound like a bad made-for-TV movie!' Elizabeth tried attempting a laugh. It came out sounding slightly deranged to her own ears.

'I need you to meet me, Bessie—'

'Stop calling me that! I haven't been Bessie in years! My name is Elizabeth!' she said.

'You'll always be Bessie to me,' the voice said. 'My baby sister.'

Elizabeth hung up, turning the phone off.

Austin, Texas
E.J., Friday

'Oh, baby, I'm so sorry,' Willis said after I told him what happened. 'Are you all right?'

'No,' I said, my voice breaking. 'Not really.'

'You want me to come there? I can get Mama to come stay with the kids.'

It was tempting. I consider myself a liberated woman, someone who is able to stand on her own two feet and do what has to be done. But the thought of having Willis here, to spoon with him in my queen-sized bed, to have him hold me and tell me everything was going to be all right, was almost more than I could bear. But I knew what he'd say when I started going through Jane's stuff, when I started asking questions, when I tried to find out what had happened. After the things we'd been through, the near misses and the tragedies, and the danger to us and the ones we loved, Willis was not big on what he considered my 'snooping into things that were none of your business'.

But he would be wrong. Again. This *was* my business. She was my friend and, damnit, I found her. I was the one who saw that broken little body lying on the cold, concrete floor. I was the one who had to call the police. I was the one who had to tell her friends. It *was* my business. So I said, 'No, honey. I appreciate the offer, but you need to stay with the kids. And you've got that meeting today.'

'I can rearrange my schedule—'

'That's OK. I'll be all right,' I said.

There was a small silence on the other end of the line. 'E.J., you're not going to go sticking your nose into something that's none of your business, are you?'

'How can it be none of my business when I'm a suspect?' I responded.

'Jesus! I knew it! I think you should really consider why you're doing this,' he said, his voice icy. 'Because we both know you're not a viable suspect. Are you doing this because Jane, a woman you didn't know that well, was your friend, or are you doing this because you like the excitement? Are you doing this because you're an adrenalin junkie who hasn't had a fix in seven or eight years?'

I couldn't believe he said that. I sat there on my queen-sized bed, stunned that my husband had just accused me of such a thing. Finally, I said, 'I'll talk to you later,' and hung up on him.

And felt very, very alone.

Black Cat Ridge, Texas
Elizabeth, Friday
It was Friday afternoon and the girls were home alone again, Dad still at work,

Mom still at her convention. Elizabeth had gone straight to
her room. She'd been in there less than five minutes when
there came a knock on the door.

'Who is it?' she called.

'Who do you think it is?' Megan said, coming in without
permission.

'I want to be alone right now—'

'Uh uh,' Megan said, flopping down on Elizabeth's bed.
'You're going to tell me what's going on. Don't deny that
something is, because you haven't been riding my ass in two
days, and that's just not you. So I know something's up and
you're going to tell me what it is.'

'Nothing's up—' Elizabeth started.

Megan rolled on to her stomach and stared up at her sister
who sat cross-legged on the bed. 'Tell me.'

Elizabeth began to cry.

Austin, Texas
E.J., Friday
The knock on the door came at a bad time. I'd just found a
sheaf of papers in Jane's briefcase and was perusing them.
One was a letter from her agent saying her long time publishing
house, Fullerton Press, had dropped her. Another was a letter
from her editor at Fullerton, obviously answering a letter from
Jane as to the reason for the non-renewal of her contract. In
essence, through all the compliments and flowery prose, it
said sales had not been as expected. Also in the stack were
print-outs of emails, one of which claimed that her latest manuscript had been plagiarized. The sender was only identified
as romance365.

I stuffed all the papers under my pillow and went to open
the door. It was Detective Washington.

'Detective,' I said, opening the door wide to allow him in.
He came in and took a chair at the table where Jerome had
been sitting earlier.

'Talked to Elena,' he said by way of greeting.

'Good,' I said, sitting down on Jane's bed, the closest bed
to the table. 'I hope she vouched for me.'

'Well, yes and no,' he said, then grinned. 'She said you
probably didn't kill anybody, but that you're a real pain in the
ass.'

'Her ass is big enough to take it,' I said, then immediately regretted the catty remark. Although Luna's ass *is* quite large.

'She said I needed to watch out or you'd try to do my job for me,' he said, the grin now gone.

'I would never interfere with a police investigation,' I said, indignant at the very thought.

'Um hum,' he said, eyeing Jane's open suitcase.

'It was already like that!' I said. 'Jane was only half unpacked.'

'Um hum,' he said, then reached in his pocket and pulled out a paper. 'Search warrant,' he said. 'Need you to vacate the premises for a little bit, Miz Pugh.'

Oh, shit, I thought, thinking of the sheaf of papers under my pillow. No way were they going to miss that. So I got up and walked to my bed, taking the papers out from under the pillow.

'I didn't know who was at the door, so I hid these for safe keeping,' I said, handing the papers to Detective Washington.

'Um hum,' he said. 'Good thinking.'

Why did I think that sounded a bit like sarcasm?

Detective Washington stood up, placing the sheaf of papers on the table. 'Thank you for safe-keeping what could be important evidence, Miz Pugh,' he said, again with that little tinge of sarcasm in his voice. 'I'll have to ask you to leave now so my people can go over the room.'

'Have you contacted Jane's family?' I asked.

'Goodbye, Miz Pugh,' he said, herding me towards the door.

'I just wondered if I should call—'

'Taken care of,' he said, as the door shut in my face.

'Sometimes I think marriage and kids are a conspiracy to keep women down,' I say. I'm in my office on a Thursday morning. The kids are in school, Willis is at work, the animals have been fed and all's right with the world – more or less.

'Absolutely!' Jane says. 'When I was growing up there were four things you could aspire to be: a teacher, a nurse, a secretary, or a mommy. And when you think about it, they're all the same thing. A teacher's just a mommy with a lot more kids, a nurse is a mommy with lots of sick kids of different ages, a secretary has to deal with the biggest kids there are – usually men! Thank God our daughters have choices now!

I've told my daughter since the day she was born: "you can do anything"!'

'So what does she do?' I ask – always the straight woman.

'Hum, well, Miranda's a mommy. My, didn't I do a great job!'

'Actually, yes you did,' I say. 'You didn't mention that she's a drug addict, an alcoholic, a sex addict or a gambler. So, yeah, Jane, you did all right!'

Jane laughed. 'Oh, so now we're talking about my son!'

'I know that's not true!' I say.

Jane sighs. 'No, it's not, but it was a good line. I think I'll write it down.'

Black Cat Ridge, Texas
Elizabeth, Friday

'So who is this guy?' Megan demanded.

'I don't know! I thought he was just a nice guy I met, but then he started this whole Aldon business—'

'Aldon?' Megan said, taken aback. 'Like your brother Aldon?'

Elizabeth simply nodded her head. Megan asked. 'What did he say about Aldon?'

Elizabeth took a deep breath and finally said, 'That he's him. That he's Aldon.'

'That who's Aldon? Tommy?'

'Yes,' Elizabeth answered.

'Aldon's dead, Liz,' Megan said quietly.

'Yes, I know,' Elizabeth said.

Megan tilted her head, looking at her sister. 'You're not sure?'

'What if . . .' Elizabeth started, then stopped.

'What if Aldon is still alive? Is that what you mean?' Megan asked.

Elizabeth nodded.

'Then whose grave is it we go visit every year?' Megan demanded.

'He said it was somebody they killed and put in his place,' Elizabeth said.

'Somebody *who* killed?' Megan asked.

Elizabeth shrugged her shoulders.

'Who did he say, Liz?' Megan demanded.

'Mom and Mrs Luna,' Elizabeth said quietly. 'And Dad, I think.'

Megan let out a heavy breath, her cheeks puffing up with the effort. 'Wow, that's pretty heavy stuff,' she said.

Elizabeth nodded, her head bent, staring at the moon and stars on the comforter that covered her bed. Megan reached out and lifted her sister's head to stare into her eyes.

'And you believed him?' she asked.

Elizabeth looked back at Megan, and shook her head. 'No, not really. I know that Mom and Dad, I mean—'

'Let me ask you something, Liz,' Megan said, her hand still on her sister's face. 'Which makes more sense? That Mom and Dad, along with Mrs Luna, conspired to kill your entire family and, failing to get Aldon, killed some poor runaway and put him in Aldon's place? Or that this asshole you met *on-line* is bullshitting you?'

Tears streamed down Elizabeth's face. 'Bullshit,' she said.

'Damn straight,' said Megan. 'Tell me exactly what he told you.'

So Elizabeth did, detailing the stuff about J. Patrick Reynolds and the gaming commission and the railroad commission, and everything else Tommy/Aldon had said.

Megan moved to the computer and turned it on.

'What are you doing?' Elizabeth demanded.

'Don't worry. If he messages you, I'll ignore him. I just want to check out his story,' Megan said, finding a link to Texas government. Sure enough, J. Patrick Reynolds was the Texas Railroad Commissioner, former Texas Gaming Commissioner. He had been instrumental in setting up the gaming commission and getting horseracing started in Texas. He was a Republican (surprise, surprise, thought Megan), and was married with two children, one a son in high school, the other a daughter in college. His wife was a homemaker and he had formerly belonged to the Knights of Columbus, the Kiwanas, the Galveston Chamber of Commerce, and was past president of the Galveston JCs. Before becoming gaming commissioner, he had owned an insurance agency in Galveston and had won the prestigious Canary Award from the American Independent Insurance Agency Association. According to Wytopia, J. Patrick was lily white and squeaky clean.

Megan checked all the other listings for Reynolds on Google and found only listings for newspaper articles mentioning him, speeches given by him and speeches given about him by his buddies. As far as Google could tell her, J. Patrick Reynolds was fiscally, socially, morally and personally conservative.

She read all this to Elizabeth.

'OK,' Elizabeth said, 'what does any of that mean?'

'Absolutely nothing,' Megan answered. 'There wouldn't be any dirt here, and if the guy was involved in this big conspiracy nine years ago, I doubt it would be mentioned on Google.'

'So what do I do?' Elizabeth asked.

'You mean what do *we* do, right?' Megan said.

'I don't want you involved in this, Meg,' Elizabeth said.

'Forget that noise. I'm involved. Where you go, I go. Got that?'

Elizabeth started crying again. Megan left the desk chair and sat on the bed next to her sister. Putting her arm around the smaller girl's shoulders, she said, 'If you don't stop the blubbering, I'm going to smack you.'

Austin, Texas
E.J., Friday

I wandered down to the bar and found Jerome, Hal and Candace at a table by themselves. I joined them. The bar, although crowded, was a lot less noisy this morning. Word had obviously spread. Jerome half stood and pulled a chair out for me next to him. I sat, feeling like it had been a hundred years since I'd done so.

'Have you heard anything?' Hal asked.

'The police are in my room now with a search warrant. Going through Jane's things.' After a pause, I added, 'And mine too, I suppose.'

Candace patted my hand. 'They'll find out who did this,' she said.

'Any word on whether the convention's going to be cancelled?' I asked.

'Ha!' Jerome said. 'Not bloody likely.'

'Angela told me there will be a moment of silence for Jane at the banquet tomorrow night,' Candace said.

'A "moment of silence"?' I said. 'That's it?'

Candace shrugged. 'We're talking about Angela here, E.J. I can't see her wearing a black armband over this.'

'No, neither can I,' Jerome said. 'But she *will* do more than a bloody "moment of silence"!' he said, standing so quickly he knocked his chair over. We all stared as Jerome marched off in a huff, on the look-out for the Beast. For half a moment I almost felt sorry for her. Almost.

Cyrus Sullivan, who had been leaning against the bar, took that moment to come to our table. Righting Jerome's fallen chair, Cyrus sat down gingerly. 'Where's he off to in such a rush?' he asked.

'He had some business to take care of,' Hal said.

Looking at us all in turn, Cyrus asked, 'Is it true? About Jane, I mean. Is she really dead?'

'Yeah, she's really dead,' Hal answered.

'What happened?' Cyrus asked, stretching out the 'happened' like a whiny child.

Hal turned to me. 'We don't know,' I said. 'We'll have to wait for the police to tell us.'

'But you found her, right?' Cyrus said. 'I mean, that's what everyone's saying.'

'I'd really rather not talk about it,' I said stiffly.

'Oh, you poor dear!' Cyrus said, jumping up from his chair and rushing around the table to my chair, putting his skinny little arms around me. 'Let Cyrus hold you!' he said.

I was beginning to understand Jerome's dislike of the little man. Gingerly removing his arms from my breast region, I said, 'Thank you, Cyrus. But I'm OK.'

'How can you be?' he cried, wrapping his arms around me again. 'What an awful experience for you! Tell Uncle Cyrus all about it!'

I pushed my chair away from the table, scooting Cyrus away as I did so and stood up. We were joined at that moment by Lydia Michaels, looking wan, wearing no make-up, her hair disheveled, wearing stretch pants and a T-shirt. She sat down in Jerome's vacated chair.

'Oh, my!' Cyrus said, looking at Lydia. 'My dear, I've never seen you look so bad!'

Lydia sent him a look that should have caused the little man to burst into flames. Unfortunately, it only inflamed his desire to 'help'. He went to Lydia and tried putting his arms around her. She took one skinny little arm and deftly twisted it behind Cyrus's back. 'Not now,' she said softly.

With his arm still bent behind him, and Lydia still holding it in that position, Cyrus said, 'Well, I know you people need your privacy. I'm just going to head back to the bar.' Lydia let go of his arm and Cyrus scooted off.

'You know old people have brittle bones, Lydia,' Hal said. 'You're lucky you didn't snap off his arm.'

'No, Hal, *he's* lucky I didn't,' she said.

'How's Mary?' I asked.

'Sleeping,' she said. 'I gave her one of my sleeping pills. I think she needed it.'

'Maybe you should do the same,' Candace said, her voice soft.

Lydia shook her head. 'No, I want to be wide awake for this. I want to find out who did this and I want twenty minutes alone with them. Just me and my Louisville slugger.'

I took Lydia's hand. 'I'm so sorry, Lydia,' I said.

She patted my hand and said, 'I met Jane twenty years ago. We were both novices. First books out and it was in Omaha. At this same convention. I was rooming with a woman whose name I don't even remember, and Jane was rooming with Mary. Mary was already well into the biz – not a queen yet, but definitely a princess. I ran into Jane in the ladies' room outside the book room. This was twenty years ago, like I said, and Jane couldn't have weighed more than a hundred pounds then. I saw this little person trying to wash her hands, and I thought it was a child. So I went over to help her.' Lydia laughed. 'Boy, did she bite my head off! She got so nasty I finally said, "It's not my fault you're so damn short!"' Again she laughed. 'Jane just stared at me for at least a minute, then she said, "Girl, you got a mouth on you!" in this thick Southern accent.' In an aside, she said, 'She hadn't been out of Mississippi long at that point. Hadn't been working on her accent. Then she said, "I like that in a friend," then held her hand out and introduced herself. We were thick as thieves the entire convention after that.' She sighed. 'When I got my second divorce, Jane's the first person I called. She took me in, gave me her spare room for a month. Fed me, stayed up with me until all hours of the night.' Tears streaked Lydia's face.

Jerome came back to the table. 'It's taken care of,' he said, pulling a chair from another table up to ours.

'What did you do?' Candace asked, her blue eyes wide in her beautiful face.

'I made a few suggestions,' Jerome said, his demeanor indicating that was the end of the discussion. 'Lydia, dear, how are you holding up?'

She shrugged. 'OK,' she said.

'Lydia was just telling us how she met Jane,' I told Jerome.

He grinned. 'Ah, yes, the bathroom incident. My first meeting with her wasn't as earth shattering, but I do remember it well,' he said. 'She was in the bar, of course,' he said, and we all laughed, 'sitting at a table with Lydia and Mary. I had known Mary for a few years and had signed with Lydia at a bookstore in . . . where was that, dear?' he asked.

'Pittsburgh,' she said.

'Ah, yes, Pittsburgh,' he said. 'And here they were sitting with the most adorable woman I'd ever seen. I swear she needed a booster chair. She looked like a miniature Sophia Loren, though. Black hair, huge dark eyes, beautiful pouty lips. And those breasts!'

'Jerry!' Lydia said.

'My dear, no straight man, or gay man, for that matter, ever looked at Jane in those days without seeing those breasts first. They might as well have been outlined in neon,' he said.

Hal shook his head. 'That was before my time,' he said. 'When I met her she'd already gained the weight.'

'It was her fifth child, my godson, by the way, that finally did her in. She had to have a hysterectomy and then couldn't get the weight off. Changed her metabolism,' Lydia said.

'But even so,' Jerome went on, 'her mouth was mightier than even those breasts. When she spoke I knew I'd be in love with her forever.'

Lydia laughed. 'I remember! She took one look at you after we told her you were Jasmine West, and she said, "Well, hell, I got a pee-paw younger'n you!"'

Jerome laughed. 'Yes, and it took me the entire convention to find out what a pee-paw was!'

Candace's big blue eyes were saucers. Finally she said, 'I give. What's a pee-paw?'

'Grandpa,' Lydia and Jerome said in unison.

'Oh!' Candace said. She laughed. 'How insulting!'

'I think pee-paws start younger,' I told Jerome and everyone laughed.

I guess it was how the room got even quieter, and how everyone in it stared at our table that made us remember why we were there talking about Jane. It can only be an old-fashioned wake if everyone's in on it.

Black Cat Ridge, Texas
Elizabeth, Friday

Megan sat at the computer, Elizabeth standing behind her, staring at the screen. They'd already emailed Tommy/Aldon and were waiting for a message. The computer had just pinged, letting them know he'd finally answered. Elizabeth had been too nervous to respond, so Megan had taken over.

T_Tom37:	E, u there?
Skywatcher75:	I'm here, A
T_Tom37:	So u B-lieve me?
Skywatcher75:	Not sure
T_Tom37:	What can I do 2 help?
Skywatcher75:	B patient w/ me – this is all so confusing
T_Tom37:	I'm sorry. I no it is – if we met n person I could x-plain it better
Skywatcher75:	I'm not sure about that
T_Tom37:	I understand. This is scary 4 u. Just no I love u, little sister

'God, this guy really lays it on thick, doesn't he?' Megan said to Elizabeth.

'But what if he is? Aldon, I mean?' Elizabeth said.

Megan turned to her. 'How can he possibly be Aldon, Liz? Do you really think Mom and Mrs Luna are in on some big conspiracy?'

'No, of course not, it's just . . .' Elizabeth started, but the computer pinged again.

T_Tom37:	Bessie, u there?
Skywatcher75:	Sorry – just thinking about what u said

T_Tom37:	I'm glad. We can meet where ever u want, whenever u want. It's up to u

'Ask him where he's been,' Elizabeth said.

Skywatcher75:	Where hav u ben 4 all these yrs?
T_Tom37:	I was hurt when it happened, but some people got me out of the house. They new what was going on and protected me. They've raised me as their own

'Coyotes, maybe?' Megan asked Elizabeth. 'I swear this is total Lifetime movie.'

'Does sound familiar, doesn't it?' Elizabeth said.

Skywatcher75:	I want 2 see u. Do u hav a pic?
T_Tom37:	Downlding now

A picture began to fill the screen. Elizabeth sat down hard on the bed behind her. 'Oh, my God,' she said. 'It's Aldon.'

The picture was of a man in his late teens, early twenties, with dark hair, fair skin and freckles. He was smiling and had a chipped front tooth.

'I remember when he chipped the tooth,' Elizabeth said softly. 'It was my fault. I was on the top bunk of his bunk bed and I wasn't supposed to be. And I was playing with his baseball bat and he told me to drop it. And I did. Hit him right in the mouth and chipped his first permanent tooth.'

'I wonder how hard it is to get age progression software?' Megan mused.

'What?' Elizabeth asked her, as if coming out of a trance.

'You know, like they use on those shows about missing kids. They show a picture of what they looked like when they went missing, then show a picture of what they'd look like now – even if it's like years later. They call it age progression.'

Irritated, Elizabeth said, 'I know what age progression means.'

'Then why did you ask?' Megan demanded, as irritated as her sister.

'But how can we tell? I mean, if this is real or age progression?' Elizabeth asked.

Megan shrugged. 'I have no idea, but I think it's safe to assume that it's age progression. Isn't that a more likely scenario than the Lifetime version he's spouting?'

Elizabeth sighed. 'Yeah. It is. But why would Tommy or whatever his real name is go to all this trouble?'

Again Megan shrugged. 'No idea. I don't think your average pervert has to try this hard, do you?'

Elizabeth said nothing, just stared at the picture on the screen. Again, the computer pinged and Megan went back to the IM screen.

T_Tom37:	Bessie, u there?
Skywatcher75:	Yes
T_Tom37:	Now do you B-lieve me?

Megan looked at Elizabeth and Elizabeth nodded. 'Say yes,' she said.

Skywatcher75:	Yes
T_Tom37:	Then let's meet
Skywatcher75:	When and where?

Austin, Texas
E.J., Friday

I'd barely been allowed back in my room for five minutes when there was a knock on my door. I should have been able to tell by the aggressiveness of the knock who it was. I opened the door to the vision in brown. A different brown shirt, possibly the same brown stretch pants, and the low heeled, sensible brown shoes.

'What can I do for you, Angela?' I asked, and not in my friendly voice. I wasn't in a friendly mood.

Brushing past me into the room, she said, 'Jane left some things for me here. I need to get them.'

'What things?' I asked, leaving the door open and following the Beast as she paced the room, looking at the surfaces for her 'things'.

'Papers. Business. Hers and mine. Where's her briefcase?' she demanded.

Gleefully I said, 'I believe the police took that with them after they searched the room.'

Angela's pasty complexion turned even paler, a feat I would not have believed possible. How can a dead fish belly look deader? More dead? Whatever. Without a word, the Beast stomped out of my room on her sensible shoes.

One of the things Jerome had managed to accomplish during his discussion with the Beast was to get the panels for the day pushed back. My eight o'clock was now set for ten. I laid down on the bed, knowing I needed to get at least a little sleep before my first panel, which would be in about an hour. I set the alarm clock next to the bed for half an hour, giving me time to wash my face, pee, put on a little make-up and get dressed. Hair was something I'd learned long ago not to worry about. It would do what it would do, and no amount of fussing would change that.

I was just beginning to relax, my eyes closed, when there came the third knock on my door of the morning. Saying an expletive unbecoming to one as ladylike as myself, I got up and went to the door, wrenching it open. Before me stood Candace Macy, her beautiful face made even prettier by red-rimmed eyes and tears. God, I hate women who look good when they cry! I look like a plague victim with splotches all over my face. She was carrying a suitcase and a tote bag over one arm.

'Candace?' I said.

'May I please move in with you?' she said, gulping back tears.

I opened the door and helped her with her bags. 'What happened?' I asked, once I had her sitting on Jane's bed.

'That horrible woman!' she cried.

'Angela,' I said. It wasn't a question.

'I was taking a nap and she came barging in there saying all sorts of hateful things about Jane! Accusing her of plagiarism! Maybella LaRue! Can you imagine? And saying she deserved what she got!' Candace began to sob in earnest. 'I just can't stay in that room with her!'

I moved from my bed to Jane's and put my arm around Candace's shoulders. 'Of course you can stay here,' I said. 'And don't listen to a word that bitch says. I think all this confirms she's a nut case!'

Candace gulped in some oxygen, then said, 'I think I just need to rest for a little while.'

'I was just thinking about a nap myself,' I said, smiling. 'Come on, let's get you tucked in.'

She took off her shoes and jeans, exposing long, firm, tan legs that I would have gladly killed for, and got under the covers. I pulled the covers over her and turned off the light between the two beds. 'Get some sleep,' I said, then crawled into my own bed.

After a very few minutes, I heard Candace's gentle, rhythmic breathing – no snoring from that girl, of course. There was, however, a tiny squeak that escaped from her perfect lips on breathing out that I knew I could find very annoying if I let myself.

And I couldn't sleep. I was wide awake. After a few minutes of lying there listening to Candace squeak, I got up, got my cellphone and went into the bathroom. Laying the Sam's thick white towels down in the bathtub, I crawled in, sans water, and dialed Elena Luna's number at the police station in Codderville. Miracle of miracles, she actually answered her phone.

'Luna,' she said in her brusque way.

'Pugh,' I said, just as brusquely.

'Cute,' she said.

'Willis thinks so,' I said.

'I'm busy. What do you want?'

'My, aren't we bitchy this morning,' I said.

'We're bitchy every morning. I repeat, what do you want?'

'Tell me about Eric Washington,' I said.

'No,' she said.

'Why not?' I demanded.

'Because,' she said, enunciating clearly, 'I do not want you to bother Detective Washington. I want you to stay away from his case and let him do his job. I want you, for once in your miserable life, to leave well enough alone.'

'I swear I won't get in his way,' I said. 'I just want to know who I'm dealing—'

'Ha!' she said. 'You get in everyone's way! That's your style, Pugh. And who you're dealing with is a detective second grade on the Austin police force. We're not talking little Podunk Codderville here, Pugh. Austin is an actual city. Stay out of his way. He *will* arrest your ass if you get in his way. And that's not a joke.'

I sighed. 'Luna, you're so dramatic!' I said. 'Look, this lady who got killed, the victim, was a dear friend of mine—'

'Yeah, right. They're always a "dear friend" of yours, Pugh. Or a relative. Or something. Let me give it to you straight: Washington will not put up with your crap! He *will* arrest you if you get in his way. He doesn't need an amateur messing in his business—'

I couldn't help smiling. 'That means you do, right?' I said.

'Shut up, Pugh. I'm hanging up now. Stay away from Washington, stay away from the case, in fact, come home, stay away from Austin all together.'

'You miss me,' I said.

She hung up.

I called Willis at his office in Codderville. 'Pugh Engineering,' Miss Juanita said. She's Willis's secretary and she's getting close to one hundred by now. She's a friend of Willis's mother and I hired her myself after we had a little trouble with Willis's former secretary.

'Hi, Miss Juanita,' I said. 'It's E.J.'

'Hello, dear,' she said. 'How's the convention?'

Willis obviously hadn't told his mother about Jane's death. If he had, Miss Juanita would have immediately asked, 'Who did it?' Vera, my mother-in-law, and Miss Juanita were the only two people in the world who supported my interest in things lethal. Vera's even helped me on occasion.

'Just fine,' I answered, adding, 'Is Willis around?'

'Just a minute, honey,' she said and switched me to Willis's line.

'Hey, babe,' he said, picking up the phone.

'Hey yourself,' I said. 'How's it going?'

He sighed. 'Graham tried to convince me he had what the girls had earlier this week, but turned out he had a fever of 107?'

'107?' I all but shouted.

'Yeah, which you can only get if you stick the thermometer under a light bulb—'

'Oh,' I said, relieved that my eldest wasn't on his death-bed.

'*And*,' Willis continued, 'he has a history test today that he's not ready for. Add the two together and we have "let's skip Friday".'

'You made him go, didn't you?' I asked.

'Didn't even let him drive. Drove him myself and watched him walk into the school.'

'He could have walked out another door,' I said.

'I didn't think walking him to class and watching him take the test was the way to improve trust issues between the two of us,' he said in that snippy voice he gets sometimes.

I decided to ignore that and check on the girls. Maybe not the best idea.

'Puddin',' he said – this was our eight-year-old mutt – 'took a dump on Elizabeth's outfit she had set out for school the night before. Turns out that is the *only* outfit she had that was good enough to wear to school on a Friday. There were some things in the dryer that she could have worn, if they'd been ironed.'

I opened my mouth to speak, but he beat me to it.

'And, no, I don't iron. She's thirteen. I figure she can learn to iron herself.'

'And how did that work?'

He sighed. 'She burned a hole in the shirt she was ironing.'

'So I take it she's home in bed?' I asked sarcastically.

'No!' he said, indignant. 'Megan loaned her a shirt,' he said. 'Shirt' is male-speak for top, blouse, T-shirt, cami, tank, or anything a female wears on the top half of her body. 'So,' he said, changing the subject, 'how goes the convention?'

I told him about my early morning visitors, up to and including my new roommate.

'Is *she* a looker?' he asked.

'Only if you're into twenty-something blue-eyed blondes with perfect bodies,' I said with disgust.

'Yuck,' he said. 'That sounds awful.'

'Good boy,' I said.

'But you're staying out of this, right?' he said.

I sighed. 'Yes. With this Detective Washington in charge, there's no way I can get involved.'

'Good,' he said. 'I'll have to meet this guy and thank him.'

'You know I could help!' I protested.

'I know you could get yourself into big trouble,' he said. 'You're not in Black Cat Ridge anymore, Dorothy,' he said. 'You're in the big city. You don't know the lay of the land—'

'I spent four years in this town—'

'A hundred years ago,' he said. 'Stay out of it, E.J.'

'Oh, for God's sake,' I said. 'I'm out, OK? There's nothing I can do.'

'Good,' he reiterated. 'I'm glad to hear it.'

'I'm hanging up now,' I said.

'You're such a baby,' he said and laughed.

'And you're a spoilsport,' I said and hung up.

I lay in my erstwhile bed, thinking. And all I could think about was Jane – her friends and family, all those people who were worse off because she was no longer in this world. And me. I was worse off for not having her in my world. Our friendship was just in the beginning stages, really, but I'd felt as if it would become something special, something I hadn't had since Terry's death. I shook myself, bumping an elbow on the hard porcelain of the tub. Don't think about it that way, I told myself. Don't think about Jane, the person. Think about the murder. It's a puzzle. Think about that.

Why had Jane left our room? It was the middle of the night; what on earth could have gotten her out of bed? Maybe she had gone to the vending machine, and someone, some serial killer stalking hotel corridors, had found her. Wrong place at the wrong time. But it didn't feel that way. Somehow, it felt personal. And why the stairwell? Had she gone in there of her own accord? Then why was her robe stuck in the door, while she was so far below on the concrete floor?

Then I remembered: I'd left the robe where it was when I went out on the landing and found Jane. So when I went back to my room to call for assistance, the robe had still been there. Been there *blocking the door*. Later, when I was dismissed by Washington and had gone back to my room, again going through the door from the stairwell to the hall, it had been propped open by the police. Did the stairwell door automatically lock? Had Jane used her robe to keep the door from locking? Why else would she have taken it off? Her gown was still on. There didn't appear to be a sexual aspect to this crime, and no one had said anything otherwise. Like Detective Washington. Or would he have? Would he tell me anything?

I wrangled myself out of the tub and quietly went through our room to the corridor outside, leaving the deadbolt out to keep our door from locking. Then I walked down the hall to the stairway door and opened it. Checking the knob on the other side confirmed my suspicions. It indeed locked automatically.

Back in the tub, I considered what I'd found out. OK, so Jane took off her robe to keep the door from the hallway to the stairwell from automatically locking. Fine. Where did that get me? Was she going downstairs for some reason? We were on the third floor. Was one of our bunch on the second floor? The fourth floor? Yes, Mary's and Lydia's rooms were on the fourth floor. Jerome, I believed, was on the second floor. Hal and his obnoxious roommate, Cyrus Sullivan, were on the same floor as my room. But what did any of *that* mean? She met Mary or Lydia or Jerome or Hal in secret in the stairwell and for some unfathomable reason one of them pushed her over?

I'll admit I barely knew any of these people, but it still seemed highly unlikely. I put my head down on my pillow, nestled into the still almost fluffy towels of the Sam, and fell asleep.

Five

Black Cat Ridge, Texas
Elizabeth, Friday

'You don't believe it's Aldon, do you?' Megan asked.

'Of course not,' Elizabeth said.

'I mean, you can't for a moment think Mom and Dad had anything to do with what happened to your family!' Megan said.

'Let's just drop it,' Elizabeth said, getting off the bed and turning the computer off at the box. 'No more IMs right now, thank you,' she said.

Megan stared at her sister. 'Mom and Dad loved your parents,' she said. 'We were all one big extended family, Mom said.'

'Let's drop it, Meg,' Elizabeth said.

Megan stood up from the computer chair, looking hard at her sister. 'If you believe any of this, Liz—'

'No,' Elizabeth said, turning to Megan and staring hard at her. 'I don't believe it.'

Megan nodded her head slowly. 'OK, then. Well, we're on for tomorrow night, right?'

Elizabeth nodded. 'Sure,' she said.

Megan left her room and Elizabeth laid down on the bed, curled into a fetal position. There's no way it's Aldon, she told herself. No way in hell. Aldon's dead. My mom and dad are dead. Monique's dead. They've all been dead for almost ten years. Dead and gone.

Her fingers reached out for the bejeweled silk drapes that passed for swags on her four-poster bed. The drapes that used to hang in the living room of their home next door. The drapes she'd use to pretend she was Princess Jasmine from Disney's *Aladdin*, the drapes she'd hide behind to sneak up on Aldon or to listen in on Monique's telephone conversations.

She'd only had them, her family, for four short years, and her memories were sporadic at best. Daddy laughing at something Aldon said, the huge sound of his laughter that shook his whole body and made everyone around him smile. Watching Monique put on make-up at her little dressing table, the care she'd take to cover every blemish, darken every lash. Sometimes she'd let Elizabeth try on some lipstick or eye shadow, once she even put the make-up on Elizabeth herself, and when Elizabeth looked in the mirror she thought her reflection was beautiful. She remembered her mother didn't think so, and Monique got in trouble. Oh, God, how she remembered her mother – holding her at night, reading her Dr Seuss or *Goodnight Moon*. She could still smell her – that scent of lemon and flowers, the cool touch of her fingers, the warmth of her lips on Elizabeth's cheek or forehead.

She tried to think of her time here, with Mama E.J. and

Daddy Willis. They'd been good times. So many more years
with them than with her real family – make that 'other family',
'birth family', whatever. Real family didn't sound right. The
Pughs were her *real* family – legally adopted. That made it
real. And they loved her. That made it real.

She began to cry, the first time she'd cried for her forgotten
family since she was a little girl.

Austin, Texas
E.J., Friday
I woke up with a sore neck. Candace was standing over me.

'You scared me to death when I couldn't find you!' she
said. 'Your alarm went off.'

I tried to get up, but finally had to stretch my arm out to
Candace. 'Help me?' I said.

She laughed. 'That'll teach you to sleep in a bathtub!' She
grabbed my hand and pulled. She was surprisingly stronger
than her lithe body would indicate.

I stood up and tried to get my bearings. 'Man, I was really
asleep,' I said.

'You have a panel or something?' Candace asked.

I nodded. 'In half an hour.'

She headed for the door. 'Take a shower,' she said. 'It'll
help wake you up.'

I stood in the bathtub on the formerly fluffy towels the Sam
provided their guests, and considered that I had not allocated
time for a shower. Too bad, I thought, bending down and
removing the towels.

Fifteen minutes later I was out, clean and somewhat
refreshed, teeth brushed, cheeks blushed, and clothes laid out.
I wrestled into my bra and considered the clothes I'd picked
out. What kind of impression would they make? I wondered.
Stretch pants and a long top. They shouted 'housewife'. I
came out of the bathroom in my underwear and held up my
selected clothes to Candace.

'What do these say to you?' I asked.

She looked at the black stretch pants and multi-colored top.
'Ah . . .' she started.

'Housewife, right?' I said.

Being a kind woman, Candace only shrugged.

'I don't have the right clothes,' I said.

'What do you think are the right clothes?' she asked.

'Something flowy. Something mysterious.'

'We're romance writers, E.J., not mystery writers.'

'Something romantically mysterious,' I countered.

'What size do you wear?' she asked.

'Fourteen,' I said proudly.

'Oh,' she said crestfallen. 'I could loan you something, but I'm a six.'

The woman was flirting with danger and didn't even know it.

I slipped on the stretch pants and pulled the top over my head. 'Let's face it,' I said, my head covered by the top, 'I *am* a housewife. Maybe this'll make the wannabes feel better about themselves.'

I got my head out and checked the clock. I had one minute to leave the room, take the elevator to the mezzanine, and find the room my panel was in. I grabbed my purse, a copy of my new book, said, 'Bye,' and fled.

Remember what I said earlier about Murphy's Law? Never leave yourself only a minute to do anything; if you do, forty-seven things will happen to slow you down. OK, maybe not forty-seven, but a bunch. First the elevator was stuck on the third floor for an hour and a half. Yes, I tend to exaggerate – get over it. Then, when I finally got in the car, there was a child standing there who had pushed every button and was gleefully happy about it. Where this child's parents were was a mystery until the car stopped on the second floor where a woman stood, arms akimbo, and snatched said child as the door opened. 'Jeremy! If I told you once I've told you a million times—' I was never to learn what she'd told him a million times as the doors mercifully closed, taking me to the mezzanine level.

That, however, was not the end of my woes. As I got off the elevator on the crowded mezzanine level, the first person to see me was Lisbet Carson, the college girl with the dirty mind.

'Oh, Mrs Pugh!' she shouted, running toward me.

I tried to duck into the nearest conference room, but she caught me. Since the room was crowded and it wasn't the room I was supposed to be in, I dutifully left it with Lisbet in toe.

'Lisbet, I'm late for my first panel—' I started.

'This will only take a second?' she said, or asked, or whatever. 'I really wanted to talk to you about the terrible events of this morning. Or last night? About Maybella LaRue!' she said breathlessly.

The last thing in the world I wanted to talk about with any reporter was Jane's demise. The thought of talking to this little girl about it gave me the shivers.

'I really can't right now, Lisbet.' Thinking quickly, I said, 'Why don't you go to the bar? The big round table is usually occupied by Ms LaRue's friends. I'm sure one of them will be happy to talk with you. All of them are much better known writers than myself,' I said. 'And two are up for Ladies.'

'I'd rather talk to you—' she started, but I interrupted her.

'Have to go! Good luck!' And I ran for Conference Room B, where my panel was to be held. I felt a little guilty, foisting Lisbet Carson on my new friends, but better them than me, I told myself, which I did find consoling.

Black Cat Ridge, Texas
Elizabeth, Friday

Friday dragged on and on, the girls spending much of their time holed up in Elizabeth's room, going over scenarios of the following evening. Each scenario ended with Megan jumping out of the bushes and pulling a mask off Tommy/Aldon's face to reveal – well, whoever they decided at that moment was the culprit – everyone from their brother Graham to Brandon Gregory, the cutest boy in school.

'Why would Brandon Gregory be doing this?' Elizabeth demanded.

'Because he's secretly in love with me,' Megan said.

'Oh. So he's harassing *me*?' Elizabeth said, with a hint of sarcasm.

'Of course. He wouldn't harass me – he loves me. Secretly—'

'Which is why he's dating Heather McDonald, to further hide his desire for you?' Elizabeth inquired.

'Duh. Anyway, he's harassing you to get my attention. He knows I'm the kind of girl to protect her sister—'

'Pro-tect me,' Elizabeth said slowly.

'Duh. And he knows I'll be there when you meet him. Then we'll get rid of you . . .'

'Do you mean that figuratively or permanently?' Elizabeth asked, raising an eyebrow.

'We'll let you drive Dad's car back . . .'

'Then you two will make out in the bushes?' Elizabeth asked.

'Oh, course not. We'll have a meaningful dialog, at which point he'll ask me to marry him. After we both graduate college, of course. Then we'll go together all the way through high school, both go to UT together, then get married, move to Houston where he'll go to med school and I'll support him as a fashion buyer for Neiman's.'

Elizabeth looked at her sister with admiration. 'Wow,' she said, 'you don't mess around with your fantasies, do you?'

'Uh uh,' Megan said. 'You wanna know the color of our bedroom?'

'No,' Elizabeth said and sighed. 'I wanna know who this creep really is who's doing this.' Sighing again, and wrapping her arms around herself, she said, 'Half of me wants to believe it's Aldon. But that would mean that Mom and Dad have been lying to me all these years, and I don't want to believe that. The other half of me knows this creep is full of crap. That he's after something else.'

'And I know what that something else is,' Megan said.

'What?' Elizabeth asked.

'Your virtue,' she said.

Austin, Texas
E.J., Friday

I'll readily admit that I had fallen in love with Jerome MacIntyre, aka Jasmine West. But that was before I had to share a microphone with him. The two of us were on a panel with three other writers, one of them serving time as the moderator. She had her own microphone. Of the four remaining panelists, Jerome was the only man. The other two women shared one microphone and Jerome and I shared the other. Or that was the plan. Other than introducing myself and stating the name of my new book, I never got to say a word. The two other women and the moderator had to interrupt Jerome to get a word in. Since I couldn't get my hands on the microphone,

I never even had a chance to do that. I was fuming by the time I got off the stage. I'd been worried about what I would say and how I would appear to an audience. Silly me. I needn't have bothered.

After the panel we went to the book room to autograph our books. Jermone's line was out the door. I had three people in mine.

'Shall we away to the bar, my dear?' Jerome asked after our hour of signing was over.

I didn't know whether to throttle him or verbally berate him. I figured I could take him physically, but doubted if I could win in a contest of wits. I decided to do neither and followed him humbly to the bar. We were the last of our crew to arrive. I was surprised to see Mary Sparrow there, freshly made-up and wearing narrow black pants and a silver and black poncho-style, see-through top over a black cami. Now that's what I should have worn. It looked great. Of course, like Candace, Mary Sparrow couldn't have been more than a size six, if not smaller. But I could buy something like that, I decided. If I ever came to one of these things again I'd do more shopping than just a dress for the banquet. I'd buy a sexy, see-through poncho, maybe a slinky caftan, and if I really lost weight, there was no end to the items I could buy to make me look more like a romance writer.

Lydia was also dressed and freshly made-up. I assumed they both had panels they couldn't get out of either. Candace was looking good in a short, red plaid, schoolgirl style skirt and off-the-shoulder red sweater. That particular outfit I couldn't get away with no matter how much weight I lost, I decided. Hal, unfortunately, appeared to be wearing the same clothing he'd worn the day before.

'How was your panel?' Candace asked me.

Looking pointedly at Jerome, I said, 'I wouldn't know. Ask him.'

All eyes turned to Jerome. 'What?' he said.

Lydia looked at me. 'He didn't share his microphone with you, did he, E.J.?'

'Not once,' I said.

'I most certainly did!' Jerome said, indignant.

'Oh, I'm sorry,' I said, sarcasm dripping from my tongue,

'that half a minute at the beginning when I got to say my name and the title of my book. Totally forgot about that.'

Jerome rolled his eyes. 'I can't help it if you're not aggressive enough, E.J.'

'Jerry,' Mary Sparrow said, 'when you have a microphone in front of you, someone would have to knock you unconscious to get it out of your hand!'

'That is not true!' he said.

'Yes it is!' Mary said.

'Um hum,' Hal said.

'Totally,' Lydia said.

'If I'd known that's what I needed to do . . .' I said.

'Next time,' Lydia said, grinning at me.

'Should I take something heavy with me if I'm ever on a panel with him again?' I asked.

'Tire iron,' Hal said.

'Ball-peen hammer,' Lydia suggested.

'I'll loan you my Louisville Slugger,' Mary said.

Candace raised her hand like a child in school – which went well with her skirt. We all turned toward her. 'I have a panel with him tomorrow,' she said. 'Mary, that baseball bat?'

'In my room,' she said. 'I'll give it to you in the morning. Instructions are on the handle.'

Jerome didn't look the least ruffled. 'If I wanted this kind of abuse,' he said, 'I could have stayed home.'

Changing the subject, I asked, 'Which of you ended up talking with Lisbet Carson?'

All I got for my question was blank stares. Finally Lydia asked, 'Who?'

'Lisbet Carson,' I repeated. 'Maybe nineteen, if that, a reporter for her college paper, curly black hair, freckles on her nose, large breasts. If it was one of you men, you'd notice that over the freckles . . .' I trailed off, still getting blank stares.

Mary shook her head. 'I didn't talk to any reporters this morning,' she said.

'Me either,' Lydia agreed.

Both men and Candace shook their heads.

'Well, I'm sure she'll be back to haunt me,' I said with a sigh. My ploy obviously hadn't worked. I knew I'd be ambushed sometime that day by the intrepid Ms Carson.

Changing the subject yet again, and knowing I didn't want

any surprises or secrets, I said, 'Candace has moved into my room.'

Lydia looked at us and Mary looked down at the table, but not before I saw the tears welling in her eyes. I felt awful for bringing up the ghost of Jane.

'What brought this on?' Lydia asked.

Candace looked at me, and I said, 'Tell them. No secrets.'

She nodded. 'This morning, while I was taking a nap, Angela came charging into the room and started saying things about Jane.'

'What things?' Lydia demanded.

Candace shook her head. 'Awful things. How she was a has-been and a never-should-have-been, how she cheated. She said she was a plagiarist.'

That brought Mary's head up and dried her tears. 'She accused Jane of plagiarism?' she demanded.

'That's what she said,' Candace said, obviously feeling uncomfortable.

Breaking in, I asked, 'Does anyone know who uses the email name of romance 365?'

'Angela,' Lydia said. 'I've gotten enough emails from her to know. Why?'

'I found an email from romance 365 to Jane, accusing her of plagiarism. The police took that and some other papers with them when they searched the room. Then later the Beast came to my room looking for "business papers" she said Jane had.'

'I knew it!' Mary said. 'Didn't I tell all of you she did it! Are the cops still here, E.J.? I need to talk to the head guy! That woman needs to be arrested!' Mary stood up, ready to take on the entire room if necessary.

I motioned for Mary to sit down. 'I think Detective Washington left,' I said. She was still standing. 'Do you have your cell? Let's call him.' Finally she sat down. I fished in my purse until I found the card he'd given me earlier, and handed it to Mary.

She dialed the number then said, 'I'm putting it on speaker-phone.'

We heard two rings then the phone picked up. 'Washington,' he said.

'Detective Washington,' Mary said. 'This is Mary Sparrow here at the romance convention?'

'Yes, ma'am,' he said.

'I'm a friend . . . I was a friend of Jane's,' she said, her voice breaking slightly. She cleared her throat and went on. 'I need to talk with you.'

'Can we do this on the phone?' he asked. 'Reason is, I got another case other side of the city, won't be getting back to the hotel 'til sometime tomorrow.'

'Ah, certainly,' Mary said. 'I know who killed Jane.'

'You do?' he asked.

'Yes, sir, I do.'

'And who would that be, Ms Sparrow?' Detective Washington asked.

'Angela Barber,' Mary said with quiet authority.

'You silly cow!' came a voice from behind us.

'Excuse me?' Detective Washington said.

Mary almost dropped the phone as we all turned to see the Beast standing behind us.

'How dare you accuse me of such a thing!' Angela shouted.

'Ms Sparrow?' Detective Washington said.

'I'll call you back,' Mary said and disconnected. She stood up, facing the Beast. Well, facing the Beast's collarbone.

Lydia was the first to stand with Mary, then we all followed suit.

'I know you did it!' Mary said.

The entire bar was quiet now, a phenomenon I thought I'd never live to see. All eyes and ears were on the two women at our table.

'Did you think no one would notice you sneaking around, trying to find the evidence that pointed directly at you?' Mary said, her face a mask of hatred. 'E.J. saw the email print out, Angela. Candace heard you accuse Jane of plagiarism. You're obviously insane. Maybe you can try that as a defense!'

'Why would I kill her? The silly cow stole my story and I can prove it! You think she was above plagiarism? She was a dried-up old hack—'

And that's when Mary Sparrow decked Angela Barber. To quote my daughters, it was way cool.

Detective Washington put off his trip across town and came straight to the hotel, which was a good thing. We were all crowded in the security room of the Sam – Mary, Angela,

Lydia, Candace, Hal, Jerome and myself, plus two security guards, the security chief for the hotel, the hotel nurse, an on-call doctor and two APD patrol officers, one male and one female. Unfortunately the room was very small and my before now non-existent claustrophobia was showing itself, although, unlike most hotels, even this behind-the-scenes room was totally the Sam: antique mahogany paneling, matching roll-top desk, polished saltillo tile, with original light fixtures of heavy glass and brass – no chandeliers behind the scenes, but plush none the less. When Detective Washington pushed his way in, the room became exponentially smaller.

The nurse and the doctor were there for Mary's hand, which appeared, without benefit of X-ray, to be broken. Angela's nose was bleeding, but it didn't appear to be damaged all that much. She was screaming at Mary, who was screaming back at her, while the security chief screamed at both of them. The noise, the closeness of the bodies, and the mixed smells of too much perfume and somebody's (I think it was the security chief's) extreme body odor, were about to do me in.

As Detective Washington shoved his way inside the room, he shouted, 'Shut up!' at the top of his lungs.

All three combatants instantly ceased, and all eyes turned to the newcomer.

'What the hell is going on here?' Detective Washington demanded, which probably wasn't a good idea. Fourteen voices, including my own, piped up to answer him.

'Stop!' he shouted. We stopped. He sighed. 'Officer Sanchez,' he said, addressing the female APD officer. 'Please tell me what's going on.'

'Yes, sir,' she said. She pulled a small spiral notebook out of her breast pocket. 'Ms Sparrow,' she said, pointing at Lydia who then pointed at Mary, 'accused Ms Barber –' she pointed at Candace who pointed at Angela – 'of killing Ms Dawson, then Ms Barber said something that pis— that angered Ms Sparrow so that she hit Ms Barber—'

'OK, OK,' Washington said, sighing again. 'Why is everyone else in here?'

'Ah,' Officer Sanchez said. 'I don't know, sir.'

The small, bald man in glasses and the white lab coat said, 'I'm the on-call physician for the hotel, Detective. Ms Sparrow appears to have broken her hand. I'll need to have her taken to the hospital.'

'She break her hand on your nose, Ms Barber?' Washington asked.

'She hit me!' Angela shouted. 'For no reason—'

'No reason my ass!' Mary shouted. 'You—'

Washington held up his hand for silence. 'Are you pressing charges?' he asked Angela.

'You bet your ass—' Angela started, but Jerome pointed his finger at her and shook his head, stopping Angela in her tracks. She sighed and said, 'No, not at this time.'

'Fine,' Washington said. 'That's very big of you, Ms Barber,' he said.

Beside me, under her breath, Lydia said, 'Big being the operative word here!'

I giggled and said 'Shhh.' Washington shot me a look, which dried the giggle dead in my throat.

'Ms Pugh. Will you please escort your friends out of here?'

Everyone looked at me and I said, 'Ah, OK.'

'Ms Sparrow, Ms Barber, Doctor, please stay.'

I opened the door and let the gang, less Mary, out of the room. The nurse, the two APD officers and the two security guards followed, the last one closing the door behind him.

Once outside and away from the guards, I turned on Jerome. 'OK, what was with the finger pointing and why would Angela listen to you anyway?'

'I was just reminding her how bad this would look for the convention. Isn't it enough that one of our best was murdered here? Should the papers now have a field day with fisticuffs between participants?'

'And she read all that from a finger point and a head shake?' I demanded.

Jerome stiffened. 'Angela is a pain in the posterior, but no one has ever accused her of being stupid.'

Lydia looked at me and I looked at her. Something wasn't right here, but I didn't know what it was.

'Mrs Pugh?' came a voice from behind me to the left. I turned. Lisbet Carson.

I sighed. 'Not now, Lisbet,' I said, trying to turn back to Lydia and Jerome, but she shoved the microphone of her tape recorder in my face.

'May I have a statement about the fight in the bar? From your perspective, as a friend of the deceased and of one of the combatants,' she said.

'Go away, Lisbet,' I said, holding on to my temper.

'My sources tell me Ms Sparrow was the first to throw a punch. Is that true?'

Jerome whirled on the college girl. 'I believe you've been told to go away several times, young lady. I advise you to do so before I call over one of the security guards! Now scoot!'

'The press has a right to know—' Lisbet started, but Hal took her by the arm and escorted her to the settee in the middle of the lobby, setting her down on it. I heard him say 'stay', as you would to a disobedient dog, then he joined us.

'Why don't we stop giving the troops a free show and go to somebody's room?' I suggested.

'Our room's the biggest,' Candace said.

Unfortunately, as the only double room, it was. I nodded my head and we all trooped toward the elevators. Horror of horrors, DeWitt Perry was waiting there for a car. He turned on hearing us troop up. I was not in the mood and was just opening my mouth to blast him when he said, 'Ms Macy,' and moved into Candace's space, grasping her hand. 'I've been dying to meet you. I stayed up all night last night reading your book, and I have to say you titillated me beyond reason.'

'How nice of you to say,' Candace said, backing up and removing her hand from his dead fish grasp.

The elevator door opened and I pushed Candace ahead of me into the car.

'Maybe we could have a drink later?' DeWitt Perry shouted, standing on his tiptoes as he called into the elevator car, the doors almost shutting on his nose.

Candace glared at me. 'I thought that was *your* stalker!' she accused.

'Equal opportunity stalker, I guess.' I grinned. 'Your turn!'

Hal did his gorilla imitation. 'You want I should hoit him, boss?' he said.

'Funny,' Candace said, turning her back on both Hal and me. Being the supportive people we are, we both laughed at her discomfort.

We all trudged into our room, taking chairs and beds at random.

'I'm totally out of Johnny,' Lydia said. 'Someone call room service.'

'Don't you think we should keep clear heads about now?' I asked.

'Don't get sanctimonious on me, E.J.,' Lydia said, her face tight. 'After all that's happened, I need a drink. Or three.'

'Ditto,' Hal said, going to the phone on the desk and dialing room service.

'Dubonnet with a twist,' Jerome called from a chair by the window.

'Diet Coke,' I said.

'Bottled water,' Candace said.

'Make mine a double, Hal,' Lydia called. 'And a double for Mary. She should be coming up soon.'

Hal placed the order and I couldn't help but wonder if there would be a drink for Mary by the time she got there.

'Is everyone through with their panels for the day?' Lydia asked.

We all nodded except Hal, who said, 'I've got one at four thirty. "The Male Perspective on Romance". Guess who's moderating?'

'Not Angela?'

Hal laughed. 'No, although she could probably pass as a male. Taylor Mitcalf.'

'Too bad *he* can't pass as a male,' Lydia said.

'Meow,' Jerome said.

'My God, why is everyone getting so sanctimonious around here?' Lydia said. 'And since when have you got the right to talk, Jerry? Why don't you answer E.J.'s question truthfully and then you can meow all you want.'

'What question?' Jerome asked, eyes wide.

'What was that finger pointing with Angela really all about?' Lydia demanded. 'She's not that smart, Jerry. And I don't think this has a thing to do with the publicity for the convention. As we all know, any mention, good or bad, is better than no mention at all.'

'I told you the truth. That's exactly what I meant. If Angela thought it meant something else, that's between her and her God. Where's my Dubonnet?'

'Are you trying to ply me with the mere thought of drink to take my mind off your indiscretion, Jerome?' Lydia shook her head. 'Won't work. It would take at least four stiff ones to do the trick.'

Hal said, 'Well, I have one stiff one,' and laughed like an idiot.

'Hal, you're a pig. Jerry?' Lydia said.

'Lydia, my darling, you are beating a dead horse. Do you think I'm going to confess and say that pressing charges against Mary will somehow open up the fact that the Beast and I conspired to do away with poor Jane?' He made a 'tsk, tsk' sound with his tongue. 'If, for some unfathomable reason, I were to want to do away with dear Jane, I would not need nor want to conspire with the likes of the Beast. I think I could have handled her by myself.'

'I wasn't suggesting—' Lydia started.

Jerome stood up. 'I have no idea *what* you were suggesting, Lydia. But I'm tired of it.' Jerome sighed. 'I'm tired of the entire bloody thing.' With that, he left the room, closing the door quietly behind him.

'Good God,' Lydia said quietly, 'I think that's the first time I've ever seen Jerry show his age. He's eighty-three, you know. But that's for our ears only. We prefer publishers and editors not know how long we may have left in the biz. Lest they decide to cut their losses early.'

'What do you think was going on between him and Angela?' I asked the room at large.

Hal shrugged and laid down on Jane's – now Candace's – bed. Candace, as in the know as myself, merely shook her head.

Lydia said, 'I wish I knew. I've never known Jerry to be particularly friendly with Angela. In fact, I thought he loathed her.' She shrugged. 'Hell, he might be telling the truth. Maybe it *was* all about bad publicity.'

There was a knock on the door and Hal got up to answer it. It was room service and when I heard Hal say, 'Just put it on the room bill,' I flinched. I was on a budget and had no idea how much two double Johnny Walkers, a Dubonnet and whatever Hal had ordered would cost.

Hal brought in the tray of drinks and placed one of the doubles in Lydia's hand, then handed me my Diet Coke and

Candace her bottle of water. He placed the extra Johnny Walker double on the night stand, knocked back a small glass of what looked like very dark iced tea, and took the remaining glass in his hand.

'Gotta get ready for my panel. I'll take this by Jerry's on the way.'

We all nodded as he left.

Six

Black Cat Ridge, Texas
Graham, Friday

All families have their little rituals, and in the Pugh household, Friday nights were for take-outs and movies. They were allowed to rent two movies – one male, as in Sylvester Stallone, Jackie Chan, or others of that ilk; the other female, as in chick flicks. A coin was tossed to see which one got watched first.

Graham's mind was not on the movie playing on the big screen TV in the family room, although he had won the toss. He was in the kitchen, staring at the phone. It was finally Friday night. This was it. The plan was all set. Why didn't the phone ring? Nine, nine thirty. Nothing. How long, he thought, did it take a drunk to drink enough to pass out? He had no idea – no experience really with that particular problem.

'Graham?' his dad called from the family room. 'You gonna come watch this movie? It was your pick!'

'Ah, yeah, Dad, be right there.' He picked up the cordless phone and took it with him into the family room.

'This movie sucks,' Megan said.

'Then go play with your dolls,' Graham said.

'Bite me,' Megan said.

'And get my mouth full of pus and snot and boogers?' Graham said.

'Oh, gross!' Elizabeth said.

'Graham!' Willis said.

Thankfully, for all concerned, the phone rang. 'I've got it!' Graham yelled, the phone still in his lap. He jumped up and ran into the kitchen.

'Hello?' he said.

'Got it!' Hollister said. 'I'm on my way. Give me ten.'

'You got it,' Graham said, hanging up and sauntering back into the family room.

'Dad, that was Hollister. We're gonna go to the movies,' he said.

'Just have him come watch this with us,' Willis said.

'Naw, we wanna see that new Jet Li at the Cineplex.'

'Good! So can we turn this, Daddy?' Megan asked.

'I'm kinda into it now,' Willis said.

'Oh, Gawd!' Megan said, slouching down in her chair, arms across her chest.

'Yeah, sure, honey,' Willis said. 'If you can find something else coming on at the hour, you can turn it then, OK?'

'Thank Gawd!' Megan said, grabbing the remote and hitting the button for the list of programs. 'Anything but Jackie Chan!'

Graham and his father looked at each other, both standing and immediately falling into a kung fu position. Both yelled, 'Jackie Chan!' at the tops of their lungs, while the two girls rolled their eyes and giggled.

'Men!' Elizabeth said, shaking her head. 'Oh, *What Not to Wear*! Megan, put it on that!'

Willis shook his head. 'I think I'll go pay bills.'

A horn honked outside the house and Graham ran for the door. 'That's Hollister! See ya!'

'Graham, in by eleven!' Willis called.

'Dad! Midnight thirty, OK?'

'Midnight! No later!' Willis shot back.

'OK. I'm outta here!'

And he was gone.

Austin, Texas
E.J., Friday
Friday night there was nothing much planned and it was going to be a free night for Jane and me. I'd planned on taking her on a walking tour of Fourth Street, maybe hit a few bars – liquor, cigar and coffee varieties – and maybe catch some

live music. Instead I was driving Lydia to Brackenridge Hospital to pick up Mary. Lydia was silent as we drove down Red River to the hospital. Finally, I asked, 'What's on your mind?'

She started then laughed weakly. 'Oh, this and that. You know, one old friend murdered, another in the hospital and almost booked for assault. The usual,' she said.

'I'm so sorry this is happening,' I said. 'I didn't know Jane as long or as well as you and Mary, but I did love her. She was a wonderful woman.'

'The best,' Lydia said quietly, then began to cry. 'Goddamn!' she finally said, hitting the hand rest of the car door with her fist. 'I hate this shit!'

'Maybe you and Mary should just leave, Lydia,' I said. 'There's no reason for y'all to stay here. It's not like either of you need it for your careers. Go to her house or yours and just veg out for a while.'

Lydia adamantly shook her head. 'I'm not leaving this town until I find out who killed Jane! If the convention ends and they still don't know, then I'll find a cheap motel and stay there and bug the hell out of the police until they find the asshole! Then just give me five minutes alone with him!'

Since this all began, Lydia had been the strength to Mary's display of emotions. This was the first I'd seen of how Lydia really felt. And in a strange way I envied Jane. To be the kind of person who could elicit this kind of loyalty must be amazing, I thought. Since the death of Terry Lester, my daughter Elizabeth's birth mother, I haven't had a friend who felt about me the way Lydia and Mary felt about Jane. At the moment, my closest female friend was my next-door neighbor Elena Luna, the Codderville police detective, and most of the time I wasn't even sure she liked me, much less that she would be capable of the feelings displayed by this kind of friendship. For a moment, driving down Red River toward Brackenridge Hospital, I felt very alone, and missed Terry more than I had in a very long time.

I pulled into the parking lot of the emergency room and drove around for a while before I found a spot, a good way from the door. Lydia and I traipsed to the entrance and found Mary sitting in the waiting room, her hand bandaged but not in a sling.

'Just a sprain,' she said upon seeing us.

'Are you ready to leave?' I asked.

'All signed out and ready to go,' she said with what looked like a fake smile.

'You OK?' I asked.

'Dandy,' she said, not looking at me as she headed for the door of the emergency room.

It was a bit awkward on the way back, as the two friends opted to sit in the back seat while I chauffeured them back to the hotel. There were whispers and tears, but I tried to keep my mind on my driving and my ears on the low volume of the radio.

As I pulled up to valet parking, I asked if they would like to go to Fourth Street with me, but they declined, heading into the hotel and up in the elevator. I wandered around for a while and spotted Hal in the bar. I thought about asking him if he wanted to go, but he appeared to be more than three sheets to the wind, so I rethought the idea. Jerome wasn't in the bar and didn't answer his phone. Candace, I knew, was at a seminar that evening on 'Keeping Romance in Your Life', so she was out as a possible companion on my Fourth Street jaunt.

I had no desire to traipse down Fourth Street by myself, so I went back to my room and took a long bath, got in my jammies, ordered something called 'Chocolate Death' from room service, with a pot of decaf, and found a movie on Pay-Per-View. I fell asleep while Denzel Washington was running from the bad guys, and woke up when the beginning credits were rolling for what I hoped was only the second time. I turned off the TV and crawled into bed. It was after midnight and Candace was not in her bed; I had no thought of looking for her, lest I find *her* dead and battered body. I was out of that business for good.

Black Cat Ridge, Texas
Elizabeth, Friday

The girls had watched *What Not to Wear*, then started their movie, but even at thirteen, both girls thought it was pretty dumb and turned it off. With no discussion about it, they both ended up in Elizabeth's room, sitting on her bed.

'Are you scared about tomorrow night?' Megan asked.

'No. Maybe.' Elizabeth shrugged her shoulders. 'You?'

Megan appeared to think about it, then said, 'Excited. Maybe a little scared. I think I'm mostly worried about Dad catching us trying to borrow the car.'

Elizabeth shuddered at the thought. 'He'd kill us,' she said.

'Yeah,' Megan said, 'and then he'd tell Mom.'

'And she'd kill us two times,' Elizabeth said.

'Then ground us for a month,' Megan said.

'Yeah, but she wouldn't do that to Graham!' Elizabeth said.

Megan grew indignant. 'No she wouldn't! All this crap about this being a liberated household with no gender roles, my ass! Graham gets away with murder, and just because he's a boy.'

'Oh, no, Megan,' Elizabeth said, imitating their mother in a sarcastic manner, 'it's only because Graham is the oldest!'

'Oh, Graham, you want to borrow the car?' Megan said, doing her own imitation of their mother. 'Here, take the keys! Shall I lie down on the driveway and let you run over me?'

Elizabeth, always fair, which pissed off her sister no end, said, 'Yeah, well, he does have a driver's license.'

Megan threw her hands in the air. 'Jeez, Liz, and just when we were bonding!'

Black Cat Ridge, Texas
Graham, Friday

They'd crossed the river into uncharted territory – Codderville. Each knew the town in small doses: Graham, his grandmother's neighborhood and the cafeteria she frequented out near the highway; Leon, the homes of his relatives, who all lived within a three-block radius of each other; Tad knew the grade school where he had gone before his family moved to Black Cat Ridge; and Hollister was familiar with his father's favorite bar where he often had to pick him up when he was too drunk to drive home.

But the bowling alley, where they were to meet the girls, was new turf, and its reputation preceded it. This was the place where the rednecks hung out, the bikers and the skinheads and weirdoes who ran meth labs out of old farmhouses. This was the place where women wore scanty clothes and had tattoos and too many piercings. This was the coolest place in Codderville.

They piled out of the pickup and stood in the parking lot. The lot was mostly full, with pickups, motorcycles and muscle cars. They had parked in the back of the lot, next to the only tree in site, a sickly pin oak whose branches were half barren. The little square of earth surrounding it was filled with beer cans, condoms and roaches – not the kind with legs, but the kind that are the end result of smoking a doobie, a blunt, a biggie, a joint, or a reefer, terminology dependant upon your geography, ethnicity, or age.

By twelve thirty Ashley hadn't shown up yet. Not her, not her girlfriends. Nothing. The guys hung out outside the bowling alley, waiting. To go inside would mean to actually be seen by the rednecks, skinheads and weirdoes who hung out inside, doing God only knew what. The images that danced in their collective brains were scenes from HBO's *Oz* and Fox's *Prison Break*. Not pretty and definitely something fifteen and sixteen-year-old boys would best avoid. They didn't speak of this, of course, but no one mentioned actually going inside.

The alley closed at one a.m., so Graham thought that if Ashley was going to show it had to be quick. Graham wasn't talking. The other boys left him alone, talking among themselves, swiping at each other, laughing, avoiding Graham as much as possible. Then the car pulled into the lot. It was Joey's car, Ashley's best friend, a brand new Jeep Wrangler her father gave her off his car lot. Talk about a lucky chick.

Graham turned to his friends and said, 'Whatja talking about?'

'Huh?' said Leon.

'Baseball,' Hollister said. 'How 'bout them Astros?'

'I don't know shit about the Astros,' Graham said. 'Cowboys?'

'Yeah,' Hollister said. 'Wrong season but what the fuck.'

So they began an earnest discussion of the Dallas Cowboys' last season, the possibilities of draft choices and the consequences of same. The discussion was so intense they barely noticed as the four girls walked up to the steps of the bowling alley. Finally, at the last possible moment, Graham turned, startled to see the girls.

'Hey, Ashley,' he said.

'Hey, Graham,' she said.

She took his breath away. Her long blonde hair was pulled to the side in a lopsided ponytail, the tail hanging over her left shoulder. She was wearing a very short skirt and a small top that exposed her belly button and the gold ring therein. Forcing his eyes on her face, Graham smiled.

The girls moved away from Ashley as the boys moved away from Graham, a tried and true mating ritual.

'Anything going on inside?' she asked.

'Naw, not much,' he said, as if he'd actually looked inside. 'Some drunks, is all.'

'I hear this place gets pretty raunchy.'

'Yeah,' Graham said. 'Me too.'

'You hang out here much?' she asked.

'Naw, not that much,' Graham said.

'So what have you guys been doing?' Ashley asked.

'Nothing,' Graham said. 'What about you?'

'Nothing. We went by Joey's house 'cause her parents are gone for the weekend, but her grandmother's there, so we left.'

'Oh,' Graham said.

Ashley sighed. 'I have to get home. I have a curfew, can you believe it?'

'That sucks,' Graham said.

'Tell me about it. My parents treat me like I'm twelve or something. You don't have a curfew, do you?'

'Oh, hell no,' Graham said.

Ashley smiled. 'Maybe tomorrow night I can tell my parents I'm staying at Joey's with her and her grandmother and you and I can meet here? Maybe earlier?'

'Yeah, maybe. Sounds doable,' Graham said.

'Then we can stay out as late as we want. Joey's grandmother falls asleep on the couch in front of the TV real early. She'll never know when I come in.'

'Sounds good,' Graham said. He smiled.

Ashley smiled. She touched his fingertips with hers. 'So I guess I'll see you here tomorrow?'

'Yeah, definitely,' he said.

'Definitely?' she said.

'Definitely,' Graham said, squeezing her fingertips.

After a second of staring at each other, Ashley pulled her fingers away and turned to her friends. 'Joey, I gotta go *now* if I'm going to make that stupid curfew.'

'Yeah,' Joey said, turning back to Hollister. 'So I'll see you tomorrow night?'

'Is the Pope Catholic?' Hollister said.

Joey laughed at his clever rejoinder and the girls gathered into their pack and headed for Joey's Wrangler, the boys watching every step as they left.

Austin, Texas
E.J., Saturday
When I woke up the next morning to pounding on the door, I quickly glanced at Candace's bed. She was there, trying to push herself up and move hair out of her eyes to see what the fuss was about.

'Who is it?' she whispered to me.

'I haven't the faintest idea,' I said, grabbing my robe and throwing it on as I went to answer the incessant pounding. I threw open the door to find Detective Washington standing there.

'May I come in?' he said, not waiting for me to answer, but pushing his way past me.

'Sure,' I said behind him, giving into my more sarcastic tendencies, 'please. Don't be shy.'

'Shut the door,' he said.

I pushed it shut behind me, not taking my eyes off the detective. 'What do you want? What time is it, anyway?' I didn't even try to suppress a yawn.

'It's seven a.m. Where were you last night?' he asked, looking directly at me.

'Here!' I said. 'I had room service and watched a movie.'

He jerked his thumb at Candace. 'She can verify that?'

'No,' I said. 'Do I need her to?'

'Where were you?' he asked, turning to Candace.

'I went to a seminar on the mezzanine level,' she said.

'What time did you leave there?'

'Ah, it was over about nine thirty, ten, something like that,' Candace said, sitting up in bed and clutching the sheet to her chest.

'And after that?'

'I went to the bar and talked to some people—'

'Your usual gang?' Detective Washington asked.

'No. They weren't there. Some people from the seminar. I don't remember any names—'

'What time did you get back to the room?' he asked.

'Eleven, maybe eleven thirty,' Candace said.

I started to correct her, then thought better of it. Why get her in trouble for a mere half an hour time discrepancy?

'Detective Washington,' I said, 'do you mind telling us what's going on?'

'Yes,' he said. 'Don't leave the hotel until I tell you otherwise,' he said and left the room.

Candace and I stared at each other for about a full minute, then she said, 'What in the hell's going on now?'

'I don't know,' I said, running to the bathroom, 'but I'm getting dressed and going downstairs.'

My first reading was at eleven a.m., so I had almost four hours to find out what was going on. Oh, and eat breakfast, read over my material and put on make-up. Not necessarily in that order. Candace and I got off the elevator at the mezzanine level, both in jeans and T-shirts, sans make-up. Somehow she managed to look like a magazine cover; well, I did, too, but it was *Mad* magazine, not *Vogue*.

There were clusters of people talking in small groups, a lot of them, even at this early hour. Angela was at the registration desk, talking to Detective Washington, gesticulating wildly. We didn't see any of our gang, but I did see the woman who'd moderated my panel the day before. Patricia? Patty? Pam! That was it.

I walked up to her. 'Pam!' I said. 'How are you this morning?'

'Weirded out,' she said.

I tried to raise an eyebrow, failed, and asked, 'What's going on?'

'You didn't hear?' she said, moving in close, that joyful yet pained looked on her face of someone who was going to get to tell someone else the bad and juicy news.

'What?' I asked, lowering my voice to her level.

'One of the fans got killed last night!' she whispered.

'A fan? My God, what happened?' I asked. Candace had moved up and was clutching my arm, fingernails digging into my flesh.

'He fell down an elevator shaft! The hotel says there's no way in hell it could be an accident. Someone would have to rig the elevators to do that.'

'Do you know who it was?' I asked.

'I don't know his name – little guy with a bad comb over?' Pam said.

I felt the bile in my stomach rise. DeWitt Perry. Someone had killed DeWitt Perry? Why? What in the hell was going on?

I felt Candace's fingernails dig deeper into my skin and looked at her. She nodded her head toward the registration table. I looked over and saw that not only was Angela pointing at me and Detective Washington staring at me, but everyone on the mezzanine level was looking my way.

The bile went back down, bounced around a little, and decided to come back up. I vomited on the floor. It would have been embarrassing if I wasn't totally terrified.

'We have you on videotape threatening him,' Detective Washington said. He had me in the little room behind the front desk, just the two of us, and I wasn't feeling my best.

'I wasn't threatening him!' I said. 'I was just being emphatic!'

'Looked like a threat to me,' Washington said.

'I swear it wasn't! He pushed the stop button on the elevator,' I explained. 'He scared me. I was just lashing out.'

'He threatened you *on* an elevator, you killed him *with* an elevator. Seems like a certain kind of justice to me,' Washington said.

I stood up. 'If I'm not under arrest, I'm leaving. If I *am* under arrest, I'd like to call my attorney.'

I didn't exactly have an attorney, but I figured I could find one.

Washington stood up, too. 'Of course you're not under arrest, Mrs Pugh,' he said. 'We're just making inquiries at the moment. I would like you to stay in the hotel, of course. If necessary, I'll put a guard on your door.'

I sighed. 'I won't leave the hotel. I don't need a guard. I have convention business to take care of today. This is my career, you know.'

'I'll need a copy of your itinerary for the day,' he said.

'It's upstairs,' I answered. 'I'll have it sent down to you.'

'Thank you,' he said formally and walked me to the door, holding it open for me. I walked out and found the entire gang waiting for me on the guest side of the front desk. Mary grabbed my arm.

'Are you all right?' she said. 'Are they going to arrest you?'

'No. Unfortunately there are cameras in the elevators and they saw me tell off DeWitt Perry when he stopped the elevator Thursday night. Somehow they interpreted my gestures as a threat.'

'Oh, for God's sake,' Lydia said. 'Do these people know nothing? How else do you deal with an amorous fan? I had to tell a twenty-one-year-old computer geek one time that I was going to emasculate him if he didn't leave me alone! I suppose they'd take that as a threat too.'

'Yeah, probably,' I said. 'If he ended up murdered the next day.'

Hal put his arm around my shoulder. 'You need a drink, girl,' he said. 'Let's head to the bar.'

'Hal, it's eight o'clock in the morning! I need food!' I said, and headed in the direction of the breakfast buffet.

'Food?' I heard Lydia say behind me.

'It's that stuff you put in your stomach so the bourbon won't eat the lining,' Hal said.

'Hal, you're a pig,' Lydia said. 'I guess I could eat.'

'Coffee,' Mary said. 'The kind with caffeine in it.'

And that's when little Cyrus Sullivan scurried past us, a bellhop behind him with a luggage rack loaded with suitcases and hanging clothes bags.

'Cyrus?' Hal called out to him. 'What's going on?'

Cyrus stopped short, the bellhop with his luggage rack almost running into the back of him. 'Hal! I tried to find you but . . . I'm leaving!' he said, his hand over his heart.

'Yeah, that's what it looks like! You said you'd be here the whole convention, man! We were supposed to share expenses!'

'Well, my God, Hal! After what's happened you don't expect me to stay here, do you? I'm next!' he wailed, tears darkening his pale eyes.

'You're next?' I said. 'Whatever makes you think that?'

'It's obvious! First Jane, then that fan! I'm obviously the next victim!' he said.

'Ah, Cyrus, I really don't see the connection,' Mary said.

'Well, I'm not going to stand here in a public place and explain it to you!' Cyrus said, hands on hips. He turned to Jerome who was standing the furthest away. 'Jerome, if you have a brain in your head, you'll leave with me!' Trying a coy smile, he said, 'We could find some place to go together where we'll both be safe.'

Jerome said, 'Oh, for God's sake!' as he turned and headed into the dining room.

'Jerome?' Cyrus called. 'Jerome!'

Sighing, Cyrus turned to the rest of us. 'You're all crazy for staying here! Everyone's going to die!'

With that he scurried out of the hotel, the bellhop hot on his heels.

We watched for a moment as Cyrus left, then trooped into the dining room and found a large round table and put down our purses, then headed to the buffet.

I would have been in heaven if I hadn't been worried about being arrested. There were about ten round tables, covered in rose-colored linen, huge bouquets of roses in the center, with all edibles known to man: your usual eggs and breakfast meats, but also smoked salmon, shrimp, cracked crab, a man making omelets, one making waffles, a table of nothing but fruits, everything from strawberries to star fruit, a table of every kind of bread, muffin, or pastry I've ever heard of and some I hadn't, casseroles, my God, it was awesome and went on forever. But because of Detective Washington I was only able to go back two times. As my mother-in-law would have said, I was definitely off my feed.

'How can you eat?' Mary said, looking at my plate as she downed her fourth cup of sugarless, creamless espresso.

'We all have our coping mechanisms,' I said, shoveling bacon into my pie hole, and wondering if I should have brought some size sixteens, just in case. The second worst thing about being the main suspect was I hadn't had the time or inclination to mourn poor, pitiful DeWitt Perry.

He had been an obnoxious little man, but that was no reason for someone to kill him. If so, half the male population would be dust. The main question, however, was why? Was this just a coincidence or did it have something to do with Jane's murder? But how could it be connected? As far as I knew,

Jane had only met DeWitt Perry that one time, when he first accosted me on Thursday. Could they have met after that? Been connected in some way? Did they both witness something neither told anyone else about? Surely not. Jane would have told me, or at least told Lydia and Mary. Unless she didn't know she'd witnessed something. Maybe they both saw some Mafioso type who was supposed to be out of the country, but here he was in this hotel, and they both had to be rubbed out lest they tell. Or, and this one I liked, maybe Osama Bin Laden was in the hotel and they saw him! That would be cool. And of course any witnesses to that would definitely have to be silenced. Or possibly they saw a land scheme going down and although they didn't realize it, the parties in question thought they could identify them and decided to have them taken care of. Yes, I watch too much television. Although the Osama Bin Laden theory was still a favorite.

But the police weren't taking any of those theories into consideration. They decided that a mild-mannered housewife shaking her finger at a man in an elevator was proof enough of murder. Now the big question was: to call Willis or not to call Willis. If he knew about this new development, he'd probably insist on coming to Austin. Where would I put him? Make Candace room with someone else? Move Willis in with Jerome or Hal? The thought of finding an empty room was out of the question. The convention had all but packed the hotel, and then there were the regular people, most of them just getting in our way.

On the other hand, could I count on any of my new friends bailing me out of jail, if it came to that? How far would these people back me up? They didn't know me well enough to know that I really didn't kill DeWitt Perry. But who did? It had to be connected to Jane. There was no way there were two homicidal maniacs running around the Sam at this precise moment. But what did Perry have to do with Jane? I kept coming back to that question, over and over.

I smiled for the first time that morning when the serious face of intrepid junior reporter Lisbet Collins came to my mind's eye. She was going to be seriously pissed when she realized she'd missed this.

'Ooo,' Lydia said, 'hunk at twelve o'clock.'

We all looked up as the man walked into the dining room. Forty-something, with blond hair dusted with gray, large blue eyes, six foot four at least, broad shoulders, not much of a gut. Oh yeah, Lydia, he's a hunk all right.

I got up from the table and walked up to the man and threw my arms around him. When he put his arms around me, I could hear the women at my table sighing.

'Washington called Luna, Luna called me,' Willis explained. 'Seemed like you might need a little back-up.'

'I don't know where to put you,' I said, tears streaming from my eyes.

'I beg your pardon?' my husband asked, still clasping both my hands as we sat at a private table in the dining room.

'Candace is sharing a room with me. We've got the only double room, and there aren't any rooms left—'

Willis laughed and squeezed my hands. 'Honey, that's the least of our worries. Hell, I'll sleep on the floor. Or in the car, or whatever. Personally, right now, I just want to have a word with this Washington asshole.'

'How are the kids?' I asked.

'Totally ignorant of the current situation. My mother's staying at the house, to the delight of Elizabeth, the boredom of Megan, and the horror of our one and only son.'

'I'm sure Puddin's excited,' I said.

'Ecstatic,' he said, grinning at me. He sobered and said, 'Tell me what happened.'

I sighed. 'Perry—' I started, and at Willis's blank look, explained, 'comb-over boy—'

'Oh,' he said.

'Anyway, he got me alone on an elevator and pushed the button to stop the elevator—'

'He did what?' my husband exclaimed, coming out of his seat.

'Sit down honey, he's already dead,' I said.

'Oh, right,' Willis said, taking his seat again.

'Anyway, I had a few choice words for him, and there was some finger pointing, and I pulled out the stop button and got to my floor, told him off and got out. Unfortunately there's no audio, just video. Detective Washington has concluded that finger-pointing leads to murder.'

'And they think you killed him over that?' he asked, incredulous.

'I know, I know,' I said sighing. 'And the thing is, he got over me. He was on to Candace by the next day!'

'Did you tell Washington that?' Willis asked.

I shook my head. 'That would have just made him suspect Candace,' I said.

Willis opened his mouth to say something, then shut it.

'What?' I asked.

'Nothing,' he said. 'Look, let's go for a walk.'

'Unless we circle the lobby four or five times, a walk is out. I'm not supposed to leave the hotel,' I told him.

He shook his head. 'This is unbelievable.' He stood up. 'Let's find Washington.'

'What are you going to do?' I asked, gingerly standing to follow.

'Don't worry about it,' he said, face grim.

'Willis, don't make this worse!' I warned.

'I'm just going to talk to him,' my husband said. And that's exactly what was worrying me.

Seven

Austin, Texas
E.J., Saturday

'And then she says, "but I was just holding it!"'

Washington laughed so hard he actually slapped his knee. Personally I was getting a little tired of 'The Perils of E.J.', as recited by my soon-to-be ex-husband, if he didn't shut his mouth.

'So Luna says, "E.J., you're getting your fingerprints all over the murder weapon!".'

Washington took out a large handkerchief and wiped his eyes. 'Oh, God, stop!' he said. 'I can't take much more!'

'I've got hours worth of this stuff!' Willis said, grinning from ear to ear.

I was sitting in a chair by the door of the little room where

I'd had my interview with Washington earlier. My arms were crossed over my chest and I was scowling, but nobody seemed to notice. 'Are we about through here?' I asked through clinched teeth.

'Yeah, baby, just a minute,' Willis said, waving a languid arm at me but not bothering to glance my way. It was a good thing Detective Washington couldn't read minds, because I was feeling very homicidal at the moment.

Washington sighed, a little bubble of laughter escaping as he did so. 'Mrs Pugh, why don't you take your husband out for a drink? There are some nice places on Fourth Street,' he said.

Damn, I could leave the hotel? I stood up. 'Why don't you call me E.J., Detective? Now that you know all my secrets?'

He stood up laughing. 'E.J., you've given me a new and healthier respect for Elena Luna!'

I smiled a tight smile. 'Yes, I *am* her cross to bear, aren't I?'

'More like her Achilles heel,' Willis said.

'Her albatross,' Washington said.

I left the room to the raucous laughter of the two male idiots, determined that Willis could definitely sleep in his car that night for all I cared.

'And then he said, and I quote, "You should really think before you speak"!' Jane sighs. 'I should get a divorce, shouldn't I?'

'Jane, you've been married to him forever. Do you really think a divorce is a good idea?'

'E.J., he told me to shut up!' Jane insists.

'Not in so many words,' I say.

'How many words do you need?' Jane insists. 'All I said was that the present administration is dumber than a sack of rocks!'

'To his boss who's Republican Party chairman of your county,' I remind her.

'You're on his side!' Jane cries.

'No, honestly, I'm not,' I say, although I do sort of see his point.

'Hey, we're out of the hotel, aren't we?' Willis demanded.

We were turning on to Fourth Street and I still hadn't said a word to him. It wasn't so much the silent treatment as it was my fear of actually opening my mouth. Once I started I was afraid I wouldn't be able to stop. And then there would be the scene, the possibility of a police presence, jail time, my kids having to come see me on visiting day – the consequences just went on and on.

'You are no longer a viable suspect,' Willis said. 'And you can thank me for that!'

I stopped dead on the sidewalk. 'Thank you?' I said, keeping my voice low and menacing. 'Thank you?'

'Ah, honey . . . ?'

'THANK YOU!' OK, maybe not so low. 'You make a laughing stock out of me and I'm supposed to *thank you*?'

Willis looked up and down the street. 'Ah, honey, not so loud—'

'Don't you tell me how loud I can be!' I screamed.

'E.J.—'

'Don't E.J. me, you . . . you . . .'

Willis put a finger to my lips. I bit it.

He jerked his hand away, shaking it. 'Ow! Why did you do that?'

'Because you deserved it!' I said, a little of the steam having died down with the bite. OK, maybe that was a little over the top. But just a little.

'You bit me!' Willis said.

'You were making fun of me!' I accused.

'You bit me!'

'Get over it,' I said, and headed down Fourth Street.

Willis caught up in two strides. 'What are you? A five year-old? You bit me!'

I was a little embarrassed. OK, maybe biting him *was* over the top. But it got his attention.

'Let's just agree to disagree,' I said, using as superior a tone as I could muster.

'Excuse me?' Willis said. 'Agree to disagree about what? The fact that a grown woman should *not* bite?' He shook his head and we walked on together – well, maybe not exactly *together*, but side by side and heading in the same direction. 'I can't believe you bit me.'

'Let it go, Willis,' I said.

He held up his finger. There was barely a mark on it. 'You bit me!' he said, his voice incredulous.

I sighed. 'And you made a fool of me. We're even.'

We got to a coffee house, went in, sat down and ordered. He was still looking at his finger.

'I have a tendency to overreact,' I said.

'Is that an apology?' he asked.

'No,' I said.

He finally lowered his finger and sighed. 'Whether you liked it or not, telling those stories, which, by the way, were all one hundred percent true—'

'They were out of context!'

'Not only got us out of the hotel, but probably got you off Washington's shit list.'

I had no argument for that. He was right. Best to forgive and forget. 'All right,' I said. 'I forgive you.'

'For what?' he exclaimed. 'I didn't bite *you*!'

'We need to figure out what happened to Perry,' I said.

'Who?' my husband asked.

'Comb-over boy,' I said.

'Oh, him. You think it's connected to your friend Jane?' Willis asked.

'How can it not be? I'm sure in its long and colorful past, the Sam has had more than its share of deaths, both accidental and intentional, but on the same weekend within the same group?'

Willis nodded his head. 'Yeah, you're right. Gotta be connected. OK, did Jane and comb-over boy know each other?'

I shook my head. 'As far as I can tell, Jane met him the same moment I did.'

'Then they had someone in common,' he said.

I slowly nodded my head. 'OK,' I said. 'Who?'

'OK,' he said. 'She's a writer, he's a fan. Connection number one. They're both at the same convention. Connection number two. They're both dead. Connection number three.'

Did I mention my husband's an engineer? As in anal? 'And this gets us where?' I asked, the skepticism in my voice quite evident.

'Do you have a piece of paper and a pencil?' he asked.

'Willis, you are not going to write this down!' I said.

He sat back in the booth and sighed. A hangdog expression on his face. 'I'm just trying to be logical and orderly,' he said.

'Yes, I've noticed over the years that murder is often logical and orderly,' I said.

'Your sarcasm is wasted on me,' he said.

'Don't I know it,' I said.

I got back to the hotel with less than five minutes to spare before my reading. I didn't have time to change out of my jeans and T-shirt, nor did I have time to put on make-up or fix my hair. My words on paper would have to do the trick with my audience because my appearance certainly wasn't going to.

The mezzanine held four ballrooms/convention rooms, each of which could be divided into three smaller rooms. Two of the ballrooms/convention rooms could be opened to make a huge ballroom. It was all done with partitions, glass and mirrors. In other words, it was magic to me. The room I was to use was one of the smaller ones, a third of a ball-room/convention room. Panels got a half room – readings a third of a room, as there was only one writer and therefore, supposedly, a smaller crowd.

Earlier I had determined not to read anything in my new book that was the least bit sensual or sexual, which would have to be the four pages at the beginning. But, walking in and seeing at least thirty women waiting, and wanting to keep my audience's attention off my blue jeans and T-shirt, I went straight to page seventy-two:

> She had never seen a man like him, so obvious in his appreciation of her. The dark eyes bore into her soul, and her eyes fixated on the bareness of his chest, the muscles of his arms rippling as he swung himself on to the bare back of his painted pony. His long black hair whipped in the wind and she no longer felt like a captive of his tribe, but a captive of her own desire.

I'll admit I was a little bit flushed after I finished my reading, as was most of my audience. Women were fanning themselves and a couple were even breathing heavily. God, I have a wonderful job! Willis has always claimed that he loved the fact that I write romances – after a good day's writing I was often, if not always, 'in the mood'. Actually there was the one time, after writing a particularly lurid love scene, when I drove to his office while his secretary was at lunch . . . Enough said.

As I was attempting to leave my third of the ballroom, I was accosted at the door by a very thin, very pert young woman with long red hair and a serious attitude.

'Are you E.J. Pugh?' she asked, her tone suggesting that if I wasn't I was in big trouble. And if I was – well, that was going to be trouble, too.

'Yes?' I said.

'Where's Lisbet?' she asked.

'Excuse me?' I queried.

With hands on hips, one hip thrust outward, and a scowl on her face, she said, 'Lisbet Carson? She was here to interview you? Right?'

I agreed that that had been the case.

'Well, where is she?' the young woman demanded.

'I haven't the faintest idea,' I replied. 'I haven't seen her since yesterday.'

The redhead sighed so hard her entire body trembled. 'Well, she didn't come back to the dorm last night and she borrowed my car to get here! My car's still in the parking lot so Lisbet's still here. Do you understand?' she said, saying the last slowly and distinctly, as if talking to a slow learner.

'I think I can follow,' I said. Then the implication hit me. Two murders and now someone was missing. Someone whose entire being revolved around asking pointed and possibly dangerous questions. I took the redhead by the arm and escorted her toward the down escalator and the lobby. 'I believe the Sam has a paging system,' I told her. 'Let's have her paged and see what happens.'

She allowed me to drag her and replied, 'Well, I suppose that will work.'

Getting to the front desk, I asked the clerk, 'Could you page someone for us?'

'Certainly, madam. Is it a guest of the hotel?' he asked in a British accent that could have been real.

The redhead and I looked at each other then back at the clerk. Simultaneously I said 'yes' while the redhead said 'no'. The clerk looked from one of us to the other.

'I see,' he said.

'I'm a guest of the hotel,' I informed him. 'And it's very important that I page someone who came here to see me. We've lost each other.'

The clerk nodded once and said, 'Certainly, madam. May I see your room card, please?'

I fished the room card out of my purse and handed it to him. Checking the number on the computer, he looked at me and said, 'Oh, my. Had a little trouble in that room, haven't we?'

'Little bit,' I agreed.

'Whom did you want paged?'

'Lisbet Carson,' I said.

'Elizabeth Carson,' he sort of repeated.

'No, Lisbet, for heaven's sake!' the redhead scolded.

'Lisbet,' I repeated. 'L-I-S-B-E-T. Carson.'

'Certainly, madam,' the clerk said, clearly losing patience with the redhead and me.

He hit a switch below the counter and leaned down. In sultry tones, he said, 'Will Lisbet Carson please contact the front desk. Lisbet Carson. Please contact the front desk.'

'Where will this be heard?' I asked.

'In all the common areas, madam.'

'Not in the rooms?'

'Certainly not, madam.'

I swear, if the guy called me 'madam' one more time, I was going to punch his lights out.

'Well, thank you,' I said, and started to walk away, the redhead in tow.

'My pleasure, madam,' he said.

I girded my loins (or attempted to gird what I thought might be my loins) and kept walking.

'Why don't you hang out here in the lobby for a few minutes and I'm sure Lisbet will be right here,' I said to the redhead.

'You think?' she asked belligerently.

'You're a prissy little thing, aren't you?' I said.

That got her dander up. 'Look, lady! I have a seminar I need to be at across town in like twenty minutes and I need my car! I got a ride here with a friend, but he couldn't take me to my seminar. I need my car. And Lisbet has the only set of keys I have here in town. Would you prefer I have my parents wire me the other set of keys? You think they'd get here in like the next twenty minutes?' All this was said with hands on hips and a sneer on her lips.

I shook my head. 'Honey,' I said, 'I don't really care. When Lisbet gets here please tell her goodbye for me.'

I turned and stalked off, but not before I heard the redhead say, 'Probably not!' behind me.

I went to the bar where I found my husband surrounded by the group. Mary and Lydia sat on either side of him, hanging on his every word, while Hal and Jerome laughed manfully at Willis's every utterance. Such suck-ups.

'Making friends?' I asked my husband as I pulled up a chair next to Jerome. Naturally one had not been saved for me.

'When were you going to tell us about this jewel of a man?' Lydia asked, touching my husband's arm and staring into his eyes, although I do believe the words were for my benefit.

'I try to keep him a secret,' I said.

'If we had a basement, she'd lock me in it,' Willis said, patting Lydia on the arm.

'Well, honey, if you were mine I'd do the same thing!' Lydia said and giggled.

'Willis, I want you to know we adore your wife,' Jerome said. 'She is a breath of fresh air in what had become a stale and stagnant existence.'

'And she's not bad to look at either!' Hal said, wiggling his eyebrows a la Groucho Marx.

'Hi!' said a voice from behind us. It was too lilting and lovely to be the Beast. And it wasn't. Willis stood up, Lydia's hand dropping from his arm as we turned to greet Candace.

'Candace,' I said, sighing, 'meet my husband, Willis Pugh.'

Candace's charms were not lost on my acutely observant husband. I thought for a moment Willis was going to kiss her outstretched hand, but he reigned himself in and shook it instead. 'Down, boy,' I said, and Willis sat.

'Have you heard anything more about DeWitt Perry?' Candace asked as Hal pulled up a chair for her. Funny, he hadn't pulled one up for me.

I shook my head, but Mary said, 'I heard through the grapevine that the Beast knew him well! He lives ... lived here in Austin and she's the one who told him about the convention.'

'Does she have any theories?' I asked.

Mary looked at me, then down at the table.

'Mary?' I asked.

She sighed. 'Well, as I understand it, she's thoroughly convinced you did it.'

I laughed. 'I did it? How? The only thing I know about elevators is if you push a button it'll take you to a floor.'

Mary looked at Willis, then at me. 'She mentioned that your husband is an engineer and isn't it convenient that he just *happened* to be here first thing this morning?'

Willis said, 'I have an alibi.'

Lydia placed her hand on his arm again. 'Of course you do, darling,' she said. 'Angela is a blithering idiot.'

'And who is she telling these things to?' I asked, getting angry.

Mary sighed. 'Everyone, as far as I can tell,' she said. 'You know Angela. She isn't particularly shy when it comes to her rantings.'

Jerome patted my hand. 'Don't worry, E.J. No one who knows Angela would ever believe a word she uttered.'

'Unfortunately,' I said, 'the police don't *know* Angela.'

'True,' he said and stopped patting my hand.

Maybe it was two nights with little sleep, or the fight with Willis earlier, or maybe it was just my own had-enough-itis, but I got up and marched to the registration table on the mezzanine level. Angela was behind the table, berating her underlings, when I walked up.

'Angela,' I said.

She looked up, started for a brief second, then frowned. 'What do *you* want?' she asked.

'I'd like to know why you've been accusing me of killing DeWitt Perry,' I said.

She squared her massive shoulders and said, 'Because I saw the tape!'

'Then you must have been surprised to find out what kind of man he was,' I said. 'Or were you already aware you allowed, or some say encouraged, a stalker into our midst?'

She was actually silent for half a second, then said, 'I don't know what you're talking about. Mr Perry was a true gentleman. I'll not have you slander his name.'

I smiled my meanest smile. I have several. 'I suppose that means he never came on to *you*,' I said.

'Whether he came on to *you* or not, Mrs Pugh, there was no need to kill the poor man!' she said, loudly.

'I didn't, Miss Barber. But I do believe whoever killed poor Jane probably killed Mr Perry. Where were you when Jane was pushed to her death?' I asked.

She sputtered. I've read about such things, but never saw it in real life. Rather disgusting, actually. 'How dare you!' she finally spat out.

'How dare *you*?' I queried. Tit for tat, and all that.

'You are a vile woman, E.J. Pugh!' she said through clinched teeth. 'No wonder you and that midget Jane Dawson were such good friends! You deserve each other!'

'So you admit you pushed Jane to her death!' I said, suppressing the 'ah ha!' that instantly came to mind.

'I admit no such thing!' she screamed.

'Ladies,' said a quiet voice behind me. I turned to see Detective Washington with an older gentleman and a younger woman in tow. 'This is David Dawson and his daughter Miranda Weaver. Mr Dawson wanted a word with you E.J.'

There was no rock for me to hide under. I couldn't help wondering how much Jane's husband and daughter had heard of the little exchange between the Beast and I.

I turned to David Dawson and took his outstretched hand, which shook slightly. 'Mr Dawson, I'm so sorry . . .'

He patted my hand and smiled faintly. 'Thank you,' he said. 'Jane held you in high regard.'

'As I did her,' I said.

He was a tall, thin man, several inches taller than I, which meant he was well over six feet. I couldn't help smiling inwardly at the 'Mutt and Jeff' comparisons that had to have been made over the years about him and Jane. My heart went out to him. Thirty-something years married to the same woman to have it come to this. They both deserved so much more.

'You have her things?' David Dawson asked.

I looked at Washington. 'We had her belongings packed up and placed in storage here at the hotel,' Washington said. 'There are a few things we'll need to keep for the time being – papers and such – but the rest you can take back with you.'

'Thank you,' Dawson said to Washington. Then to me, he added, 'May I speak with you a moment?'

I excused myself from Washington, not bothering to say a

word to the Beast – what could be said anyway? 'We'll continue with the accusations later' hardly seemed fitting.

I led David Dawson and his daughter to an area outside one of the conference rooms. There was a sofa, loveseat and two chairs, all of butter soft camel colored leather. I took the sofa, David the loveseat and his daughter Miranda opted for one of the armchairs. She was a pretty young woman with dark hair streaked with blonde, big brown eyes like her mother's, that were now red-rimmed from crying. I knew from my many conversations with Jane that Miranda was recently divorced and had moved back home with her two children. I assumed either the ex or one of her siblings was now caring for her children while she and her father were on this horrendous errand.

'I don't know what's going to happen,' Jane says with a resigned sigh. 'I'm actually surprised she asked – although of course she asked her father, not me.'

'What happened between the two of you?' I ask her.

'The teen years,' Jane said. 'Most of the time you live through it, but Miranda and I didn't. She discovered when she was thirteen that she hated me and she hasn't changed her mind since.'

'Jane, that's not true,' I try.

'E.J., how would you know? You say that to placate me, but I was there, you weren't. I'm here now, you aren't. She still comes home for Christmas and Thanksgiving, but she goes out of her way to make sure she and I are never alone together, and the only time she actually talks to me is when I ask her a direct question.' She sighs. 'And I have two grand-children I barely know.'

'If she moves in with you,' I say, 'that's going to have to change.'

'One way or another, it's going to!' Jane says, and by her tone of voice, I believe her.

'Please tell me what happened,' David Dawson said quietly. So I did, taking them through the evening and on into the night and wee hours of the morning when I'd stumbled on Jane's broken body.

'Do you think she suffered?' Miranda asked, her voice choked.

I shook my head. 'No way,' I said. 'It had to be instant-aneous.' I knew that I was lying to the girl. The amount of blood around Jane's head indicated that she had been alive for a while after hitting the concrete floor. A dead body doesn't bleed; only a live body does. It would do no one any good for these two people or the rest of the family back home to know this fact. I hoped Jane had been at least unconscious after hitting the floor, never privy to the fact that her life's blood was spilling out around her.

I smiled at the two of them. 'I feel like I know you both, you and your whole family. Jane told me so much about you. We'd been emailing for quite some time.'

David patted my hand and smiled. 'I know what you mean. Jane told me all about you. She was really . . . really looking forward to . . . this convention. To meeting you in person.'

I laughed. 'Did she tell you what she did to me?' I asked, then went on to tell them about my shock on seeing the petite older woman at the door, instead of the buxom brunette on the book jacket.

Even Miranda managed to laugh. 'Mom loved to do that to people who only knew her through her books. Sarah Anne – my sister-in-law, the one who modeled for the book jacket – actually got stopped in the supermarket all the time. I think that's why she dyed her hair blonde. She was getting tired of it.'

David sobered and asked, 'Do you have any idea . . . who . . . I mean, well . . .'

'Who killed her?' I asked, getting the hard question out for him. He nodded. 'No,' I said. 'But Detective Washington is on top of this. He'll find out.' With my help, I thought but didn't say.

'I heard you and Angela Barber arguing. I know Jane didn't like her much, which made me wonder why they'd been communicating so much lately.'

I perked up. 'Communicating? How do you mean?'

'Phone calls, email. Jane hung up on her a couple of times when she called. When I asked her what it was about, she wouldn't say,' David said.

'Do you have access to Jane's email account?' I asked.

He nodded. 'I have her password. Why?'

'Would you be willing to come upstairs to my room with

me? I have my laptop and we could look at those emails. See what was going on. If the Bea— If Angela Barber had anything to do with Jane's death, I want to know. And I want to know now.'

David stood up, a determined look on his face. 'You and me both,' he said. 'Where's your room?'

'Well, we had it out,' Jane says when I pick up the phone.

'How bad?' I ask.

She starts to cry. 'I'm too old for this shit, E.J.! I just want my life back! The one where I could walk and talk and sit and stand without someone second guessing my every move!'

It's the third week since Miranda and her children had moved back home. Things obviously weren't going well. 'Have you talked to her?' I ask.

'That's what I tried to do this morning,' she says, sniffing back tears. 'All I got for my efforts was this shoulder-heaving sigh and "What now, Mother?".'

'Have you talked to David?' I ask.

'Ha! Tell David his little darlin' is abusing her mother? No, he wouldn't believe me,' Jane says. 'Besides,' she sighs heavily, 'this is between Miranda and me. It's not fair to involve David.'

'You said you had it out,' I remind her.

'Yeah, I guess I lied. She said "What now, Mother?", and I said, "We need to talk," and she rolled her eyes and said, "And what good would that do?" and I said, "Probably none," and she said, "So why bother?".'

'What would you say to her if you could say anything at all?' I ask her.

Jane is silent for a moment, thinking, I hope. Then she says, 'I'd say "I love you and I forgive you, and I hope you forgive me."'

My turn to be silent. Finally I say, 'That's all that needs to be said. So say it.'

Long pause. 'Yeah,' Jane finally says. 'Yeah, you're right.'

Black Cat Ridge, Texas
Graham, Saturday

It has already been established that not all, but some, fifteen-year-old boys can be incredibly self-absorbed. Graham Pugh fell into this category. He was feeling many things that Saturday morning when the phone woke him up: relief that his excursion into Codderville the night before had not resulted in mayhem of any kind; confidence that he could easily do it again, pride in the fact that he was obviously braver than he'd ever given himself credit for; and, of course, horny. When he picked up the phone and listened for mere seconds, he felt something else: incredibly lucky.

At first he thought it was criminal that someone would call the house before eight in the morning, but when he listened to the conversation between his neighbor Mrs Luna and his dad, with Mrs Luna telling him what had happened at his mother's convention, and heard his dad say he was on his way to Austin, he realized it was a gift from the gods. A fact that a friend of his mother's had died, and someone else, too, and his mother was being questioned as a possible suspect in one if not both murders, was not something that really entered his thoughts. His mom had been there before. She always got out of it. But the main thing, the all encompassing thing was: he was going to be free to stay out as late as he wanted. No curfew!

His parents knew better than to leave him in charge of his sisters; which meant his grandmother would be coming to stay at the house. When they were little they would go stay with her, but now, with all their activities and friends and stuff, she came to their house.

Which was perfect. Joey's grandma wasn't the only one who fell asleep early. Grandma Vera didn't watch TV – but she actually went to bed no later than eight thirty. Which meant the girls on their computers as late as they wanted – and no one would know when Graham got home. Or even if he went out for that matter. His sisters rarely spoke to him and never worried where he was or what he was doing. Which worked out well on most occasions.

So tonight was the night. Ashley had no curfew and he had no curfew. He knew without a doubt that tonight was the night: he was gonna get laid.

Austin, Texas
E.J., Saturday
The emails between Jane and the Beast went back ten or so months. Hoping to gain insight into what was going on,

I decided to read them chronologically, going back to the beginning.

> 3 June 2005
> Romance365: Jane, thanks so much for agreeing to read my book. It means so much to me that someone of your stature would agree to read it. Ha! Ha! Sorry, I meant your stature as a writer, not your physical stature! ☺ Please take your time and let me know what you think.
> Best,
> Angela

I opened the attachment and read a few pages. Obviously the Beast had written a romance novel and was getting one of the best to give her advice. I closed the attachment, not interested in Angela Barber's witless prose, and looked for Jane's reply.

> 31 June 2005
> Mitylarue: Angela, I've read your pages and they're not bad. They of course need work. What pages don't? But I think you've done a good job. Kudos.
> Best,
> Jane

I didn't see how this was going to get us anywhere, but I kept going.

> 5 August, 2005
> Romance365: Jane, I've made all the changes you suggested. Would you mine reading it again?
> Hugs,
> Angela

There was another attachment, presumably Angela's reworked pages. I didn't bother to open it. It was the next email that got my attention.

6 November 2005

Romance365: Jane, thank you for your phone call last night, but do you really think three months is that long? I've heard so many stories about how long it takes to get an agent's or publisher's interest, and I'm just not sure if your plan wouldn't be jumping the gun. If you don't mind, I'd like to keep that in reserve.

Hugs,

Angela

10 November 2005

Mitylarue: Angela, you've sent this out to every reputable house there is! And how many agents have you sent it to? Dozens! It's too good not to see the light of day! If I sent it to my agent as mine, and through her to my editor, it would be on the list in a New York minute! You get 90% of the take, I get 10%. I just want you to get your voice out there!

Best,

Jane

11 November 2005

Romance365: Jane, I see the practicality of your suggestion, but I do want my name associated with my work! How do we solve that dilemma?

Hugs,

Angela

11 November 2005

Mitylarue: Angela, no problem. As soon as it's published and out, you start going to signings with me and we tell the world! The joke, of course, will be on the publishers!

Best,
Jane

11 November 2005
Romance365:   Jane, OK, I'll do it. But I want some-
                thing in writing and notarized!

12 November 2005
Mitylarue: What, you don't trust me?

12 November 2005
Romance365:   Not with my baby. I don't trust
                anyone!

13 November 2005
Mitylarue: Angela, you've obviously never given
                real birth. It's definitely not the same
                thing. One is painful but rewarding for
                the rest of your life. The other is sort
                of fun, then goes off into oblivion. Try
                to understand the difference and
                lighten up!

14 November 2005
Romance365:   Jane, you're right, I've never had a
                child and I doubt if I ever will. So
                this book is as close to a real baby as
                I'm going to get. I hope you can
                understand my paranoia and over-
                protectiveness.

15 November 2005
Mitylarue: Angela, of course I understand it! I
                just want to make sure you don't look
                at this as a life or death situation.
                There's always the possibility that they
                won't publish it, even under my name.

16 November 2005
Romance365:   Jane, I'm not worried about that! With
                some of the stories you've had out

lately, this will be like a breath of fresh
air for your publisher!

I almost laughed out loud. No matter what, Angela couldn't
help being Angela.
Why Jane would even consider doing such a thing – which
basically amounted to fraud – was beyond me.

8 December 2005
Mitylarue:　　　Angela, please stop calling me. I
　　　　　　　　haven't heard anything from my agent
　　　　　　　　yet. I'll call you the minute I hear
　　　　　　　　anything. As I told you, she's sent it
　　　　　　　　to my publisher. New York is always
　　　　　　　　slow. They don't work on the same
　　　　　　　　timetable as we mortal humans. Please
　　　　　　　　have patience.

14 December 2005
Romance365:　　Jane, Why aren't you answering your
　　　　　　　　phone? Every time I call your husband
　　　　　　　　says you're not there! I know he's
　　　　　　　　lying! Surely you've heard back from
　　　　　　　　NY by now. Call me immediately!

20 December 2005
Mitylarue:　　　Angela, I heard back from my agent.
　　　　　　　　I'm very sorry to say my publisher is
　　　　　　　　not interested. She felt the story was
　　　　　　　　amateurish (her word). I'm so very
　　　　　　　　sorry. Why don't you table that story
　　　　　　　　for now and start on another? Think
　　　　　　　　of that one as practice. We all have
　　　　　　　　one or two novels sitting in a cabinet
　　　　　　　　somewhere that never saw the light of
　　　　　　　　day. Again, Angela, I'm sorry this
　　　　　　　　didn't work out. It could have been
　　　　　　　　fun for both of us.
　　　　　　　　Best,
　　　　　　　　Jane

20 January 2006

Mitylarue:	Angela, I'm informing you in writing that I'm having my phone number changed. Please do not try to contact me again. I did everything I could to help you, and this is the thanks I get! Angela, you need help. Please leave me alone. Jane

22 February 2006

Romance365:	Jane, you bitch! I know what you're doing! I know you haven't written a decent book in years! You're trying to steal mine! Do you think I'm stupid? Well, I'm not! You can change the title, change the main characters' names, do whatever you think you can do, but I'll know it's my book and so will everyone within listening distance! And so will my attorney! You can't get away with this! And if you try to go through with it, you'll be very, very sorry!

David and I looked at each other while Miranda finished reading it. 'Dad!' she said when she was done. 'My God, she's threatening Mother! What is this all about?'

'It appears that Angela didn't believe your mom when she said the publisher didn't like the book,' I said. 'Angela obviously believed that they were going to publish it under Jane's name – and that Jane was going to take credit for it.'

'My mother would never do that!' Miranda said indignantly.

'No, she wouldn't,' I agreed. 'But Angela would. And I'm afraid Angela believes anything she's capable of doing anyone else is also capable of doing. She doesn't understand that other people have ethics.'

'Why in the world would Jane even offer to do this for that woman?' David asked. 'She never liked Angela.'

'But maybe she thought the book was good,' I said. 'That would mean a lot to Jane. Even if she didn't like Angela, she *did* like talent, and she would go out of her way to see that that talent was appreciated.'

'And that bitch killed her for it!' Miranda said, bursting into tears. David turned away from the computer to comfort his daughter.

I couldn't take my eyes off the computer, the last entry from Angela, that last threatening entry. Should I turn this over to the police? You bet your sweet ass.

Eight

Black Cat Ridge, Texas
Elizabeth, Saturday

It was nine a.m. when the two girls found out Dad was going to Austin to be with Mom, and that Grandma Vera was coming to spend the night.

'It's divine intervention!' Megan said.

Elizabeth just shook her head in wonder. 'It's amazing!' she agreed.

'Taking Grandma's Valiant will be a piece of cake!' Megan said, grinning.

'She goes to bed at eight thirty!' Elizabeth said, grinning back.

'We couldn't have planned this better ourselves!' Megan said.

The smile faded from Elizabeth's face. Maybe it wasn't divine intervention; maybe it was demonic intervention, she thought. Maybe all this was conspiring to lead them into something that wasn't such a good idea.

Elizabeth shook off the thought and looked at her sister. She smiled back as they did a double high five. 'We're gonna kick some ass!' Megan said.

'You bet!' Elizabeth said, pushing her reservations to the far corners of her mind.

Austin, Texas
E.J., Saturday

　'We left the kids with David and went to the mall,' Jane tells me. 'I haven't had so much fun in years!'

'I'm so glad,' I say.

'Who knew Miranda had such a diabolical sense of humor? I sure didn't!' she says, laughing.

I smile on my end of the line.

'This doesn't prove anything,' Washington said.

'No, but you finally have someone with a motive!' I said.

He was quiet as he reread the words on my laptop. Turning to a small, Hispanic woman who always seemed to be at his side, he said, 'Guzman, please ask Ms Barber to step in here a moment.'

The woman left, leaving Washington and me alone in the small room behind the front desk. I took a seat in one of the two available chairs.

'What are you doing?' Washington asked.

I raised my eyebrows. 'Sitting,' I said.

He shook his head. 'No, you're not. You're leaving.' He stood up and took the two steps to the door, opening it wide, presumably so that I could pass through. I'm not that dumb. Once out of this room, I was out for good. If I had to I'd hide under the desk.

My turn to shake my head. 'Nope. I'm not budging. I'm a fly on the wall. Ignore me.'

'Let's see,' he said, looking hard at me. 'A six foot buxom redhead. Little hard to ignore.'

'I'm only 5'10",' I said.

The slightly pleasant look on his face disappeared behind a scowl. 'I don't care if you're 3' 7". You're leaving.'

'If I were 3' 7" I could easily hide under the desk—'

'Out!' he said, pointing with one long finger towards the door. I got up slowly, heading for the door, just as Guzman came back with the Beast in tow.

'What have you accused me of this time?' Angela said, a mean look on her face. Of course, she had no pleasant facial expressions with which to contrast, so it actually could have been her friendly look for all I know.

'I only deal in the truth, Angela,' I said. OK, a little self-righteously, but it's hard not to be self-righteous around a woman like that.

'You wouldn't know the truth if it bit you on the ass!'

Angela said, at which point I determined that was definitely not her friendly face.

'Ms Barber,' Washington said, ushering the Beast into the room. 'Good day, Ms Pugh,' he said as he slammed the door, practically taking off part of my ample bottom – a weight-loss regime I hadn't thought of until then, but it did seem like a painful way to go.

Passing through the lobby on my way to the bar, I was again accosted by Lisbet Carson's skinny, redheaded roommate.

'Mrs Pugh,' she said, pointedly staring at her watch. 'I've missed my seminar and Lisbet still isn't here!'

'Did you have her paged a second time?'

'I tried, but he wouldn't do it!' she said breathlessly, giving me the first hint of concern on her part for her missing room-mate.

My earlier musings on two murders and a missing nosy reporter came back. Sure, she was just a college kid, doing a fluff piece for her school newspaper, but did the killer know that? With the questions Lisbet was bound to ask regarding Jane's murder, she could have stumbled on something big and scary. I looked around me at the Sam's lobby. This was a huge hotel. I had no idea how many guest rooms, but there were a lot, then there would be the numerous common rooms, and then the not so common rooms – all the places where the actual work of the hotel was done: the kitchens, the laundry rooms, the basements, etc. We needed more than just the two of us.

I found the troops in the bar – surprise, surprise – and the redhead and I went up to the table. 'What's your name?' I asked the redhead.

'Carrie Winston,' she said.

I introduced her around, then said, 'Carrie is Lisbet Carson's roommate. Lisbet was the young lady interviewing me for her college newspaper. Did any of you speak with her at all yesterday?' I asked.

Jerome said, 'She caught Hal and me at the bar here around, what was it, Hal, noonish?'

Hal shrugged. 'Maybe later?'

'Possibly,' Jerome agreed.

'She tried to follow me into the elevator,' Lydia said, 'but I let the doors close on her. Sorry. What's the problem?'

'She's got my car keys!' Carrie Winston said, hands again on hips, belligerent tone again in voice, scowl again marring pretty brow.

'I think she may be missing,' I said.

'Well, that's a little dramatic!' Carrie said, giving me the evil eye.

The others instantly caught my drift.

'Maybe she asked a few too many questions,' Mary said.

'Of the wrong person,' Lydia added.

'At absolutely the wrong time,' Jerome said.

'Ah, shit,' Hal said, standing up.

The others followed suit, Willis coming over and putting his arm around my shoulders.

'Where do we start searching?' Candace asked.

'What's going on?' Carrie asked, the puzzled look on her face much more appealing than her former visage.

'I've already had her paged, which covers all the common areas,' I told the gang. 'That leaves the rooms and the service areas.'

'Are there any empty rooms left in the hotel?' Mary asked. 'I thought the convention had filled the place up.'

'And the service areas are used constantly by the employees of the hotel,' Jerome said. 'Surely they would have noticed her.'

'No, look, it's OK. I can call a friend to take me back to the dorm . . .' Carrie started.

I turned to her. 'Carrie, there have been two murders in this hotel in the past twenty-four hours. Now your friend, a reporter who was asking questions, is missing. Do you see where I'm headed here?'

Carrie's pale, freckled complexion whitened, then was infused with blood, turning her face a dark pink. 'Oh my God!' she breathed. Then she screamed. 'Oh my God! Oh God! Oh dear Lord! Oh oh oh!'

I grabbed her by the shoulder as heads began to turn. 'Carrie, cut it out! You need to get a hold of yourself!' I shook her slightly, my right hand prepared to slap her face if necessary. Actually, the girl got on my nerves and the thought of giving her a good slap (for medicinal purposes only, of course) wasn't an unpleasant one. Unfortunately she calmed down.

'You think Lisbet's dead?' Carrie whispered.

'No, I don't,' I lied. 'But I'm afraid she might be in trouble.'

Carrie pulled herself together, straightening her shoulders and standing tall. 'What do you want me to do?' she asked.

I shook my head. 'Just let me think.' Finally I turned to Jerome. 'You're my candidate for asking the desk clerk how many empty rooms there are. And get a pass key for them. Willis, would you go with him?'

Jerome threw me a mock salute and headed for the front desk.

Willis kissed my cheek. 'Sure, honey,' he said, following Jerome.

'There are storage rooms on each floor, by the vending machines. I know the doors are unlocked because I stole some extra toilet paper yesterday. Mary and Lydia, y'all take the lobby, the mezzanine and the second floor, Hal, you and Candace take floors three through five.'

'And what are you going to do?' Mary asked.

'Carrie and I are going to take the garage,' I said.

'The whole thing?' Carrie whined. So much for her earlier concern and conviction.

'Yes,' I said, then turned toward the front desk. Jerome and Willis were standing there by themselves; the desk clerk was gone. Seeing me, Jerome gave me a thumbs up sign. I waved back and Carrie and I were off.

The garage was three stories, hot and smelled like exhaust fumes. We walked against the walls, checking in front of cars and between them, and any crevices used for service. We checked the stairwells. We started with the first floor; an hour later we were on the third floor with no results.

'Where's your car?' I asked Carrie.

'It's here,' she said. 'On the third floor.' We'd already checked in front of the cars, now we walked down the wide driveway, checking out the backs. She slapped her small Toyota Camry on the trunk. 'This is mine,' she said. The trunk slapped back.

Carrie jumped back as if shot; I just stood there, as if waiting for the trunk to speak. It did. 'Help!' it said.

Carrie and I both ran to the trunk. 'Lisbet?' I yelled. 'Is that you?'

'Yes!' she said, her voice weak. 'Please help me!'

'Keys!' I yelled at Carrie.

'She's got them!' Carrie yelled back, pointing at the trunk.

'Is the car unlocked? Do you have anything in there—'

'It's locked! Hold on, Lisbet! Hold on!' she yelled at the trunk.

Another car was pulling out a few cars down. I ran to it as fast as I could, slapping the side of it as it began to take off. The driver slammed on his brakes and turned to look at me. 'This a carjacking?' he asked.

'No! We've got someone locked in a trunk back here and no key! Do you have a tire iron?'

The man got out of his car. He was in his fifties, soft around the middle but still big. A linebacker gone to seed. He popped his own trunk and got out a nice heavy tire iron and followed me to Carrie's Camry.

Seeing the tire iron, Carrie said, 'Ah, you're not going to break my car, are you?'

'Got a better way to get her out?' I asked.

'Jeez!' she said, then, speaking to the trunk, 'Lisbet, you're paying for the damage to my car!'

The man stuck the beveled edge of the tire iron in the small space between fender and trunk lid and leaned. Nothing happened. I got on the other side of the tire iron and, on the count of three, the two of us leaned together. The lid popped open.

Lisbet tried to sit up, but I had to help her. There was a gash on her head.

'Oh my God! You spilled blood everywhere!' Carrie yelled, hands on hips again.

Helping Lisbet out of the trunk, I said, 'I suggest you put in for a new roommate.'

'No shit,' Lisbet said, leaning on me heavily, right before she passed out.

I was back at Brackenridge Hospital, awaiting word on Lisbet Carson's condition. Her parents were driving in from a suburb of Dallas and would be there in about another hour. Carrie, the caring roommate, had insisted someone tie her trunk down for her and then drove off, muttering under her breath as she left something about irresponsible roommates. Detective

Washington kept me company, of sorts, pacing back and forth in the hallway.

'You really can leave, Mrs Pugh,' he said for the third time.

'I'll wait to find out how she is,' I said, for the third time.

'You will not go in with me when I interview her,' he said, for the third time.

'Never entered my head,' I replied, for the third time.

Yes, it was getting monotonous. Not only our verbal intercourse but being in the emergency room of Brack, as the hospital is known in the city. Before today, the last time I'd been at Brack had been seven or eight years ago when I'd been in the morgue to identify the body of my husband. Obviously it hadn't been my husband, as he was now back at the Sam, probably swilling beer and being hit on by Lydia, as I sat in an uncomfortable chair and was berated by Detective Washington. Finally, after forty-five minutes of anxious waiting, a scrub-wearing personage came out the door and said, 'Family of Lisbet Carson?'

Washington and I ran up together. He looked from one to the other of us then said, 'Whatever. She has a severe concussion and a cracked skull. Her condition is serious but stable.'

Washington flashed his badge. 'I need to ask her a few questions,' he said.

'She's asleep right now—'

'You're not supposed to let someone with a concussion sleep,' I said. Then muttered, 'At least that's what I've always heard.'

'She's on medication and fluids. How are you related to her?' he asked me.

'She's not,' Detective Washington said. 'She's just leaving.'

'No, I—' I started.

The doctor, or whatever he was, interrupted, 'Ma'am, if you're not related, you'll have to leave.'

I turned tail and left. What's a girl to do?

I went in search of the troops, once again finding Willis holding court in the bar. He had a beer in front of him, two empties next to it. 'Whoever wants to allow Willis to share their room tonight,' I said, 'I just want to warn you that he snores like crazy after a couple of beers. Drools, too.'

'Hey, sweetness,' he said, cupping my butt with his hand,

something he rarely does in public unless he's several sheets to the wind, as they say.

'Honey, I don't care if you talk, walk, or hopscotch in your sleep,' Lydia said, her words slightly slurred, 'I'm more than willing to share my king with you.'

'Nope,' I said. 'Next offer. From a gentleman, please.'

It was finally agreed that a cot would be ordered from the desk to be placed in Jerome's room. 'I don't snore,' Jerome said, 'but I do make a certain amount of noise in my sleep. I prefer to think of it as creative, yet unintelligible, verbal musings.'

'How's the kid?' Hal asked.

'Cracked skull and a concussion. Washington's interviewing her now.'

'Maybe we'll find out what the hell's been going on,' Hal said.

'Wouldn't that be nice?' I agreed.

'What are you wearing tonight, E.J.?' Mary Sparrow asked.

'Tonight?' Then it struck me. 'Oh, my God! Tonight's the banquet!'

Mary sighed. 'I know. It hardly seems fitting to go on with it, doesn't it? I had a chance to speak with David before he left. Miranda seemed . . . distraught.'

I nodded. 'Yes, she's pretty upset.'

Mary looked around her, then, leaning closer to me, said in a whisper that everyone leaned forward to hear, 'David said you found something on Jane's computer that points directly at Angela! Is that true?'

I leaned forward, too, nodding. 'Washington interviewed her earlier, but I don't know what he found out.'

The look on Mary's face was frightening as she said, 'If she did this, I will hurt her. Badly.'

I believed her. I was hoping the gang wouldn't grill me about the emails, because I didn't want to go into Jane's basic fraud attempt. Silly me. This gang not grill me? Fat chance.

'I'd really rather not go into it,' I said primly after Mary, Lydia, Hal and Jerome all asked in slightly different ways what had been in the emails.

Mary slammed her fist on the table and everyone blinked but got extremely quiet. 'How dare you not share this with us?' she said, her voice soft but deadly. 'We were her best

friends. We've known her for years! I'm not saying you're
not one of us, E.J., but you are very new to the group. You
barely knew Jane. And for you to keep something this important from us is unconscionable.'

Willis drained his third beer and wiggled his eyebrows at
me. Ah, the support I get from my dearly beloved.

I sighed and said, 'Then let's go to my room. I'm not talking
about this where other ears can hear.'

We all stood up except Candace. I looked down at her and
said, 'You coming?'

She shook her head. 'I'm not really part of the group,' she
said quietly. 'I'm just here by accident.'

'Get your ass up and get to your room,' Lydia said, swaying
against my husband's arm. 'Now!'

Candace got up and we all headed for the elevators.

It was one of the harder things I've ever done, telling these
people what I found on Jane's computer. Telling these people
that their funny, spirited, but ever moral and ethical friend had
attempted to commit fraud. Sometimes in our lives, more than
once if we're lucky, we have someone we put on a pedestal.
Someone we look up to, admire, know in our hearts is beyond
corruption, immoral thought, word, or deed. Someone to whom
we aspire to emulate, and when we can't achieve their lofty
goals, feel a little less about ourselves. Unfortunately, having
that someone fall off the pedestal we've placed them on does
not raise our own value; it just makes us terribly sad.

'Why would Jane do that?' Mary asked. 'I mean, it's fraud!
As soon as she and Angela proclaimed to the world that it
was Angela's book, her publisher would drop her like a hot
potato, if not press charges!'

Lydia sighed. 'They'd already dropped her, Mary,' she said.

'No, no they hadn't. They didn't take her last book—'

'Her last *two* books, ' Lydia corrected. 'I think Jane thought
Angela's book was good enough to get her back in.' She sighed
again, tears in her eyes. 'I'm just not sure if she was doing
this for Angela or for herself. What if she *was* going to steal
the book?'

Mary stood up. 'Jane wouldn't do that and you know it!'
She walked to the window and looked out on to Sixth Street.
'If anything, she was going to embarrass her publisher. Have

them publish the book under her name then do just as she told Angela she would – tell the world it wasn't even hers.'

'Isn't that fraud?' Hal asked.

'Not technically,' Jerome answered. 'The publishers would pay for a book, which they would get, the actual author would get her money, and Jane would get what amounted to a finder's fee. Agent gets her cut.' He shook his head. 'I don't see anything criminal here. Unethical, yes.'

'No house would touch her again,' Mary said.

'No house would touch her period, Mary,' Lydia said. 'Her last two published books lost money, and then two rejections from a house who'd published her for years?'

'Oh, God,' Mary said, sitting down on the edge of one of the queen-sized beds. 'She told me she was thinking of changing agents. She'd been with Rita for years and I couldn't understand . . .'

Lydia and Mary looked at each other, then Lydia said, 'She wasn't dumping Rita, Rita was dumping her.'

'I just don't understand,' I said. 'Jane was one of the best romance writers out there! Her heroines were feisty before feisty was cool – she was an innovator!'

'Did you read her last book?' Mary asked and I shook my head. 'I never said this out loud to anyone, but it was a rehash of her second novel. She changed the names and the setting, but basically it was the same book.'

'Oh, my God! *The Bride of Rune Castle*!' Lydia said. 'I just thought I was having a very long *déjà vu*!'

'So what does any of this mean?' Jerome asked. 'How does this prove that Angela killed Jane?'

'It doesn't, Jerry!' Lydia said impatiently. 'But I for one needed to know why my very good friend would go off the deep end and get involved with the Beast to begin with!'

'I'm sorry, Lydia,' Jerome said, bowing his head. 'I didn't mean to offend.'

Lydia got up from her chair and walked over to where Jerome was sitting on the second bed, sat down beside him and hugged him. 'I'm sorry,' she said. 'I didn't mean to yell at you . . .' Then she burst into tears.

I felt like crying myself. How hurt must Jane have been to come up with such a scheme? To be on the top of the heap as she'd been for years, then to have everything come tumbling down. Writers have to have large egos, how else would one even think that anyone else would want to read their work? The praise she'd gotten over the years, the awards, the kudos, were all going away. Maybe the muse had left her high and dry, but maybe someday it would come back. We'd never know now, because someone had killed her. Was that someone Angela Barber, the person Jane had tried to use to get back at her publishers? What would such a revelation have done to Angela's budding career? After the scheme became public, would any publisher ever want to touch Angela's work? I doubt if Angela had thought further than the publication of that first book.

'Mary, you said Jane's agent was named Rita?' I asked.

'Rita Slinger with the Wrightman agency,' Mary answered.

'Do you know her?'

'Not personally,' she said.

'I do,' Hal said. 'I was with her for a couple of years before I went with Paul.'

'Could you get her on the phone?' I asked. 'I'd like to talk to her. She may not even know about Jane, and we can use that as an excuse to call her.'

'What are you going to say to her?' Lydia asked.

'With Jane gone, there won't be a confidentiality agreement. And if she somehow gets the impression I'm with the police . . .'

Lydia grinned. 'Hal, call!'

Black Cat Ridge, Texas
Graham, Saturday

That Saturday stretched before Graham like a long Texas highway. No end in sight. His father had left instructions, which unfortunately his grandmother was aware of. Mow the lawn, clean out the garbage cans with the hose and soap, roll the hose back up and sweep off the patio. Graham couldn't help but notice that the yard had never looked this good before he was old enough to be told what to do. It was unfair, he realized, but it's what he got paid for. He would eventually become a good employee, knowing his worth and enjoying the monetary fruits of his labors.

It was after lunch when the phone rang. 'Graham? Man, I got the truck tonight! Legit,' Hollister said. 'The old man said

I could borrow it if I put gas in it. You got enough dough to do that?'

'I'll find some,' Graham said, and hung up, thinking hard. Where to get cash? Megan just had a birthday and their grand-mother in Houston always sent cash. All he had to do was get in her room and find it. He grinned to himself. Piece of cake, he thought.

Austin, Texas
E.J., Saturday

Hal was smoother than I thought possible for someone who wore the same Penney's stay-press pants three days in a row. He was able to finagle Rita Slinger's home phone number from his agent and called her, sadly informing her of Jane's demise.

'The police are investigating and they have questions,' he said, which wasn't a lie. 'There's someone here who needs to ask you a few things.' Again, not a lie. He handed the phone to me.

'Ms Slinger, this is Elena Luna,' I said, using that name instead of my own, which, of course, was a lie. Romance is a small community and I've had some success. This agent who specialized in romance writers might know my name. 'I'm so sorry about Ms Dawson.'

'Thank you,' said the whiskey voiced woman on the other end of the line. Age, cigarettes and good Scotch had done a job on her vocal cords. 'She was a valued friend and client.'

'I have just a few questions for you,' I said.

'I'll do anything I can to help,' she said.

'I understand Ms Dawson recently sent you a manuscript that was rejected by her publisher,' I said.

'Yes,' she said, making the small word three syllables.

'Did you read that manuscript?' I asked.

'Of course,' she said indignantly. 'I read all my writers' work!'

'Did you notice anything different about this manuscript?'

'No,' she said, 'not really.'

'Then there was something?'

She was quiet for a second, then said, 'Well, the story line was fresh, which was something . . . well, something I

hadn't been seeing from Jane for a while. But the prose was
. . . well, just not Jane. It was, well, just not up to her usual
standard.'

'Were you aware that someone other than Jane Dawson
wrote that book?'

There was a silence on the other end of the line. After a
full minute, Rita Slinger said, 'What?'

'It was actually written by a woman named Angela Barber,'
I said.

'The Beast?' Rita Slinger exclaimed.

'You know her?' I asked, surprised. Looking around the
room at those present, I noticed several shocked faces.

There was a long, heartfelt sigh on the other end of the
line. 'Oh, God, yes,' she said. 'She's been trying to get me to
represent her for years! Buttonholes me at every convention!
That's why I didn't go to this one, since it was in her home
town.' She sighed again. 'That was *her* book?' Her voice both
incredulous and sad at the same time.

'Yes,' I answered. 'Do I understand correctly that Ms
Dawson claimed this book as her own?'

There was a pregnant pause before she said, 'Yes.'

'And her publisher rejected it?' I asked.

'Well, not right off the bat. They wanted a full rewrite and
Jane refused. She said they had to take it as is.'

'And that's why her publisher rejected it?' I asked.

Rita Slinger sighed. 'To tell you the truth, I don't think her
editor even read it. Her old editor retired a few years ago, and
this new one, who's like twelve,' she said, in that aggrieved
tone that only someone over forty can have about someone
under thirty (believe me, I know), 'has rejected the last two
manuscripts of Jane's that I've sent! Granted, her last published
work didn't do as well as usual, but that's no reason to just
ignore someone of Jane's caliber!'

'But you were letting her go,' I said.

'That is absolutely not true!' Rita Slinger said. 'It's true
she asked me to shop that newest manuscript around, but I
told her I didn't feel comfortable doing that.' There was a
short silence, then she said, 'I mentioned she might want to
take it to another agent.'

I thanked her for her time and hung up, telling the group
what I'd found out.

'Take it to another agent?' Candace said. 'You can't have two agents, can you?'

Mary shook her head. 'No, honey, you can't. That was Rita's way of saying she was taking herself out of the equation.'

'Sayonara, cupcake,' Hal said.

'Don't let the door hit you in the rear,' Willis said.

'Don't leave in a huff, just leave,' Jerome said.

Mary stood up. 'Are you gentlemen, and I use the term loosely, through?'

The guys shut up, which was nice. The room was silent, then I heard something – a slight sound, barely more than a whisper. I turned to Candace sitting next to me. Her head was lowered and tears were streaming down her face, her shoulders shaking.

'Candace!' I said, putting my arm around her. 'Honey, are you all right?'

'It's just so unfair!' she whispered, the sobs getting louder. 'This is such a mean business!'

None of us had an answer for that. We all just sat there, quietly, and let her cry.

Nine

Black Cat Ridge, Texas
Graham, Saturday

In Graham's book of rules to live by, stealing did not count if one stole from one's sibling; thus, sneaking into Megan's room to take her birthday money was not only permissible, but downright honorable. The sneaking part was only necessary because Megan's book of rules to live by did not have this particular chapter.

Grandma Vera had both girls in the kitchen, helping her make dinner. It was now or never, Graham thought. He went to the door of Megan's room, ignoring the KEEP OUT sign posted on the door, opened it and went in. He'd been in

Elizabeth's room lately; this wasn't Elizabeth's room, that was obvious. Where hers was decorated with weird pillows and girly drapes and stuff, Megan's was wall-to-wall clothes. There wasn't any place to put your foot that wasn't on top of some shirt or jeans or, yuck, underpants. Jeez, did the girl have absolutely no couth or what? The only thing that was the least bit neat were her shelves over her desk, and that's where the big pink elephant piggy bank was. He vaguely remembered her getting that for Christmas one year. It was a big deal because it was breakable and she was too young at the time to have breakable things – still was, as far as Graham was concerned. So that's why it had been stuck up on this shelf. Was it too high for her to use? Would she keep her money in it or was it just for decoration? As if it did anything to improve this pigsty of a room. Graham was no neat-freak, that was for sure, but this was too disgusting even for him.

He went to her desk and reached up for the piggy bank. At six feet, four inches, just like his dad, he had no trouble reaching it. He shook it and heard a muffled rattle. He liked the muffled part. If it was just change, it would have been a louder rattle. Muffled meant there was paper money in there. Had to be.

He pulled the piggy bank down and peered inside the slit at the top. Looked like paper money in there. He turned it over and found the stopper on the bottom. It took a good five minutes to work the stopper out, and the entire time he worried that Megan would come into the room. She didn't though, and he finally got it out, spilling coins all over the desk and floor. Reaching inside the elephant, he pulled out a wad of paper money. Two tens, a five, and a wad of ones. He counted the ones. Seven. Thirty-two bucks. Would she miss it? Not right away. If he picked up all the coins that had fallen, she'd never notice. He'd get it back to her – sometime. He shoved the paper money into his pocket and picked up the coins.

Downstairs the girls were setting the table for dinner. He stuck his head in the kitchen and said, 'Grandma, I'm going out.'

'No, you're not! We're fixin' to sit down to dinner, young man!' Vera said, shooting him a look.

'I'll get something while I'm out—'

'You're not gonna eat some fast food nonsense when you can eat a good decent meal here! Now you go sit!'

Graham sighed. There was nothing to it but to do it. 'Yes, ma'am,' he said and headed into the dining room.

He looked at the spread before him. Good decent meal my ass, he thought, looking at the home fried chicken, mashed potatoes, green beans and new potatoes, corn on the cob, homemade biscuits and the apple pie sitting on the side board. His mouth began to water and he decided that he had a few minutes he could spare for a good decent meal.

Austin, Texas

E.J., Saturday

'I'm thinking of hanging it up,' Jane says when I pick up the phone.

'Hanging up what?' I say, always Dean Martin to Jane's Jerry Lewis.

'The biz. The writing biz. It's just not what it used to be,' she says.

'When is anything what it used to be?' I say.

'Point E.J. But really, I'm irritated with my agent, pissed off at my editor – the new one. Audrey was a wonder, the bitch. Why she had to retire, I'll never know.'

'Because she was seventy-four years old, Jane.'

'So? She's too old to retire and do anything fun! She should stay my editor, which is easy.'

'You have a mean streak,' I say.

Jane sighs. 'That's true,' she says. 'But what has that got to do with anything?'

It was time to start getting ready for the banquet. I had finagled a ticket for Willis and he had borrowed a jacket from one of the male writers Jerome knew. It wouldn't be great, but it would be presentable. The best I could hope for tonight – or any night, to be truthful. Willis, although wonderful in many ways, is not what you'd call a clothes horse. He's not even a clothes pony. If anything, he's more a clothes donkey, if I may run this metaphor into the ground.

Candace was asleep in her bed and I didn't wake her as I began my preparations for the evening. I figured she didn't need as much time as I did, and any disadvantage I could give

her in the looks department would only help Mary, Lydia and
myself look better. I began with a leisurely shower two hours
before the beginning of the banquet. Then, while my hair dried
partially on its own, I began the Hippie-on-the-Beach rubdown.
This was so christened by my daughter Megan for what will
become obvious reasons.

I discovered a year or so ago, while reading a woman's
magazine, that all these expensive firming and moisturizing
lotions were basically just cocoa butter with added perfumes.
So, being the clever and or cheap person I am, I started buying
the store brand cocoa butter and mixing my favorite perfume
into the mixture. However, it's difficult to find scent-free cocoa
butter, so I got as far away from the coconut smells as I could,
ending up with what essentially smelled like, well, cocoa butter.
I mixed this with my favorite perfume (you can take the girl
out of the Seventies but you can't take the Seventies out of
the girl), which is of course patchouli. Mixing the scents
together you come up with, voila, Hippie-on-the-Beach. If
anyone ever compliments me on the scent, I'll think about
bottling it.

After slathering my body with lotion, I began the painstaking
make-up regimen I call the Number Three. Number One is
lipstick and blush, Number Two is Number One with an addi-
tion of mascara. Number Three is The Works: foundation,
concealer, blush, three kinds of eye shadow, eyebrow pencil,
eye liner, mascara, lip liner and lipstick. Then came the hard
part: my hair. I got the Sam's built-in blow dryer and began
the process of straightening my hair. As we were staying in
the hotel, never venturing outside, there was the faint possibility that my hair might stay frizz-free for an hour or two.

Candace woke up when I turned on the blow dryer and
watched for a minute while I attempted to straighten my hair.
Then she went to her own bag, brought out a round brush,
and took over. When she finished my hair looked like Lauren
Bacall's in *To Have and Have Not*. Gorgeous. I slipped on
the green and gold dress, clasped my mother-in-law's gold
chain with the one-carat pear-shaped diamond drop, slid on
the gold shoes and looked at myself in the mirror. I have to
say it: I was a knockout. I pulled a little at the bodice of the
dress, hoping to conceal some of the cleavage. Candace slapped
my hand.

'Stop!' she said. 'If I had boobs like yours, I'd have a dress split down to my navel! Now leave it alone! You look stunning!'

I looked at the clock on the bedside table. 'We have less than half an hour! You'd better hurry!'

Candace sighed. 'Do we really have to do this?' she asked.

'Honey, we're the floor show. It's gotta be done.'

She sighed again and headed to the bathroom. I sat at the dressing table, alternately picking out earrings and staring at myself in the mirror. With five minutes to spare, Candace came into the room wearing a white, one-shoulder designer dress, silver strappy sandals with four-inch heels, her blonde hair tousled like someone on TV, and her make-up impeccable. I shunned the mirror. I wanted to remember the way I *thought* I'd looked five minutes before.

Black Cat Ridge, Texas
Elizabeth, Saturday

Graham tried to leave early, but Grandma made him stay and eat supper. Elizabeth's good hygiene included eating right, and looking at the meal in front of her she knew it was all unhealthy. She also knew her grandmother made the best fried chicken in Texas. Hygiene be damned, she had seconds of the mashed potatoes and cream gravy.

Pushing herself away from the table, she and Megan did the dishes while Graham, whose turn it actually was, was allowed to leave the house with his friends. Grandma was like that: rather misogynistic, if a woman could be that. She decided to look that up.

After the dishes, they sat in the family room and watched TV with their grandmother until, at eight o'clock, Grandma Vera announced, 'Well, it's been a long day. Gets that way when you're up at five thirty like I am every morning,' she said.

To Elizabeth's ears it sounded like she was bragging, but Elizabeth couldn't figure out why anyone would be proud of that. It seemed silly to her. But, since it worked to her advantage, she just smiled and said, 'Good night, Grandma. Sleep tight.'

'Don't let the bedbugs bite,' Megan finished, which was the refrain Grandma used with them when they were little and spent the night with her.

Grandma Vera smiled and said, 'You girls lock up, OK?'
'No problem,' Megan said.

They sat in front of the TV until nine, then crept upstairs
to make sure Grandma was asleep. Opening the door of the
guest room resulted in hearing the sounds of Grandma's
snoring, snorting and heavy breathing, an indication she was
well into REM sleep. Her purse was on the dresser and Megan
quietly crept in and lifted it, taking it into the hall. Finding
the keys, she gingerly crept back in and put the purse back
on the dresser.

It was show time.

Austin, Texas
E.J., Saturday

As planned, we met the gang on the mezzanine level. Luckily
(for him) my husband only had eyes for me. The look he gave
me assured me I looked hot. Red hot. I smiled.

'You like?' I asked.

'Sweet Jesus!' he said.

'Good answer,' I said, slipping my arm into the crook of
his elbow.

As a group, we took the elevator down to the main lobby
and the ballroom. The lobby was jam-packed with beautiful
people. A jewel thief would have been in hog heaven.

I was happy to see that Hal had put on a suit; Jerome was
in a tux, the style of which indicated he'd probably bought it
sometime in the Thirties. Willis looked acceptable in his
borrowed navy blue blazer and gray slacks.

Mary and Lydia had gone all out. Mary was wearing a
silver sequined tank-style gown that looked great on her slim
frame, with a three-strand of black pearls around her neck.
Diamonds dripped from ears and fingers. Lydia's dress was
a flowing lavender chiffon over a silk slip dress, with one
giant lily-of-the-valley covering the entire skirt in the front.
A 'simple' chain of diamonds hung from her neck. We stood
in the lobby for a while, complimenting each other on how
gorgeous we were, then headed into the ballroom.

The hotel had gone all out in the decorating of the ballroom. A large table in the middle of the room was draped in
white silk with shimmering faux jewels, with the largest
arrangement of white roses I'd ever seen jutting out of an

enormous crystal vase. All the tables were covered in white bejeweled silk with white rose arrangements at each table. The room sparkled with the huge chandeliers bouncing light off the bejeweled table drapes. Sconces of white roses and white silk swags hung from the walls and all the chairs were covered in white. It felt like being in the inner chamber of the ice princess's castle, ready for all the mystery and romance to begin.

The first hour was cocktails, so the seven of us stayed pretty much together, mingling as little as possible. Angela Barber was the first person we all spotted on walking into the ballroom. She would have been hard not to see. The Beast had foregone her basic brown of the past three days for hot pink taffeta. Frighteningly, it was a strapless gown, held up with a vengeance by Angela's large bosom. The dress was several sizes too small, causing ripples of flesh to escape at her armpits, rolls to appear at her waist, and for all who saw it to worry about the seams across her buttocks. Even for Angela's height, the dress was exceedingly long, with a train of sorts falling behind her. She stumbled crossing the room and the poor husband of one writer actually took a tumble into a table as his feet got caught in her train as she passed by.

When it came time for the dinner, our group had to split up. The three nominees, Candace, Jerome and myself, were sitting at tables sponsored by our publishers. My editor, her boss, my publicist and three other people, were at the table. When I asked if Willis could join us, a young woman, presumably the lowest on the totem pole, was ejected from the table to fend for herself. Looking around, I saw that Mary and Lydia had found seats at a table with Mary's publisher, but saw Hal standing alone by a wall, looking for a place to sit. The Susan Lucci of the romance writing biz seemed to be persona non grata at this particular dinner. No nomination, no table.

After a few minutes of talking to my editor, I looked up again and couldn't find Hal. Scanning the tables, I finally found him sitting at a table in the back with some first-time writers and some wannabes – this man who'd been nominated four times for the top award couldn't find a decent seat. This sad reminder of how quickly fame could fade in the writing world tempered my elation at my own heady state of affairs.

Angela was seated at the head table and I couldn't help staring at her. And it wasn't the hot pink taffeta dress that was holding my attention. This woman had written a book that Jane felt was good enough to be published under her own name. Did Angela kill Jane because of it? But if she did kill Jane, what did that have to do with DeWitt Perry, comb-over boy? Had they conspired together to kill Jane? But why? Why would DeWitt Perry involve himself with that? And I couldn't see Jane leaving our room to meet either of them. Had DeWitt Perry seen what the Beast had done and did she kill him to keep him quiet? My mind was slogging through all these possibilities when Willis touched my arm, bringing my attention back to the table.

The food was good, better than the rubber chicken dinner the first night, when Jane was keynote speaker. Being a red meat eater whenever my children weren't around, I'd opted for the bacon-wrapped filet, which was a little overdone but still very good, served with asparagus tips and tiny new potatoes in their skins. Willis got the dinner of the young woman who'd been ejected from the table. Unfortunately she was a vegetarian, so he ended up with pasta alfredo and buttered carrots. He kept eyeing my filet, which I moved to the opposite side of me, shielding it with my body.

My husband is nothing if not a smooth talker. So whenever I got flustered talking to my editor or her boss, or lost in the possibilities of who had killed Jane, comb-over boy and attacked Lisbet, he'd take over, smoothly extolling my virtues while I simpered quietly. All in all, the meal went quite well, with me not dropping a thing on my green satin gown, nor trying to cut up the filet on my editor's plate.

As dessert was being served, Angela Barber stood up and walked to the podium. I thought this thing was supposed to be MC'd by David Barton, one of the few male romance writers who wrote under his own name. I couldn't understand why the Beast was taking the microphone.

'Ladies and gentlemen,' she said, her voice booming through the room. Angela really didn't need a microphone. 'In a lot of ways this has been one of the best conventions ever,' she said, then waited until a smattering of applause started up in the silence, then quickly faded. 'But it has also been one of our most tragic conventions. People come to these conventions to meet their favorite authors, to get books autographed, to meet like-minded people. They don't come to get thrown down elevator shafts,' she said. 'I would like to take this time for a moment of silence for our fallen brother, Mr DeWitt Perry.'

Oh, there was silence all right. A stunned silence. Which made the dropping of Jerome MacIntyre's chair on the carpeted banquet hall floor sound ominously loud. He was standing and marching for the dais, a look on his face I would not want pointed in my direction.

Once on the dais, he wrestled the microphone from the Beast's hand, and said, 'While we're thinking of Mr Perry, let us not forget our fallen comrade Jane Dawson, aka Maybella LaRue, the first to die at this convention, by the hands of an unknown assailant.' This last part he said while looking directly at the Beast. I wanted very much to kiss him at that point.

'Jane Dawson was a personal friend of mine, and one of the finest women I've ever known. She was also, and second-arily so, a wonderful and unique writer. She will be tragically missed by her family and her friends, and by her fans. By all things holy, this convention should have been cancelled the moment Jane's body was found. If it had been,' he said, again looking directly at the Beast, 'then maybe Mr Perry would not have suffered the same fate.' Looking back at his audi-ence, he said, 'I will miss dear Jane with all my heart, and I pray to the gods of good sense that she has a special place in heaven, reserved for the angels that spent time here on earth.' With that, and with tears streaming down his face, Jerome left the dais.

I heard clapping to my left and looked to see Mary and Lydia standing and applauding. I stood, too, quickly joined by Willis and then the rest of my table. Soon the entire room was standing and the applause was thunderous. Amidst this outburst of support for Jane, the Beast quietly took her seat on the dais.

After the thunderous applause had died down, it was time for the awards and the filet, asparagus and baby red potatoes threatened to make a return engagement. I'd never seen a Lady, the award given out at this convention, and seeing the first one being held by one of the presenters, I knew in my heart I had to have it. A crystal statue of a woman in flowing gown, head bent in a prayerful attitude. It should be mine, I couldn't help but think. I wanted it! But as the program wore on, with award after award, my stomach settled down and I actually began to get a little bored.

An hour after the awards started, the MC announced, 'And now for the highlight of the evening. I'd like to announce the nominees for Best Romance of the Year. Kella McReynolds for *Meet Mr Right* –' a scattering of applause – 'Jasmine West, aka our beloved Jerome MacIntyre, for *Lyrics for a Swan Song* –' the applause was deafening, with Willis and I joining in loudly – 'E.J. Pugh for *The Devil's in the Details* –' my table erupted in applause – 'and Candace Macy for *A Woman's Favor*.'

The MC stepped back from the microphone as he opened the envelope.

Willis was grasping my hand so tightly my fingers were turning white, but I hardly noticed.

'And the winner is . . .' he said, taking a pregnant pause, 'Candace Macy for *A Woman's Favor*.'

As Willis let go of my hand so we could both clap loudly, there was a crash at the back of the ballroom. Still clapping I looked around to see what it was. Hal Burleson was standing up at his table – the crash having been his chair as it fell over in his rush to stand up to applaud. He was beaming as if he himself had just won the award. I smiled, thinking for maybe the hundredth time, what a great bunch of people I'd found.

The festivities wound down, the lights dimmed, and Rafe Conte and his band tuned up for their 'big band' sound. Willis and I danced to a poor rendition of Sinatra's *I Did It My Way*, an even poorer rendition of Tony Bennett's *I Left My Heart in San Francisco*, and finally decided to opt for the bar when the same bad singer started in on *Stardust*.

We found the group at a large table in the bar (surprise, surprise), with Hal standing up, holding his glass high. 'To Candace,' he announced, 'for the first in a long line of winning books!'

'Here, here!' said Lydia with Mary joining. Jerome held his glass up but was just silently smiling. No 'here, here' from that quarter. If he was feeding on sour grapes, he was at least being graceful about it.

I went up to the table and hugged Candace. 'Bitch!' I said, kissing her on the cheek.

Candace laughed. 'As long as there are no hard feelings!' she said.

'Just don't go to sleep tonight,' I warned with a grin.

Willis leaned around me and kissed Candace on the cheek. 'Congratulations,' he said. 'You know I'm going to pay for your win, right?'

I dug my elbow in his ribs and he said a loud, 'Ouch, she's starting already!'

We all sat down at the table while Hal poured champagne. He waved to the bartender, yelling, 'Another bottle over here!'

'Hal, be careful!' Mary warned. 'Can you afford it?'

Hal shot her a look and she shut up.

'So, Jerome,' I said, covering the slight awkwardness, 'shall you and I get blotto and drown our sorrows?'

'Thank you, my dear, but I already am,' he said, raising his glass. 'I had two, count them, two, bottles of wine with dinner.'

'Then I,' I said, raising my glass toward Hal for a refill, 'am at a distinct disadvantage.'

Hal filled my champagne glass with the second in what turned out to be countless glasses of champagne.

Black Cat Ridge, Texas
Graham, Saturday
In the Pugh home, chores were not divvied by gender, but rather by ability; thus, Graham, as the eldest and strongest, mowed the lawn, Megan vacuumed, and Elizabeth changed linens. Daily chores, such as setting the table for meals, clearing meals, dishwashing, garbage/trash disposal and feeding the animals were done on rotation, with each offspring getting a chore for the day.

All of this changed when Grandma Vera was in charge. Old fashioned in many ways, Grandma Vera would never entertain the thought of having a male offspring doing the 'womanly' chores of dealing with meals or the cleaning up after same. This, of course, would elicit strong concerns from both Megan and Elizabeth, while Graham wholeheartedly concurred with his grandmother.

And so it was with great joy that Graham ran to the door after hearing the bleating of Hollister's pick-up's horn, forestalling the

usual argument with his sisters regarding his elitist and misogynistic tendencies. He ran to the truck and shoved his way in.
It was an old truck, and big, but barely big enough for four boys
on the one bench seat. No seatbelts, of course.

They drove straight to the bowling alley in Codderville.
Joey's Jeep Wrangler was already there, the girls leaning
against it, talking. Hollister pulled the truck up next to the
Wrangler and the boys piled out.

'Hi,' Graham said to Ashley as he came up to her. She
looked even hotter tonight: her long blonde hair loose down
her back, eyes all smoky with make-up, a thin sweater so tight
he could see her nipples through the top and her bra and jeans
that cupped her magnificent ass like he wished his hands
could.

'Hi,' she said. 'You made it.'

'Said I would,' Graham said.

'Hey,' Hollister said coming up and drawing Graham
aside. 'Me and Joey are leaving in my truck. I'll see you
back here around midnight.'

'Ah . . .' Graham started, but Hollister was already gone,
heading for his truck.

'Here! Lindsey!' Joey said, tossing her keys to one of the
other girls. 'Don't hurt it!' And she and Hollister were off in
the truck.

'Sweet!' Tad said. 'Come on Linz, let's boogie!' To Graham
and Ashley, he said, 'Y'all coming?'

Graham took Ashley's arm, but she pulled back. 'Let's don't
go,' she said, smiling at him. 'I'd rather be alone, wouldn't
you?'

Oh, God, yes! Graham thought, but only said, 'Yeah sure.'
To the rest of the group, he called out, 'Y'all go ahead. Ashley
and I are going to stay here.'

'Whatever, dude! *Asta lavista*, baby!' Tad shouted, sitting
on the top of the Wrangler's shotgun seat, holding on to the
roll bar.

Lindsey peeled out and then there was silence.

Ashley put her hand on Graham's chest. 'I'm glad they
left,' she said, her voice soft and throaty. 'They get awful
rowdy.'

'Yeah,' Graham said, his voice husky. He wasn't sure what
she'd said, but at that point he would have agreed to anything.

Ashley lifted her face to his and he leaned down to kiss her. It wasn't the first time he'd kissed a girl, but it was the first time he'd kissed a girl he really liked. He put his hands on her back, pulling her closer and her arms slipped around his neck. He went for some tongue, surprised at how easy it was to slip it in her mouth. She tasted like peppermint and Cheetos.

She pulled away, her head resting on his chest. Graham took a deep breath, afraid he might have forgotten to breathe for a few seconds there.

'Hey, Ash! What the fuck!' came a voice from the steps of the bowling alley.

Graham let go of Ashley and turned. A guy was striding down the stairs toward them, his face looking mean. He was an older guy, maybe twenty, twenty-one, wearing ripped jeans and a black leather motorcycle jacket, a large silver chain going from his side pocket to his back pocket. His hair was as close to a mullet as you could get and he had a soul patch under his bottom lip.

Ashley turned her body away from the newcomer, but turned her head to address him. 'What do *you* want, Lee?' she asked.

'Who the fuck is this?' Lee demanded, pointing at Graham, who just stood there unable to move at this point.

'A friend,' Ashley said, her arms across her chest, her cute little bottom sticking out as she arched her back.

'Yeah, you suck face with all your friends, do you, Ash?' Lee demanded, his voice belligerent.

'What I do is none of your business, Mr "I'd Rather Go Out With My Friends"!'

'I go out one night with my boys, and you decide to fuckin' cheat on me?' Lee screamed.

'One night!' Ashley screamed back. 'What was last night? Rehearsal?'

'Who the fuck *are* you?' Lee demanded, turning to Graham.

'Just a friend,' Graham said, getting nervous now. The guy was shorter than him, but broader and Graham figured, rightly so, that Lee probably had more experience pulverizing an opponent than Graham did.

Back to Ashley, Lee demanded, 'Did he do anything to you?'

Ashley cocked her eyes at Graham, then back to Lee. 'He tried to touch my ass,' she said, a quiet smile on her face.

Graham never saw it coming. One minute he was standing there with a pain free face, the next he was on the ground, his jaw on fire. When his vision cleared, he looked up to see Lee holding his right hand and screaming, 'Ow!' over and over.

Ashley moved close to Lee, taking his hand in hers. 'Oh, baby, did you hurt your hand?'

Lee pulled away from Ashley, looking at the ground covered by Graham. 'You fuckin' broke my hand!' he said.

This time Graham saw the steel-toed motorcycle boot coming his way and he rolled on the ground to avoid it. He jumped to his feet and began to run, never seeing his cell-phone as it fell out of his pocket on to the ground.

Austin, Texas
E.J., Saturday night/Sunday morning

'I'm fat,' I say.

'Then go on a diet,' Jane says.

I hadn't thought about that. 'Just for this?' I say, thinking hard.

'Sure,' she says. 'Lose twenty pounds, then you can gain it back after. Just think of the fun you'll have eating your way back up.'

'That's terribly clever,' I say, light dawning as I think of the bakery next door to the grocery store and all the goodies I haven't allowed myself in years.

'I'm a terribly clever woman,' Jane says. 'Why do you think they pay me the big bucks?'

It was after one on Sunday morning by the time Candace and I got back to our room. We were holding each other up, with the help of Willis who was supporting both of us to our room. Willis made sure we both got inside, kissed me good night and left. Candace and I fell on to our respective beds. It was at that point that Candace burst into tears.

I managed to sit up and lean towards her bed. 'Hey,' I said. 'It's OK. What's the matter?'

'It's not fair!' Candace wailed.

'What's not fair?' I asked.

'I shouldn't have won!' she said.

'Oh, pashah!' I said, the first time to my knowledge I'd ever used the word. 'No biggie! You did good,' I said, lying down again.

'But Jane's dead!' she wailed.

'I know,' I said. 'That really sucks.' I turned over on my side, facing her bed. 'Jerome was good tonight, huh?'

This started a whole new batch of tears. 'Yes!' she wailed. 'He was very good!'

Turning back to lay on my back, I said, 'You need to stop crying. You're going to puke.'

'Uh huh,' she said, stumbling off the bed to the bathroom. As my eyes closed, I could hear her retching.

Black Cat Ridge, Texas
Graham, Saturday night/Sunday morning

There were a million stars in the sky, but no moon to light his way. The street lights were few and far between in this section of the old town. Disoriented, nauseous and slightly pissed off, Graham had no idea where he was. He'd run so fast and so far that he was totally lost. Codderville was the town closest to his family's subdivision of Black Cat Ridge. But it was across the Colorado River from home. There was one bridge that crossed the Colorado and that was the freeway bridge, and you couldn't walk on that, even if you had a mind to.

Graham looked around him, trying to get his bearings. His grandmother lived in Codderville, but she was at his house now in Black Cat Ridge. And his dad had an office here in town, but he was in Austin with his mom. He wasn't sure what time it was, but figured it would be a while before Hollister got back to the bowling alley. Personally, Graham wasn't sure he ever wanted to step foot in the bowling alley parking lot again, not after what just went down. He reached into his pocket for his cellphone, ready to call Hollister to come get him. The cellphone wasn't there. Panic set in and Graham determinedly sent it away. He shouldn't be scared, he told himself. What he should be is pissed.

Jeez, and he thought she liked him. What an idiot! Why would a girl like Ashley Davis give him the time of day? Except as an excuse to piss off her boyfriend! He was just a male body to her, someone to show Lee he wasn't the only fish in the sea.

Truthfully he didn't want to see Hollister and the rest of his pack any time soon. How was he supposed to explain what the hell happened? He kept walking, not sure what direction he was going – north, south, whatever. Not sure what direction home was. He didn't really care if he was going the wrong way. Just so long as he was moving. That was when the skies opened up and it began to rain.

Austin, Texas
E.J., Saturday night/Sunday morning
I woke up with the full-blown knowledge that if I didn't get out of bed immediately I was going to: 1. puke all over my beautiful green dress; or 2. pee all over my beautiful green dress.

I stumbled out of bed, vowing once again never to touch alcohol of any kind ever again, and made my way into the bathroom. The toilet was blocked by the prone body of my roommate, Candace Macy, still in her beautiful designer dress. I kicked her. She grunted. I kicked her again. She grunted again.

'Get up!' I said. 'I have to puke!'

'Ummmmmmmmm,' she said, or words to that effect.

I stepped over her, lifted my ton of green satin and sat on the seat, thinking peeing was a better idea than puking. I know, too much information. If so, you don't want to read further. It was at this point that I puked, all over the skirt of my beautiful spring green satin gown. Which made me cry.

I'm not sure if it was the peeing, puking, or crying that did the trick, but Candace woke up.

'Where am I?' she said, like a heroine in a made-for-TV movie.

'On the floor of the bathroom,' I said, through my sobs.

'Are you crying?' Candace asked, trying to lift her head up off the floor.

'No,' I sobbed.

'Yes you are!' she said, managing to sit up. 'Why?' she asked.

'I puked on my dress!' I said, bursting into tears once again.

'Oh no!' she wailed and she too began to cry. Looking at

her own sorry state of affairs, she said, 'I think I puked on mine too!'

At this point one of us giggled. Then we were both laughing like the idiots the devil grape had made us.

We managed to pick each other up, discard our evening attire, and make it back into the bedroom where we dressed for bed.

'I don't drink much,' Candace confided in a near whisper.

'Me either,' I admitted.

'I'm thinking I'll probably never drink again,' she said.

'I think that's a very good idea. Wanna make a pinky pack?' I suggested. We were sitting cross-legged on our respective beds. When we both leaned forward to wrap pinkies, someone lost their balance and almost ended up on the floor. OK, it was me. Candace pushed me back up and we giggled about that some more, and at some point we both passed out. Which was probably a good thing.

Ten

Black Cat Ridge, Texas
Graham, Saturday night/Sunday morning

In Central Texas there are two kinds of rain: the one you get in the winter that's more of a drizzle, and the one you get in the spring – which is a torrential downpour. The spring rains would swell creeks and ditches, flooding backyards and streets and sending any cars driven by people too incompetent to understand the phrase 'low water crossing' down stream, often drowning said incompetent drivers and their unfortunate passengers.

The month in question being April, and April definitely being a spring month, Graham was caught in one of Central Texas's more classic torrential downpours. This one came with lightening, thunder and, as Graham ran to the nearest tree for shelter, hail. At first the stones were pea-sized, but it didn't

take long for the inevitable golf ball-sized hailstones to start
to fall. His less than sheltering tree was only a few feet from
an old house that had its lights off. Hoping no one was home,
Graham ran for the front porch, crawling under it into the
high space of the pier and beam house. It was muddy but no
hailstones could reach him there. He sighed and leaned his
head on his outstretched arms. This night was turning into a
nightmare, he thought. All he wanted at this point was to get
home to his warm house and take a hot shower and crawl into
his bed. If he never got laid the rest of his life, he figured he
could live with that.

The horrible sounds of the golf ball-sized hailstones hitting
the aluminum siding of the house under which Graham huddled
soon slacked off. With the absence of the pounding of the
hailstones Graham was able to hear a more subtle sound: that
of a low growl. He gingerly looked around him. It was pitch
black under the house and he could see nothing. Then a car
drove by on the street in front of the house and the ambient
light glowed from a pair of eyes not a yard in front of him.
The glowing eyes growled again, soft and menacing. Then he
could see the light reflecting off shiny white and very pointed
teeth. They appeared to be moving closer. Graham began to
slowly scoot his way toward the opening into the yard. As he
moved, so did the glowing eyes, the growl getting just a little
bit louder and lasting just a little bit longer.

Graham rolled for the opening just as the glowing eyes
pounced.

Austin, Texas
E.J., Sunday
My dreams were chaotic. My children were in them and of
course Willis. And Jane was there. She was telling my girls
how they should never, ever write anything. 'Not even school
work,' she told them. 'They'll take it from you. Sell it to the
highest bidder. Then they'll eat you for lunch.'

Megan, my daughter, said, 'I prefer pimento cheese.'

'A salad is healthier,' Elizabeth said.

Willis said, 'Nobody's going to have anything to eat if you
don't finish your band aids!'

'Band aids?' my dream self screamed. 'They can't finish
their band aids! Jane is dead!'

Graham patted me on the arm. 'No, Mom. You are.'

Willis chuckled and shook his head. 'Jeez, E.J., honey, you died last week, don't you remember?' he asked.

I shook my head. 'No,' I said. 'I don't remember.'

'We ran out of band aids,' Megan said, then began to cry.

'Gawd, Mom, see what you did?' Elizabeth said, taking her sister in her arms 'My other mom Terry never came back after the band aids!' She shot me a recriminating look.

'Don't back talk your mother,' Willis said. 'Even if she is dead.'

'Well, shouldn't she stay dead?' Graham argued.

Willis shrugged. 'You'd think,' was his answer.

Black Cat Ridge, Texas
Graham, Sunday

Once out from under the protection of the house, Graham kept rolling as fast as he could, until he ran into the tree that had sheltered him earlier. He stopped and looked. The glowing eyes had pursued him and he could now see the muscular pit bull that went with those eyes. Fortunately the dog was on a chain and the chain only extended to less than three feet from where Graham lay huddled by the oak tree. The dog was barking and straining at the chain. Holding on to the tree, Graham righted himself, keeping both eyes securely on the dog and the chain that was his only saving grace. He backed away slowly until he reached the sidewalk, then began to run.

He was three blocks away when he stopped running. It was then that he noticed it was no longer hailing or even raining for that matter. The one good thing about a Central Texas torrential spring rain was that it was very often over quickly. Graham sighed in relief and began to ring out the bottom of his shirt, now covered in mud and water. All he had to do, he told himself, was get to a phone. Then he could call Hollister and have him come get him. That was all he had to do.

'Hey, dude,' a voice said. A car had pulled up beside him, a low rider, filled with guys. 'Where you going, man?' the guy riding shotgun said. 'Hey, I know you, man! You go to Black Cat Ridge, right? I seen you around.'

'Yeah,' Graham said. 'You're Manny Esparza, right?'

Manny laughed. 'Yeah, man! Hey, whatja walkin' for, man? Hop in, we give you a lift.'

Graham could see that the other guys in the car were older, maybe all of them, and there were a bunch. 'Doesn't look like you have room. And 'sides, I'm just headed to my grandmother's house.' He pointed. 'It's right up there.'

'Hey, man, we'll give you a lift,' Manny said.

'Thanks, but—' Graham started, but then Manny pointed the gun at him.

Graham sighed and got in the back.

Austin, Texas
E.J., Sunday

I slept like the dead. A small bladder and too much booze woke me up around five in the morning, my mouth tasting like the bottom of a birdcage and so thirsty I could have gratefully drunk from Austin's semi-polluted Town Lake. Unfortunately I remembered my dream. Feeling slightly disoriented and more than a little afraid, I stumbled into the bathroom, sticking my head under the faucet and letting the cold water run into my mouth, gulping large mouthfuls of blessed water. I used the facilities then headed back into the bedroom. And there it was: déjà vu all over again. There was no one in the other bed. Was it Jane's bed? I asked myself. No, that was a couple of days ago. It's Candace's bed now, right? I looked around for my new roomy. She wasn't in the room. My stomach twisted in knots and I walked slowly toward the door to the hall. It was locked, but the deadbolt and chain lock weren't on. I opened the door and looked outside, seeing no one in either direction. Then I heard voices – coming from that damned stairwell.

Black Cat Ridge, Texas
Graham, Sunday

'Y'all can just let me off at the corner up here,' Graham said, trying to get his arm up to point, but unable to as there were five guys in the back seat, counting him, and he couldn't move his arms.

'No, we gonna ride around some, dude,' Manny said. 'Hey! Where are my manners?' He pointed at the driver of the car. 'This is my brother Eddie, and this –' he pointed at the guy in the middle between Manny and his brother – 'is my cousin Ramon. In the back seat we got, from left to right, my cousin Rey, my other cousin Bug, my uncle Ernesto and my other cousin Tonio. Guys, meet Graham.'

'He one of those rich boys go to your school?' the one referred to as Uncle Ernesto asked.

'Yeah, I think so,' Manny said. 'You one of them rich boys, Gray-ham?' Manny asked.

Graham shook his head. 'No. Middle class all the way,' Graham said, trying out a laugh for size.

The rest joined in, laughing a little too loudly for his attempt at a pretty dumb joke.

'Hey, man, middle class sounds rich to us,' Manny said. ''Cause we ain't got no class at all!'

And they all laughed again. Graham tried to join in, but both arms were going to sleep and he was very nervous. They'd passed his corner, or the one he claimed to be his, several blocks ago and the car just kept up its slow but steady pace.

Uncle Ernesto leaned forward, looking toward Graham. This was definitely a good news/bad news situation. The good news was that when he leaned forward, it gave everyone a little more space, which allowed Graham to wiggle his arms a little in an attempt to get the circulation going again. The bad news was that Uncle Ernesto was looking directly at Graham.

Uncle Ernesto was a little bit older than the others, but not by much. He had thick black hair in a braid going down his back, pockmarked cheeks and a large mustache. He was dressed in baggy shorts and a rugby shirt.

'You got any money on ya, man?' Uncle Ernesto asked Graham.

Graham sighed and brought out the money he'd liberated from his sister's piggy bank.

'Awright!' Manny said, turned around in the front seat. 'Let's hit it!'

Eddie did, taking the low rider up to a dizzying thirty-five miles an hour. Graham was terrified. He had no idea where they were going or what his money was going to buy them. Crack? How many rocks could you get for thirty dollars? Moonshine? He'd heard that went on around here, especially in the barrio. Another gun to rob a convenience store to get enough money for meth?

Eddie pulled the car into a Stop-N-Shop. Manny grabbed the thirty dollars Uncle Ernesto held out to him and opened his car door. 'Whatja want?' he asked.

'Yahoo and a moon pie,' someone said. Someone else called out, 'Pork skins and a Dr Pepper.' Still someone else cried out for a cherry Pepsi and a Little Debbie anything.

Manny turned to Graham. 'Whatja want?'

'Ah . . . ?' Graham said, trying to adjust his thinking.

Manny laughed. 'Hell, I know! A Diet Coke and a graaaa-no-la bar!' Everybody laughed, except Graham.

'Hell no!' Graham said. 'Gimme a Big Red and a Twinkie.'

'Cool,' Manny said, then brought out the gun. He pointed it in Graham's face and pulled the trigger. Luke warm water dripped down Graham's face.

'Man, that's funny,' Graham said, not cracking a smile.

Manny nodded his head, gave Graham his fist, which Graham gave back, then went in the store in search of sustenance.

Austin, Texas
E.J., Sunday

I turned the deadbolt so the bolt itself was sticking out, keeping the door from closing, and slowly, on bare feet, headed toward the door to the stairwell.

I moved to the stairwell door, listening to the voices beyond.

'Are you finally happy?' a woman's voice asked. I could tell she was crying. 'Here! Take the damn thing! I don't want it! I didn't earn it! It's yours, OK? You paid a high enough price for it!'

'Don't be like that, honey! You know how important this was to me,' a man's voice said.

'Important enough to kill two people?' The crying started in earnest now and I could barely discern her words. '. . . dead and for what? . . . can't take it . . . I just want to get out . . . don't touch me . . . stop!'

I slammed the door open and stared at the sight before me. Candace in her lacy nightgown standing in front of Hal Burleson, his hands on her arms, wearing nothing but a T-shirt and boxer shorts.

'Let go of her!' I shouted.

He put his hands down at once and smiled at me. 'E.J., it's not what you think . . .'

'I think you killed Jane and that poor fan!'

'Oh!' he said, the smile vanishing. 'It *is* what you think.'

He grabbed my arm, pulling me into the stairwell, the door slamming shut behind me.

'Dad! No!' Candace shouted. 'Just stop! Enough!'

'Candy, you be quiet,' Hal said. 'Let Daddy handle this.'

'Dad?' I said, looking from one to the other as best I could, with Hal grasping my body close to his. 'Daddy?'

Hal hustled me down the stairs, past the lobby entrance, down flights leading to the garage, with Candace crying and grabbing at his arm the entire time. As we passed the door to the lobby, I tried crying out. Hal didn't seem to have a weapon; he hadn't threatened me with a gun or a knife. But I'd barely gotten a squeak out before Hal grabbed me around the throat, choking off any sound escaping my lips.

'Daddy, don't!' Candace wailed. 'Stop! Haven't you done enough? You can't hurt E.J.! She hasn't done anything to you! Let her go!' She grabbed his hands as he dragged me further into the depths of the Sam. He let go of my neck, but not my arm. I could breathe, sort of, but I couldn't help tripping as he hightailed it down the stairs.

'Hush, Candy. Let Daddy handle this,' Hal answered, his voice at odds with the hard grip on my arm and the fast hustle down the stairs. He sounded as if he was talking about a broken toy or a box of cereal spilled on the floor. Not the deaths of two people and the possible death of a third – namely me.

'Hal, come on,' I said, trying to keep my voice as low-key as his. 'You don't want to hurt me. I'm your friend.'

'Really, E.J., I barely know you. Jane and I had been friends for years, and look what I did to her! And, by the way, I'm really sorry about that. There was nothing else I could do.'

'And what about DeWitt Perry?' I asked, more to keep him talking than anything else.

'Who? The fan?'

'Yes. Hal, you're really hurting my arm—'

'Well, I can't say I'm exactly sorry about him. I mean, I didn't really know him, did I? And he was basically stalking my Candy, and we just can't have that. But I will say I'm regretful. Much better word in this case than sorry. Not nearly as loaded, you know what I mean? As a writer, you understand the difference? E.J.?'

'Ah, yeah, sure,' I said, trying to keep from slipping on the stairs as we went lower and lower, past the hotel garage and into the sub-basements.

'Regretful,' he repeated. 'Yes, I think that is the best word in this case. But I will admit I'll be sorry about you, E.J. I've enjoyed your company.'

'Daddy, stop!' Candace said from behind us, the tears and the run down the stairs robbing her of breath, the words coming out barely above a whisper. 'Please, Daddy!'

'Oh, honey bear, why don't you go on back to bed?' Hal said. 'I can do this by myself.'

'Daddy, E.J. has children! You don't want to leave them without a mother!' Candace tried. I looked back at her, willing her to keep at it.

'I raised you without a mother, and look how well you turned out,' Hal said with a smile. 'Didn't she turn out well, E.J.?'

'Swell, Hal. Great kid,' I said.

'Ah, here we are,' Hal said, stopping finally at the bottom of the staircase in front of a door marked 'Hotel Personnel Only'. He pulled a card key from his pocket and swiped it, the door popping open as he did so. 'It's so convenient the way the maids leave their card keys just lying on their carts, don't you think, E.J.?' he said and laughed. 'Grab an extra towel, some shampoo and, oh, don't forget the card key!'

He finally let go of my arm as he pushed me through the open door. It was just like in the movies. Lots of pipes and plumbing-like fixtures, just no steam. I always thought the whole steam escaping stuff in the movies was hooey. I mean, that stuff burns, you know?

I stumbled into the depths of the Sam, my bare feet crunching on dirt and gravel and probably dead bugs. I tried not to think about it. Dead bugs were the least of my worries at the moment. Candace wasn't in the room with us. The door to the stairwell had closed with Hal and me on one side and Candace on the other. She didn't seem to have much influence over her father, but at this point I'd take anything. And now I didn't even have her.

Black Cat Ridge, Texas
Graham, Sunday
Graham sat on the curb in front of the store, drinking his Big Red and eating his Twinkie. Manny sat beside him drinking from a can of green tea and eating from a bag of potato chips.

'Green tea?' Graham asked.

'Hey, man, it's good. Good for ya, too.' Manny took a big swig and asked, 'You used to hang with Luis Luna, right?'

Graham nodded. 'Yeah. He lives next door.' Graham laughed. 'Didn't so much hang with him as he let me tag along. He thought of me as a little brother.'

'Hey, that's nice,' Manny said. 'That mean he liked to beat the shit out of you?'

'Oh, yeah,' Graham said.

Manny shrugged. 'That's what big brothers are for, man. Keep you straight.'

'Umm,' Graham said.

'So what's he up to now?' Manny asked.

'He's at A&M, but he's thinking about joining up.'

'Oh, man, that's crap! Bad time to do that!' Manny said.

'Yeah, but his dad's Army and so's his mom, so, you know,' Graham said, shrugging.

'Yeah, got a brother in the Marines. He's over there. My mom cries every night, prays all the damn time.'

'That's rough,' Graham said.

'So, you gonna tell me what you were doing out walking around in Codderville when you live in Black Cat Ridge?' Manny asked.

Graham shrugged.

Manny said, 'Hey, man, don't make me shoot you again.'

So Graham told his story. In gory detail. About Ashley and thinking he was going to get laid, only to find out he was only there to make her boyfriend jealous.

'That where you got the shiner?' Manny asked.

'Shiner?' Graham said, touching his eye.

'Other one,' Manny said. 'Not too bad now, but it's gonna be great in the morning.' He grinned at Graham.

'Oh, shit. How am I going to explain this?' Graham said.

'Ran into a door?' Manny suggested. Then he said, 'Man, you asked me, I coulda tole you: that Ashley Davis is a prick tease. Know a guy went out with her once, she had him dancin', then she says, "no, I'm not that type a girl". Can you believe it? Girl looks like that, says she's "not that type of girl"?' Manny shook his head at the injustice of it all.

'Man, I don't even wanna talk about it,' Graham said, staring at the cigarette butts and other trash on the driveway of the convenience store.

'Yeah, man, I unnerstand. Gotta be humiliatin',' Manny said.

'That's about the size of it,' Graham agreed.

They were back in the low rider, riding around, looking at whatever there was to see. Graham said, 'I gotta be at the bowling alley to meet my ride.'

Uncle Ernesto said, 'It's five to twelve. We better hoof it. We gotta pick up Lotta by midnight.'

Manny turned in his seat. 'You know Lotta, right, Graham? My cousin? She goes to Black Cat. She's in the same class as you.'

'Lotta Esparza?' Graham asked.

'Yeah, she's my cousin,' Manny said.

Graham laughed. 'Man, you got a lot of cousins!'

Nobody else laughed, and Manny said, 'Yeah, I do.'

'Yeah, I know Lotta,' Graham said. They'd had Spanish together junior year. A tall, long-legged Latina who was always correcting the teacher's pronunciation.

'She works at the Dairy Queen,' Uncle Ernesto said. 'That's on the way to the bowling alley.'

They pulled into the parking lot of the Dairy Queen just as all the lights were switched off, leaving on just the emergency lights. Lotta Esparza came out the front door wearing her Dairy Queen uniform.

Manny reached out the window and behind him, opening the back door. 'Here, Lotta. You know Graham, right? Sit on his lap. He ain't kin!' And he laughed like an idiot.

Lotta rolled her eyes. 'Hey, Graham, can you scoot over?'

Graham shook his head. 'Sorry. No room. Would you rather sit on somebody else's lap?'

Lotta sighed. 'You'll do,' she said, and got in, sitting on Graham's lap, her arm around his neck, head bent in an attempt not to bump it on the ceiling, long legs stretched across her cousins' laps.

Graham had never noticed before, but Lotta was round in all the right places. And he couldn't help noticing her eyes when she looked down at him. Big and dark and full of mischief and mystery.

'What are you doing with these losers?' she asked him.

'Losers!' Manny shouted from the front seat. 'Who's a loser?'

'You are, *pendejo*! Riding around all night doing nothing when you could be studying or making money! *Culo!*'

Uncle Ernesto laughed. 'That's all this girl thinks about is studying and making money!'

'Yeah, and I'll be the first of this bunch to go to college, *culo*! You hide and watch!'

'Where you planning on going?' Graham asked her.

'UT,' she said. 'I should be able to get some scholarships I keep my grades up. And maybe a grant or two.'

'Yeah? Me too!' Graham said. 'I mean I'm planning to go to UT. No scholarships or grants or anything. I'm not that smart.'

'You don't apply yourself,' Lotta said. 'Me? I apply myself. I'm gonna live up to my potential!'

'Damn, you sound like every report card I ever got! Doesn't apply himself, not living up to his potential!' Graham said.

Manny laughed. 'I don't apply myself neither. But I'm afraid I *am* living up to my potential!'

As they passed the Pizza Garden, Graham saw something out of the corner of his eye. When it registered what it was, he yelled, 'Stop!'

The low rider came to a shuddering halt.

'Back up!' Graham yelled.

Manny's brother Eddie, the driver of the car, muttered an obscenity, but Manny said, 'Back up, man!' so Eddie did.

'Whoa!' Manny said, upon seeing what had gotten Graham's attention. 'She'd be hot if she wasn't crying,' he said.

'Shut up, man!' Graham said through clinched teeth. 'That's my thirteen-year-old sister! Let me out!'

Graham opened the door and Lotta got out, letting him out. He ran to Megan who threw her arms around him, sobbing.

'He got her! He got her!' Megan screamed.

'Who?' Graham demanded. 'What's happened?'

'In Grandma's car! Hurry!' Megan ran to the low rider and jumped in, Graham and Lotta following. Megan straddled the hump in the middle of the back seat, leaning through the bucket seats toward the middle of the front seat. The cousin riding in the middle of the front seat had been shoved to the side so Manny could 'help' the newest arrival.

'Go fast!' Megan wailed. 'They got like a three-minute lead!'

'Megan, what in the hell's going on?' Graham demanded, trying to pull her back from the front seat, either to get her attention so she'd tell him her story, or to get her away from Manny, not even Graham was sure of his actual motive.

'First make him go fast!' Megan shouted, 'then I'll tell you what's going on!'

'For God's sake, *culo*!' Lotta said, 'make this piece of crap move!'

Eddie stopped the car, did something under the dash, and the low rider moved upward, into the position of a normal car.

Hitting the accelerator, the Chevy pulled several g's, knocking those in the back seat against the rolled leather upholstery.

Graham grabbed his sister's arm. 'What's going on?'

'He kidnapped Liz!' she said.

'Who did?' Graham demanded.

Megan looked at her brother for a long moment. Then, sighing, she said, 'Aldon.'

Austin, Texas
E.J., Sunday

I moved as far away from Hal as I could get, and said, 'Hal, before you do whatever it is you're going to do, I think it's only fair that you tell me what's going on. I mean, I really don't understand why you're doing this.'

Hal sighed. 'E.J., this –' he used one arm to gesture widely at the room we were in, encompassing both of us – 'was never my plan. Hurting Jane was never my plan. It just all got . . .' He seemed to search for the word, then smiled. 'Complicated,' he said. 'Complex, even.' The smile faded and the look on his face was a little scary. 'All I ever wanted was my due,' he said. 'You know what it feels like being nominated four times for Best Novel and never winning? Losing to people who can barely compound a sentence? You know what those winners had that I don't have? Vaginas!' he said triumphantly. 'Ever single time I was nominated the winner was a woman. If you look at the records, E.J., you'll discover that a man has never won the top award! Ever! And even of the women who win, it's usually the best dressed or best-looking woman! Never really on merit! Most of those winners couldn't write their way out of a paper bag! I'll admit Jane was the exception to that. Not only was she not the most attractive when she won, but the woman could write!' He sighed. 'Unfortunately, she could also read. That's what happened that night. She told me she needed to talk to me, so we went into the stairwell to talk, and she told me she'd read Candy's book and knew that I'd written it.' He looked at me, a tear in his eye. 'What was I to do? Let Jane ruin everything? I was on the brink of winning! I knew I was going to finally win it this time! After all these years! And here Jane was, getting ready to blow the whistle! I . . . I just . . . couldn't let her do it.'

I was aghast. 'You killed two people because of a stupid award?'

'Three,' he said, 'if you count you. Which I do. And it's not a stupid award! You just say that now because you lost it! I won! You didn't! But try going through tonight three more times! Four times of getting your hopes up, feeling the tension, feeling all eyes on you, knowing that this time . . . But then it doesn't happen. Again, and again, and again, and again. Well, not this time. This time I won!'

'No, you didn't, Hal,' I said, keeping my voice as calm as possible. 'Candace won. Maybe you wrote the book, but you weren't the one up on the dais. She was. You weren't the one everyone was looking at. She was. Your name won't go in the record book. Candace's will. Another woman.'

'Not this time!' he shouted. 'This time the whole world is going to know! Tomorrow morning at the farewell breakfast, I'm going to stand up and announce it to the whole room! Then see whose name is going in the record book!'

I shrugged. 'I guess you'll be able to appreciate that while you're waiting for the needle in Huntsville,' I said.

'What are you talking about?' he said, eyeing me.

'You tell the room what you did, you think the police won't figure out that you killed Jane and DeWitt Perry? Not to mention me. They'll have found my dead body by then, probably.'

He was speechless for a moment. Which was bad. I needed to keep him talking. There was a slight possibility I could get away if I kept him talking – distracted. He had no weapon, except his hands, but I have to admit that the way my throat felt at the moment his hands had been plenty of weapon. But I could run. I was lighter than Hal, maybe I could run faster. True, I knew nothing about the ins and outs of this boiler room, or whatever it was, and Hal presumably did, since he had a key card to the area. He could probably find me with no problem, but what else was I to do? Running would buy me time. Time was the only thing on my side at the moment. But I needed to get him talking again.

'But why DeWitt Perry?' I asked. 'What did he do, besides "stalk" Candace?'

'Isn't that enough?' he asked belligerently. 'Let's just say he was in the wrong place at the wrong time. Following my Candy, trying to . . . to . . . Well, whatever. I don't even want to think about it. I've always had problems with men and Candy. She's so beautiful, you see. Just like her mother,' he said, smiling in remembrance. 'I couldn't believe she even wanted to go out with me, much less marry me,' Hal said. 'She was a dancer, at one of those gentlemen's clubs. They made her take her clothes off. She didn't want to do it . . .'

His eyes clouded over as his thoughts went to Candace's mother, and that's when I made my move. I bolted to the left, away from the door, toward the depths of the steam room and the twists and turns therein.

Eleven

'Who's Alton?' Manny asked from the front seat, not taking his eyes off Megan.

'Aldon,' Graham corrected. 'Nobody really,' he said, also staring at his sister. 'Used to be my best friend when I was a kid. That was before he died, though.'

'Huh?' Manny said, finally turning to Graham. All eyes and ears in the car were on Graham, except Megan, who looked to her lap.

'Where'd hell I'm going?' Eddie, the driver, asked.

'Straight ahead. It's an '84 Dodge Valiant. Blue. Vanity plates that say "Granof4",' Megan said.

'That's a dumb ride to kidnap somebody in,' Uncle Ernesto said, honestly disgusted at the ineptitude of some people.

'He stole our car,' Megan said.

'Grandma's car!' corrected Graham, letting himself get off track. Shaking his head, he said, 'Tell me. Who the hell is this guy?'

'Can you go faster?' Megan pleaded to Eddie as his ride began to pick up speed.

'Sure, *chica*. Calm down,' Eddie said.

'Megan! What is going on?' Graham insisted.

So she told him – about Tommy, about the messages, about him suddenly changing his tune and saying he was Aldon. About the accusations against their mother and Elena Luna.

'And Liz believed this shit?' Graham said, incensed.

'No, of course not. I mean, not really,' Megan said.

'You mean she did!' Graham accused.

'No! She was so confused, Graham,' Megan said, tears stinging her eyes. 'Someone claiming to be a part of her *real* family—'

'We're her *real* family!' Graham said.

Megan turned to the driver. 'Do you see it?' she asked.

'No, *chica*. No blue Valiant. I don't think I've seen one of those in a hundred years!'

'Well, it *is* a blue Valiant! Trust me!' Megan said, letting her temper show.

Manny patted her hand. 'It's OK, Megan,' he said. 'We'll find her.'

Graham removed Manny's hand from his sister's. 'Thirteen!' he said, glaring at Manny.

'So who's this chick we're looking for?' Manny asked, keeping his hand on the back of the seat, just inches from Megan's.

'My sister,' Graham said.

'I thought *she* was your sister?' Manny said, pointing at Megan.

'She is, dumb ass! I have two.'

'How old is the one we're looking for?' Manny asked.

'Thirteen!' Graham said, shooting Manny a look.

Manny turned around in his seat. 'Well, somebody's got an attitude!' he said under his breath.

'And you two thought you'd just come confront this guy, right?' Graham said, glaring at his sister.

Sinking back on to Uncle Ernesto's lap, Megan said, 'It seemed like a good idea at the time.'

'Graham, I think you're missing the big picture here,' Lotta said from his lap.

'You know, I really don't need y'all's help here—' he started, but Lotta interrupted.

'You need *somebody's* help, buster,' she said, glaring down at him. 'First off, Megan, are you OK?'

Megan shook her head. 'No, not really. But thank you for asking,' she said, shooting a look at her brother.

'Did he hurt you?' Graham demanded, moving forward so fast Lotta fell between his feet and the back of Manny's seat.

'Hey, *pendejo*!' she yelled. 'Pick me up!'

'Sorry,' Graham said, pulling her back on to his lap. To Megan he asked, 'Did he?'

'Not really. He threw me on the ground and I might have scraped my hands . . .' She looked at them and they were indeed scraped. Manny grabbed one while Uncle Ernesto grabbed the other.

'Oh, poor *chica*!' Uncle Ernesto said. 'We need to get these cleaned out!'

Graham hit both men's hands away from Megan's.

'But mostly I'm just scared for Elizabeth,' Megan told Lotta. 'She's not real strong,' Megan said, as tears began to fall down her cheeks. 'She's little. A lot smaller than me. If I'd seen him, maybe—'

Lotta reached over and put her arms around Megan. 'Honey, you did what you could! The guy blindsided you!' She held Megan's face up and with a finger wiped away her tears. 'But we're going to find her. And when we do, with all these macho guys we got here, the asshole's not gonna know what hit him!'

Megan smiled for the first time in an hour.

Austin, Texas
E.J., Sunday

The boiler room wasn't as big as I thought it was. I only made one turn before I was up against a blank wall. Cornered. No way out. I turned, determined to make another run for it. Hal was blocking my exit.

'You were just trying to distract me, weren't you, E.J.? Getting me to talk about Candace's mother, but I'm not going to tell you about her! You think you're so smart, but you're not! You're just like the rest of these women! Thinking you're better than me, but you're not! I'm smarter than all of you! All you think about is how someone looks! Well, I fooled you with Candy, didn't I? Yes, she's beautiful, but she's as dumb as her mother was! And just as venal. She betrayed me just like her mother did! And I'll take care of her just like I took care of her mother!

'Don't you know beauty is just on the outside, E.J., don't you know that? Don't you know that it's what's on the inside that counts! And I've got it inside! I'm more talented than every last woman upstairs put together! I should be on the bestsellers list. You stupid women have wet dreams about my books! That's how good I am! But you don't like the way I dress, and you don't like that I'm bald, and you don't like that I'm fat! As if any of that mattered! Candy's mother didn't like that either, and look where that got her! But I'm not telling you about that, am I? It's none of your business!

It was a long time ago! I'm sorry, E.J., but you're just one of them. You're not worth the trouble you could cause me.'

He moved in closer to me, and as he got nearer, his hands outstretched for my neck, I brought my knee up. He moved at the last minute and my knee only made contact with one testicle. But it was enough. He doubled over and I clasped my hands together and whacked him on the back of the neck. He went down and I ran for the door.

I slid on the dirt on the concrete floor as I rounded the corner, falling to one knee. Hal hadn't been as out of it as I'd thought. He had me around the throat before I'd gotten completely up. I lost my footing, falling backwards on top of him, but he didn't let go of my neck. We rolled, and as we did, I got my knee up again. Still my aim was off a little, but close enough for horseshoes and hand grenades. He rolled over groaning; unfortunately, one hand was in my hair and wasn't letting go.

'So, Hal, my man! How did you find this place?'

We both stopped struggling, but Hal didn't let go of my hair. He sat up, pulling me by the hair toward him, shielding himself with my body. Jerome MacIntyre stood a yard or so in front of us, wearing a red and black plaid silk dressing gown over black pajamas.

'Jerry, you need to leave,' Hal said.

Jerome smiled brightly. 'But I just got here, Harold! Hi, E.J.'

'Hi, Jerome,' I said.

'Harold! Would you believe I found out what the E.J. stands for? Eloise Janine! Do you blame the poor girl for going by initials?'

'I was named after my grandmother!' I said through gritted teeth, thinking if I ever got out of this Willis was in for it.

'My God, two poor women with that name!' Jerome laughed. 'Although, I don't suppose you and I can say much about that, can we, Harold?'

'Jerry, you need to leave,' Hal said again.

'No, you need to let go of my wife,' came a voice from behind us.

The way Hal had me pulled to him, I could see slightly behind us. One of the Sam's blow dryers was pressed into Hal's back. Willis was holding it.

I suppose it's entirely possible that the end of the Sam's

blow dryer felt larger than the end of a normal gun. And who knew that an overweight, bald man in a T-shirt and boxers could move so fast?

All I know for sure is that one minute Hal was holding a hank of my hair and Willis had a blow dryer at his back, the next Hal had swung around, using his free hand to swipe the blow dryer out of Willis's hand. He took two long steps toward the door, still holding tightly to my hair. At the second step he let go, flinging me to the floor as he rushed the door to the boiler room, bowling over Jerome on his way. He was out the door, slamming it shut behind him.

I turned toward my husband, who was lying on the concrete floor of the boiler room, his feet tangled in the cord of the blow dryer.

'Get to the door!' he shouted and I ran in the opposite direction of my husband.

Jerome was gallantly trying to stand as I ran past him. I grabbed the door and pushed. Nothing happened.

'It's stuck!' I yelled.

Jerome was the first to reach me, putting his bony shoulder into the door. All that accomplished was the bruising of a nice old gentleman. Willis caught up to us as Jerome was rubbing his shoulder.

He pulled and tugged, pushed and swore. The door didn't budge.

'He's locked us in somehow,' Willis said. Reaching in his pocket, he brought out his cellphone.

'Maybe it would have been nice to use it before you came down here,' I suggested. Then it dawned on me. 'Oh my God! He's going after Candy! He's got to be! We've got to stop him. He thinks she betrayed him!'

'You're welcome to my saving your life,' Willis said, then uttered an emphatic string of curse words. 'I can't get a signal in here!' he said.

He walked away from the door, staring at the read-out on his digital phone, muttering, 'No, uh uh, nope,' as he tried spot after spot.

I ran to the door and started hammering, yelling 'Help!' at the top of my lungs.

Slowly, through the din of my own voice, I heard another's: Jerome talking to someone.

'Yes, we're stuck in the boiler room. And please send any police presence still in the hotel up to room 515 immediately. Hal Burleson is going to kill someone else.'

Willis and I turned to him. Jerome shrugged and pointed. 'It's an intercom. I figured it couldn't hurt to try it.'

It took less than five minutes for a custodian to reach us and remove the blockage from the boiler room door, but it was the longest five minutes of my life. We ran for the service elevator and took it up to the third floor of the hotel, running to my room. It was full of police, but Candace wasn't there.

Detective Washington grabbed my arm. 'What the hell's going on?' he asked.

So we told him. In detail. And then sat down on the beds to worry about Candace.

Black Cat Ridge, Texas
Elizabeth, Sunday

'Let me out!' she yelled for what felt like the millionth time. She was on the floor of the back seat of Grandma's old Valiant, her hands and feet bound with duct tape. He hadn't taped her mouth, and she was glad for that. She never saw his face. He'd shoved Megan down and grabbed Elizabeth's head, burying it in the seat, and holding it there as he got in the driver's seat and spun out of the Pizza Garden parking lot. They were several miles down the road before he stopped the car and bound her hands and feet with the duct tape and threw her in the back of the car, the entire time keeping her face turned away from him. He also hadn't said a word.

He was driving moderately, probably the speed limit, Elizabeth thought, not wanting to draw the attention of the police. If she'd been in the trunk, she thought, she could kick out one of the tail lights like she saw on *Oprah* that time and get the police to stop them. But lying on the floor of the back seat, she had no options.

Finally she decided to try some finesse. 'Aldon?' He didn't answer. 'Why are you doing this?' Still no answer. 'I want to see you. I want to talk to you about what's happening. I don't understand why you've thrown me back here! I'm your sister!'

It was as if the car was driving itself. There was no sound, no movement from the front seat. Elizabeth tried again. 'Is it because I brought Megan with me? I'm sorry about that, but I don't drive. She had to drive me here. Is that what you're mad about?' Still only silence met her words. 'She doesn't know, if that's what you're worried about. She thinks I was meeting a boy. I mean, you know, like a boyfriend. I didn't say a word about you, Aldon! You told me not to. And I've always done what you told me to do, haven't I, big brother?'

Softly, from the front seat, he said, 'You were a good baby sister.'

Elizabeth felt her skin crawl. Was it better having him answer her? At this point she wasn't sure. 'And you were a good big brother,' she said.

'I tried,' he said. 'I saved you that night.'

Mama E.J. had told her that her real mother, Terry, had fallen on her when she was shot, keeping her safe with her dead body. She said Aldon had been found on the stairs, trying to run away. 'Yes, I know,' Elizabeth said. 'I always knew it was you who saved me.'

'I've changed, Bessie,' he said. 'Physically and emotionally. I'm not the same Aldon you knew.'

'How could you be?' Elizabeth said. 'After what you've been through.'

'I've had work done to hide my appearance,' he said. 'That picture I sent you on email was taken right before I had everything done.'

'Oh,' she said. And she knew in that moment, although she'd thought she'd known all along, at this point she really knew: This was not Aldon. Aldon had been dead for the past nine years, just as she'd always been told. Tears sprang to her eyes as the half-hope left her. She really hadn't known which to hope for – that her brother Aldon was alive and that her adoptive mother and father were evil, or that her world was just as she'd always thought it was, and still without Aldon.

Something in her tone must have alerted the driver. He said, 'You don't believe me.'

Trying to control her thoughts and tears, Elizabeth said, 'Of course I do, Aldon.'

There was a laugh from the front seat. 'No, you don't. But that's OK. I don't really care. You ever see *Aliens*?' he asked. 'The second one. Where that Marine gets scared and he yells, "Game over, man, game over". You ever see that?'

'Yes, I saw that,' Elizabeth said, remembering parts of that movie that had scared her so badly she had nightmares.

'Well, Bessie,' he said, pulling Grandma's Valiant to a stop. 'Game over.'

Austin, Texas
E.J., Sunday

Jerome felt it only prudent to call both Lydia and Mary, knowing that in the morning, had they been left out of this part of the drama, they would have boiled him in oil. So the five of us sat in the room I shared with Candace, formerly with Jane, and wondered if I would again lose a roommate to the hand of Hal Burleson.

I rubbed my head where Hal had been holding my hair. 'Here, let me look,' Mary said, getting up from Candace's bed to come inspect my scalp.

'How bad is it?' I asked as she gingerly fingered my hair and scalp.

'There's some missing, but if you back-comb it a little, no one will ever know,' she said.

'I need to get a real gun,' Willis said, apropos of nothing.

I just looked at him and shook my head.

'If I'd had a real gun, he wouldn't have swiped it away like that!' Willis insisted. 'And even if he'd tried, it would have been a smaller target and I'd have had a better grip on it.'

Jerome patted Willis on the shoulder. 'It's not your fault, Willis. Hal's insane. It's not your fault.'

Jerome was looking all of his eighty-three years, his shoulders bent, his face dejected. 'I've known Hal for over thirty years,' he said quietly. 'I thought he was my friend, but I didn't even know he had a daughter. Obviously I didn't know he was homicidally insane.'

'None of us did, Jerry,' Lydia said.

'Jane was reading Candace's book that night,' I said, remembering. 'I'd just bought it at the bookstore. That must have been when she realized it was Hal's work, not Candace's.'

'But why would she approach him about it?' Willis asked. 'She had been planning on doing just about the same thing.'

'Maybe she realized how foolish her plan had been,' Mary said quietly. 'Maybe she didn't want to see Hal make the same mistake she'd almost made. Before all this with Angela, Jane was always a very ethical person. I think seeing what Hal was doing, knowing she'd almost done the same thing, finally got through to her. She finally saw how futile and unethical it really was.'

'I should have tripped him as he ran for the door,' Jerome said. 'I didn't even try.'

'It all happened so fast . . .' I started.

Jerome shook his head. 'When you get old, E.J., you get . . . afraid. Afraid of people hurting you, afraid of breaking a hip, falling down, eating the wrong foods and getting constipated. Afraid of everything.' Jerome stood up. 'I'm also afraid, ladies and gentleman, that I'm done. It's time to retire. This is my last convention, my last book. My last hurrah.' And with that he was out the door.

Black Cat Ridge, Texas
Graham, Sunday

They were in the country now, having left Codderville behind. Still no sign of the Valiant. Giant oaks and pine lined the sides of the two-lane blacktop, no shoulder for emergencies. The asphalt was still wet from the earlier storm, slick and dangerous, with potholes hidden by pools of black water. The Chevy rolled along at a fairly fast clip, all eyes out the windows, searching for Grandma Vera's car. As they made a sharp turn they saw taillights up ahead.

'Is that it?' Megan asked, leaning into the front seat.

Manny patted her shoulder. 'Let's get closer, Eddie,' he said. To Megan, he added, 'We'll find out.'

Eddie hit the accelerator and Megan could feel the g's pulling at her face. Eddie shone the extra lights and they could see the car ahead. An antique Valiant. There could be only one in the Codderville area.

The car in front put on the brake lights, slowing. 'I think he wants you to go around,' Graham said from the back seat. Thinking fast, he said, 'Do it. Pass him. Everybody down,' he said, pushing Megan's head toward the floor.

They could feel the Chevy accelerate once again, could feel the wheel turn slightly as they moved into the oncoming lane, then back.

'Stay low,' Graham ordered, 'but you guys try to keep an eye out.'

'You got it, *el jeffe*,' Uncle Ernesto said.

'Slow down,' Graham told the driver, 'we need to keep 'em in sight.'

'Got it,' Eddie said, taking his foot off the accelerator and slowly letting the speed lessen.

They were approximately four car lengths ahead of the Valiant when there came another tight corner. Eddie applied the brake, slowing the Chevy down even more to make the turn. A straight away was ahead and he coasted into it, keeping his eye on the rear-view mirror.

All eyes were staring out the back window of the Chevy. Nothing happened. Eddie let the car slow more. Finally Graham said, 'Stop. We lost 'em.'

'No, man, they turned off!' Manny said. 'Eddie, back up! We gotta see where they turned off, man!'

Eddie put the car in reverse.

'Jesus, Mary and Joseph!' Lotta said from Graham's lap. 'Don't back up, you idiot! Turn around! What if somebody else decides to use this public road? Gawd!' she said, leaning back against Graham. Turning to him, she said, 'You see where I come from? You see the adversity I've had to overcome? A family of complete idiots!'

'You're a strong woman,' Graham said, his hand on her tiny nipped-in waist.

'Graham!' Megan said, turning his attention back to the problem at hand.

Driving down the correct lane in the correct direction, Eddie eased the Chevy around the bend. There they saw an almost invisible dirt road, leading off to the left.

'Cut the lights!' Lotta ordered.

'I'm gonna hit something!' Eddie protested.

'So we hit something! Get over it!' Lotta ordered.

'But my Chevy . . .' Eddie wailed.

'Just do it, man,' Manny said. 'Or you know she's gonna hurt you.'

Eddie turned off the headlights of the Chevy and turned on to the dirt road. All could feel the Chevy slipping and sliding in the mud caused by the heavy rain.

'We're gonna get stuck!' Eddie protested.

'Try to drive like you know what you're doing!' Lotta ordered.

'There it is!' Megan yelled, pointing at the tail end of the Valiant peeking out of some bushes to the right of the road. In front of where the Valiant had pulled off was a mud puddle the size of Dallas.

Eddie put on the brakes. 'I ain't driving through that!' he said, arms across his chest. Eddie had taken a stand.

'Everybody out,' Graham said, 'and be quiet!'

Black Cat Ridge, Texas
Elizabeth, Sunday

It was so dark Elizabeth could barely see her hands in front of her face; that is, if she could have gotten her hands in front of her face. But since they were duct-taped behind her back, that was pretty much an impossibility.

Tommy/Aldon had stopped the car and come to the back, pulling her up on the seat and untaping her feet. 'We walk from here,' he said. 'We're almost home, Bessie.'

Now she followed him, or tried to. She could barely see him in the dark, could barely hear his footfalls for the sound of the cicadas coming from the woods, louder than she'd ever heard them.

'Wait, Aldon,' she said, forcing herself to use that name. 'I can barely see you!'

He stopped and she bumped into him. 'Please untie my hands!' Elizabeth pleaded. 'I can't get my balance with them tied behind me.'

She could see him now. Definitely not Aldon. No amount of plastic surgery could have changed the shape of his head, the texture of his hair. She may have only been four years old when her brother had been murdered, but she remembered him. She remembered all her family, everything about them. The touch of her mother's skin, the way her father's early morning beard had tickled her cheek when he kissed her, the sound of Monique's laugh, the feel of Aldon's hand in hers. Aldon had been a tease, loving to play jokes on his sisters and his parents. Some had been in bad taste, as only a ten year old could conceive. Others had been just plain funny. Elizabeth had loved to follow him around, take his toys and hide them, elicit his ire, which usually led to running, to laughing, to tickling, to fun.

This brown-eyed blond was not Aldon. Aldon had looked like

their father and would have grown to look even more like him. His build had been a miniature of their father's – short and stocky with slightly bowed legs. This guy was tall and thin and, if anything, was knock-kneed. Not Aldon. Aldon's hand had felt safe and welcoming when she held it; when this guy grabbed her hand to lead her further into the woods, it felt anything but.

This was not Aldon. Tears sprang to her eyes. *This was not Aldon.*

Austin, Texas
E.J., Sunday
We sat there quietly, none of us looking at each other or saying anything. Just waiting. And not even sure what we were waiting for. For Hal to be caught? For the police to find Candace's lifeless body? For this to be over once and for all.

There was a commotion from the hallway, and then the Sam's fire alarm began blaring. We all looked at each other and ran for the door.

There was no smoke in the hall. Only Candace pressed up against one wall and Hal prostrate on the carpet before her. Jerome stood over him with the metal end of the fire hose in his hand, wielding it like a baseball bat.

'Would someone turn off that infernal racket?' Jerome called loudly. 'And get Detective Washington up here. Or an exterminator. Whichever you find first.'

'You're going to have so much fun at the convention, E.J.,' Jane says. 'Wait until you meet my friends! They're going to love you.'

'I hope so,' I say cautiously. 'I'm not great at making first impressions.'

'Honey, screw first impressions. I've never even met you and you're one of the best friends I've ever had,' Jane says.

I sit there with the phone at my ear, a tear in my eye. How funny, I think, I'd never met her, but it was true: she was a great friend.

Black Cat Ridge, Texas
Vera, Sunday
Vera Pugh woke up, slightly disoriented. She had to go to the bathroom, that much was for sure. But where was she? Then

she remembered: in Willis and E.J.'s bed. Which meant the bathroom was right here in the room. She found it, used it, then decided to go upstairs and check on the kids, wondering what time it was and whether Graham was home yet.

Leaving the bedroom she passed through the family room, noting the time on the digital clock of the cable box. Two a.m. Graham would be home by now and asleep. She pulled herself up the stairs, wondering why anyone in their right mind would buy a two-story house. First you had to climb stairs, and then you had to vacuum them. Vera, who vacuumed every day, thought having stairs was an excessive waste of time and energy.

She got to the upstairs landing and turned left towards Graham's room. The door was shut, but Vera opened it to peek in. Her night vision was still very good, thank you very much, and she had no need for a night light. She could see quite well that Graham was not in his bed. Had she given him a curfew? She wondered. She didn't remember doing it. Which meant he thought he could come in whenever he wanted, forgetting what his parents usually told him. She smiled. Such a willful boy, that one. Just like both her boys had been.

Deciding to check on the girls to make sure they were covered properly, she went back down the hall, stopping first at Elizabeth's room. Opening the door, she discovered Elizabeth was not in her bed. Hoping her granddaughters had decided to sleep together this night, she hurried to Megan's room. Through the piles of clothes on the floor, Vera could see the bed, stacked high with something. Was it the girls, she wondered. Flipping on the overhead light, she discovered that it was just more clothes. Neither Megan nor Elizabeth was here.

Vera went back downstairs to the front door and opened it. Sure enough, her Valiant was not in the driveway. She went to the family room and grabbed the cordless phone. She didn't really care what time it was; an emergency was an emergency, period. She dialed Elena Luna's number.

Black Cat Ridge, Texas
Graham, Sunday
'Be quiet!' Graham hissed.

Everyone stopped talking. 'Just listen to me, OK?'

All eyes turned to Graham. 'Eddie, you and Uncle Ernesto stay with the car, in case they double back.'

Eddie and Uncle Ernesto nodded.

'Lotta, you take these two,' he said, indicating cousins whose names he'd forgotten, 'and fan out,' he said, pointing to the right. 'Manny, you and Megan come with me. We're taking the path.'

'You'd do better taking me than Manny!' Lotta said, hands on hips.

'Somebody's gotta control these guys,' Graham pointed out in a whisper.

Lotta thought for a moment then nodded her head. 'You're right. Without a babysitter they'll end up driving back to town for tacos!'

'Listen for me,' he told them. 'I'll holler out if I need you.'

They all nodded and he, Megan and Manny hit the trail.

Twelve

Austin, Texas
E.J., Sunday

'Somebody call Washington,' I said, staring at Hal who sat on the floor, leaning against the Sam's tasteful wall. He was conscious, just not going anywhere. To continue that condition, I said to Jerome, 'May I borrow your fire hose, please?'

'Certainly, my dear,' he said, handing me said implement.

I held it menacingly. 'OK, give,' I said to Hal. 'I know why you killed Jane, stupid as it was, but why comb-over boy? I mean, DeWitt Perry? And why did you assault Lisbet?'

'Who?' Hal asked, squinting up at me.

'The girl from the college paper that you put in the trunk of the car,' I said.

'Huh?' Hal asked.

'Ah . . .' Came from behind me. I turned. It was Candace, still holding up the other wall.

'Hal, Daddy didn't do that . . . I did,' she said softly.

I turned on her, and as I did, Jerome took the fire hose out of my hand. 'You deal with her, I'll keep an eye on him,' he said.

Releasing the hose, I said to Candace, 'What in the hell are you talking about?'

With tears streaming down her face, Candace hiccupped, then said, 'She was asking all these questions of Daddy. And . . . and I saw that look . . . that look he gets. I knew he was going to hurt her, like he did Jane and Mr Perry . . . I wasn't sure that he had, you know, hurt Jane and Mr Perry, but I thought . . .'

'So you cold cocked Lisbet Collins?' I said, or squeaked, or whatever.

'I told her I needed a ride and, if she'd give me one, I'd . . . I'd tell her everything she wanted to know, you know?'

I nodded my head. I felt a presence behind me and turned my head slightly to see Detective Washington standing there. He put a finger to his lips and I turned back to Candace. 'OK,' I said to her.

'And . . . and when we got to her car and she unlocked it, there was this book there, this heavy textbook, and I . . . Well, I just hit her with it.' Finally Candace looked up at me. 'It was either that or let Daddy kill her,' she whispered.

'Daddy?' Washington asked softly in my ear. I pointed at Hal still sitting on the floor with Jerome standing over him with the fire hose. Hal's head was bleeding and Jerome looked for all the world like Clint Eastwood in a Dirty Harry movie.

'You can put the hose down, Mr MacIntyre,' Washington said.

Jerome turned around, seeing the detective for the first time. Breaking into a large full-watt smile, Jerome said, 'My pleasure, Detective. He's all yours.'

Black Cat Ridge, Texas
Vera, Sunday
They were in Luna's personal car, a black Chevy Tahoe with all the bells and whistles, including a magnetic bubble light with siren that could adhere to the roof of her car if need be. At this point Vera felt it needed to be.

'I'm not going to run lights and siren through Black Cat and Codderville, Vera, so just get over it,' Luna said.

'The kids are in trouble!' Vera insisted.

'You don't know that! The girls decided to raid whatever party Graham had going, for their own amusement. At the most, they're standing around screaming at each other as we speak.'

'We need to call Willis and E.J.,' Vera said.

'No,' Luna said. 'Now's not a good time.'

Vera sighed. 'I know they have sex, Elena! They have three children, for God's sake. Well, two children that they had to have sex for. Anyway, I think it's OK to disturb their little love nest to let them know their children are missing!'

'We can't call them,' Luna said. She sighed. 'Look, there've been a couple of murders at this convention thing Pugh's at—'

'Really?' Vera said, perking up.

'And as usual your daughter-in-law is in the thick of it, causing all sorts of problems for the police.'

'Who got killed?' Vera asked, almost forgetting her missing grandchildren.

'Her roommate—' Luna started.

'Oh, my God! Maybella LaRue? I love her books!'

'The kids, Vera, the kids,' Luna reminded.

'They're probably OK,' Vera said. 'Just having fun.'

But somehow, in her gut, Vera didn't believe that. Jeez, she thought, Maybella LaRue, murdered!

Black Cat Ridge, Texas
Elizabeth, Sunday
Tommy/Aldon led her to the door of a shack in the middle of the woods. A poor excuse for a driveway led up to it, but she couldn't imagine anything but a four-wheel drive making it. The shack was just a black outline to Elizabeth, but she could smell mildew and dust and old. Inside was pitch black until Tommy/Aldon lit a candle, then she could see a bit of her surroundings, but mostly she could see him. His hair wasn't really blond so much as light brown, or what they called dirty blond. More like beige, really. All of him. His skin, his hair, his eyes, even his clothes, various shades of beige. His eyes were like glass doll's eyes. No spark of spirit or soul. His lips were thin and his nose pointed. She noted all this, memorizing it, ready for the sketch artist she would describe him to. Because Elizabeth knew she would get away from this

man, knew that she would live to tell her tale. And hopefully live to beat the living shit out of him!

'Sit down, Bessie,' he said, indicating a neatly made-up cot in the corner. She moved to it, gingerly sitting down. The bedding was new; it didn't smell like the rest of the room; it smelled like Downy fabric softener, the smell of home. This brought tears to her eyes that she willed away. Don't break down, she told herself. Don't give him the satisfaction!

'What now, Aldon?' she asked.

He looked at her for a long moment, a look on his face that scared Elizabeth. It wasn't a mean look, a dangerous look; it was a blank look. A look that said he had not thought beyond this point. From now on, Elizabeth knew, he would be playing it by ear. Which meant her living through the next few hours could be totally up to her – up to what she said, how she reacted, how she played his game.

Memories were flooding her, of playing Candy Land with Aldon, with his made-up rules that always let him win; of throwing the gingerbread men from the Candy Land game at her brother, hearing him laugh, hearing Mom say, 'You make a mess, you clean it up!' Same thing Mama E.J. said.

Mama E.J. God, how she wanted her now. If she'd been here, this wouldn't have happened! Elizabeth thought. Nobody could have gotten to her if Mama had been here. Tears threatened again, and she pushed away the thoughts.

Tommy/Aldon had turned, moving into the small kitchen area, such as it was: a camp stove on a counter by a sink, and an ice chest next to it.

'You hungry?' he asked.

Elizabeth said, 'Yes.' Keep him busy, she thought. She was totally untaped now, both her hands and feet. With his back to her, she looked around the small cabin, looking for something heavy she could use to bash his skull in – some kind of weapon, anything.

She saw the door opening before the creaking of its hinges sounded, making Tommy/Aldon swing around, a sharp knife in his hand. Graham stood in the doorway.

Elizabeth saw him smile at her abductor. 'Hey, Aldon,' Graham said, 'remember me, man? It's Graham! Your best friend! Remember?'

Tommy/Aldon just stared at him, the knife pointed in his

direction. 'God, I couldn't believe it when Megan told me you were alive!' Graham said. 'Man, I'm so glad! I really missed you, man! Hey, Liz . . .' he started, turning toward his sister.

Tommy/Aldon said, 'Bessie. Her name is Bessie.'

Graham nodded. 'Yeah, right, man. Bessie. You OK, kiddo?' Graham asked her.

Elizabeth nodded.

'She's better than OK,' Tommy/Aldon said. 'She's with me now, so she's where she belongs.'

'Man, that's cool,' Graham said, keeping the smile plastered on his face, trying to keep his demeanor non-threatening, his hands at his side. 'She's really missed you.'

'You were part of it!' Tommy/Aldon said, taking a threatening step towards Graham.

'Part of the conspiracy?' Graham asked. 'Man, how could I be? I was like only six at the time, remember?'

'Six?' Tommy/Aldon said, confusion on his face. 'But I was ten.'

'Yeah,' Graham said, smiling bigger now. 'You were my hero.'

'Yeah,' Tommy/Aldon said. 'Yeah, I remember. You followed me around.'

'Sure did,' Graham said. 'Went everywhere you went. Our moms called me "the shadow".' Graham forced a laugh.

'The shadow,' Tommy/Aldon repeated. 'You were the shadow. Not me.'

'That's right, Aldon,' Graham said. 'I was the shadow.'

Behind Tommy/Aldon was a window and Elizabeth could see someone at it. She had no idea who it was, a Hispanic boy she didn't recognize. Who was he? Was he with Graham or with this man who held them both at knifepoint? She looked to Graham, who smiled and nodded at her. She hoped he meant the guy at the window was with him. But she wasn't sure what good it would do. The window was closed and it looked as if it had been painted over a thousand times. No way was that window coming open.

The face disappeared from the window and seconds later a heavy branch crashed through the glass. Tommy/Aldon whirled around, and when he did, Graham jumped forward, yelling, 'Liz, run!' as he did so.

She ran through the door, but stopped on the shallow porch, unable to move further as she watched through the open door as Graham tried to wrestle the knife from Tommy/Aldon. Behind her someone grabbed her. Elizabeth swung around, ready to take on whoever it was, but found Megan pulling at her. She threw her arms around her sister.

Just as she did, Tommy/Aldon came running out the open door, almost knocking over both girls.

'I got him!' yelled the Hispanic kid who took off after him. Megan and Elizabeth ran into the shack.

Graham lay on the floor. Elizabeth could see no blood. 'Are you all right?' she demanded, kneeling by him. 'Did he cut you?'

Graham lifted his head. 'Naw. Just knocked the wind out of me. Where is he?'

'Manny ran after him,' Megan said.

'Who's Manny?' Elizabeth asked.

'Long story,' Graham said. To Megan, he said, 'Go shout for the others.'

Megan got up and ran out of the cabin while Elizabeth asked, 'What others?'

'Come here,' Graham said.

Elizabeth moved to him and he took her in his arms 'You OK?' he asked, kissing her on the forehead.

'Yeah,' she said, curling up in his arms 'But I think you saved my life.'

'Yeah, well, we superheroes are like that, ya know,' her brother answered.

Megan came back in, a limping Manny with his arm around her shoulder.

'You better be injured, bro,' Graham said, 'or I'm cutting your arm off.'

'Hey, man, I fell down. Think I broke my foot!' Manny said.

'It's probably a sprain,' Megan said.

Graham stood up, pulling Elizabeth to her feet. 'Let's get out of here,' he said.

Once outside, as Manny limped toward his cousins who were coming up the trail, Graham pulled both girls into his arms, hugging them to him. After a few seconds, Megan touched the top of her head, bringing back moisture on her hand.

Looking up at her brother, she said, 'Are you crying?'

Graham pushed both girls away, holding them at arms' length. 'If you ever mention this to anyone, I'll kill you both. Severely.'

'Mention what?' Elizabeth said.

Graham smiled at her, holding up his hand for a high five. Elizabeth reached up, slapping his hand with hers.

Megan said, 'I know what. Graham cry—'

Elizabeth elbowed her sister in the ribs. 'Ow! Jeez, can't a girl have any fun?' she wailed.

Putting his arms around the shoulders of his sisters, Graham led them down the trail and out of the woods. 'I think we've had enough fun for one night,' he said.

Austin, Texas
E.J., Sunday

'Before you take him away, Detective Washington,' I said, 'I'd really like to know why he killed poor comb-over boy.'

'Who?' Washington and Hal said in unison.

I sighed. 'DeWitt Perry,' I said.

'Well, that's just cruel,' Washington said.

'That fan?' Hal said, still squinting as blood was now dripping into his left eye. 'It wasn't my fault. The idiot tried to run from me. He heard Candy going on and on about Jane! She kept accusing me of having done something to Jane—'

'You did!' I said. 'You killed her!'

'I know that!' Hal said. 'But Candace didn't! Anyway, that creep was in the hallway trying to come on to my baby girl, and he heard her, and he got all excited and then *he* started accusing me!' Hal looked totally exasperated at this turn of events. 'I mean, who was this guy to say such a thing to me? Well, I sent Candy to her room and I started to talk to him, this fan, and he turned and started running for the elevator! He's pushing the button over and over like it's going to get the elevator there faster! I hate when people do that! You push the button once. That's it. Once! But he's pushing it over and over and looking at me over his shoulder and I say, "If you want the elevator that badly, here, let me help!" And I pulled the door open. It was easier than I thought it would be. The Sam really should have someone look at that,' Hal said.

'And then you pushed him?' Washington asked.

'Well, he wanted to go downstairs, now didn't he?' Hal said.

And who could argue with that.

Black Cat Ridge, Texas
Vera, Sunday

They'd driven around the usual teen haunts of Codderville: the pizza parlor, the MacDonald's, the video game arcade, no sign of the kids.

'I've got one place left to check,' Luna said, 'and if they're there, I'll beat them myself.'

'Where? A bar?' Vera asked.

'Worse,' Luna said. 'The bowling alley.'

As they drove by, Luna noticed about twenty cars parked close to the entrance in the big parking lot, but there was one pickup and a Jeep parked close to the street, away from the other cars, under a pitiful specimen of an oak tree. Several teenaged boys were standing around the two vehicles.

Driving closer, Luna asked, 'Vera, you know any of these guys?'

Vera leaned forward, squinting through the windshield of the Tahoe. After a second she said, 'Yes! That's Leon, Graham's friend! The skinny one with the glasses!'

Luna pulled into the parking lot.

Black Cat Ridge, Texas
Graham, Sunday

'Where are the keys?' Graham demanded, looking at Elizabeth.

Hands on hips, Elizabeth said, 'I wasn't driving, numb nuts! *He* was! I suppose he still has them!'

'Shit!' Graham said.

'Language!' Megan said, then seeing her brother's glare broke into a wide grin.

'OK,' Graham said, 'everybody back in Eddie's car.'

'How?' Lotta said, hands on hips, staring at Eddie's car.

'OK,' Manny said. 'Eddie, Ramon and me in the front, with Megan on my lap—'

'Manny, I swear to God I'm going to bust your ass if you don't—'

'I should go in the front,' Elizabeth said. 'There's less room and I'm the smallest.'

Manny grinned. 'Hey, that's fine too!' he said.

Glaring at Manny, Graham said, 'Liz, if he so much as looks at you funny—'

Lightly touching Manny's shoulder, Elizabeth said, 'Manny would never do such a thing, Graham. He knows the kind of trauma I've just been through and he's too nice a guy to take advantage of that.'

Both Elizabeth and Graham looked at Manny. Manny's grin vanished, he said, 'Well, shit!' and got into the front seat of Eddie's car. Behind her back, Elizabeth held out her palm for a low five from her brother, which he dutifully fulfilled.

The rest piled into the back in basically the same order as before. 'Where to?' Eddie called out, starting his engine.

'Back to the bowling alley, please,' Graham said, Lotta firmly on his lap.

Black Cat Ridge, Texas
Vera, Sunday

'Leon, you get your butt over here right now!' Vera said, having pulled herself out of Luna's Chevy Tahoe and taken the hard drop to the ground.

Leon, Tad and Hollister all came to attention, Leon paling at the sound of his name being called. When he saw who it was, he was afraid he might soil himself. He wasn't afraid of his own grandmother, but there was something about Graham's that scared the crap out of him. And now here he was, without Graham to defend him.

Hesitantly Leon walked toward the Tahoe, with only a couple of pushes from behind by Hollister and Tad.

'Yes, ma'am?' Leon said, noting his voice was higher than it had been since he'd gone through puberty.

'Where's Graham?' Vera demanded.

'Ah . . .' Leon started.

'And the girls?' Vera demanded.

Leon blanched. 'The girls?' he squeaked. 'How do you know about the girls?' Desperately he looked back at what was left of his pack for back-up and noted they were both getting in Hollister's dad's truck.

Luna had gotten out of the Tahoe and noticed the same thing Leon did. 'Get down now!' she said, pointing at the two boys.

Legs stayed in mid-air, doors halfway open. Slowly the two boys climbed down from the cab of the truck. 'Over here!' Luna said.

Heads down, the two boys obeyed.

'What have you done with the girls?' Vera demanded.

Leon looked at Tad and Hollister, both of whom refused to look back, finding something fascinating about their running shoes.

'Nothing!' Leon finally managed to get out. 'We just left them on the side of the road.'

'You did what?' Luna demanded.

'When we found out what they were really up to, what they were going to do to Graham, well, gosh, surely you understand . . .'

'What the hell are you talking about?' Vera demanded.

Leon began to cry. 'It wasn't my idea! It was Tad's! And Hollister left Joey, too!'

Vera and Luna looked at each other. 'Who's Joey?' Luna asked.

Hollister pulled himself up to his full height and held his head up high. 'Ma'am, we know where they are and we'll go get them. We didn't mean them any harm, we just wanted to make sure Graham was OK.'

'And Megan and Elizabeth are with this Joey? Is that a boy or a girl?' Vera demanded.

The boys exchanged glances. 'Huh?' Hollister asked.

They were saved from any further confusion by the arrival of the 1976 Chevy Impala low-rider, as it noisily entered the parking lot.

Black Cat Ridge, Texas
Graham, Sunday
'Whoa shit!' Graham said as they entered the parking lot.

'Who's that?' Lotta asked.

'The little one's my grandmother. The big one is Detective Elena Luna of the Codderville Police Department.'

Eddie slammed on the brakes, throwing the car into reverse.

'Jeez, Eddie, what are you doing?' Graham shouted.

'Ah, Eddie's got a few violations against him, man,' Manny said.

'Let us out first, Eddie!' Graham said.

Lotta leaned forward and slapped her cousin in the back of the head. 'Stop the car, *pendejo*!' she said. The brakes were applied. 'Now, let them out, for God's sake!'

Graham and Manny both opened their doors and Lotta, Graham, Elizabeth and Megan piled out. As Lotta started to get back into the car, Graham caught her wrist. 'Ah, so, Lotta, it's been an interesting evening,' he said.

She grinned at him. 'Call me. We'll go out next Saturday. I have the night off.' With that she slid into the back seat and the Chevy went rapidly in reverse out of the parking lot.

Graham turned to his sisters and the three of them looked at the group approximately one hundred yards ahead. Putting his arms around their shoulders, Graham said, 'Well, my sisters, we're in for it now.'

Black Cat Ridge, Texas
Vera, Sunday

'There they are!' Vera exclaimed, pointing to her three grand-children walking towards their group. She marveled that Graham had his arms around his sisters' shoulders and didn't even seem to be trying to choke them or anything. Something was definitely wrong.

Vera walked as fast as her seventy-year-old legs would take her to meet her grandkids. 'What happened?' she demanded.

'Everybody's OK,' Graham said. 'Can you get Luna over here? We have something we have to report to the police.'

Black Cat Ridge, Texas
Elizabeth, Sunday

They were back in Black Cat Ridge, back in the Pugh house, sitting at the kitchen table. Vera had made a pot of coffee and given cups to herself, Luna and Graham. The girls were allowed hot chocolate, which they gratefully took. Elizabeth held the cup in both hands, warming them. She was colder than she should be, she knew that. Possibly a little bit of shock was setting in.

Her grandmother had insisted the kids be taken back to their home, rather than to the police station, and Mrs Luna had agreed. So now they were supposed to tell their story, in all its detail. Elizabeth was embarrassed. How many times had she heard about Internet predators? How many TV shows and movies had she seen about Internet predators? Heck, there was even that one magazine show that relished setting these guys up and then busting them. Which was always fun to watch. So she knew, intellectually she knew, about Internet predators. So how had she fallen for Tommy? What made her just assume he wasn't one? Heck, the idea had never even entered her head! She felt so stupid.

She was holding her cup, eyes downcast, getting a little mini-facial from the steam off the hot chocolate. When Luna said, 'Elizabeth?' she was forced to look up.

'Yes, ma'am?' she said.

'Start at the beginning,' Luna said.

And so she did, slowly at first, trying to feel her way into the story, trying to discover at what point she'd become such a blithering idiot as to just accept this guy for who he said he was. When she got to the point where Megan became involved, her sister jumped in, holding Elizabeth's hand as she confessed to their scheme of catching him.

'We thought if we could get him in a public place, and see him, that would prove he wasn't Aldon,' Megan said.

'And prove that your mother and I didn't conspire to kill Elizabeth's family?' Luna said quietly.

Both girls looked into their hot chocolate mugs.

Finally, Elizabeth looked up. 'I'm sorry, Mrs Luna,' she said. 'I never really thought—'

Luna nodded her head, a slight smile playing at her lips. 'I know, honey,' she said. Turning back to Megan she said, 'Go on.'

'Well, we got to the Pizza Garden and we sat at a front window and waited and waited, and then it started to rain, really bad, hail and everything, so we thought maybe he wouldn't show. So we waited some more and he didn't, show I mean, so we decided to just go home,' Megan said.

'And who's driving my car all this time?' Vera demanded.

Both girls looked at each other, then in unison they turned to their grandmother. Both said, 'I did.'

Looking at Luna, Vera said, 'Is this what they call bonding?'

Luna shrugged. To Megan, she said, 'Keep going.'

Elizabeth listened to her sister tell her side of events, of having been thrown to the ground, scraping her palms and her knees, of running into the Pizza Garden for a phone, but not knowing who to call. Of coming back out to the parking lot, of just standing on the curb, crying, not knowing what to do, when Graham showed up in the low-rider.

All eyes turned to Graham. Graham took a deep breath, turned to one of his sisters and said, 'Megan, I stole thirty-two dollars out of your piggy bank.'

'You what?' Megan yelled.

Sheepishly he turned to Luna. 'Figured I might as well get all the confessions out of the way.'

'Thirty-two dollars isn't a felony,' Luna said. 'But would you like to press misdemeanor charges against him, Megan?'

Megan threw herself back in her chair, arms across her chest. 'No,' she finally, grudgingly said.

Graham leaned over and kissed the top of her head. Megan swatted at him. 'Oh, gross!' she said.

Graham laughed, then sobered. 'OK, here's the deal,' he said to Luna and then began to recite his portion of the evening.

Austin, Texas
E.J., Sunday
My cellphone was as dead as I felt, so I left it on the charger in my room as I blundered my way down to my nine a.m. panel, entitled, 'Keeping the Heroine Fresh', which translated to mean what, I had no idea. I had no idea when I was signed up for the panel, and even less of an idea that morning, after the night and early morning I'd just endured. By the time I left the convention room where the panel was being held, I still had no idea what it was supposed to be about as the discussion had quickly segued into a discussion of various sexual positions and what the actual line was between romance and pornography. The panel was half and half on the last question, my half squarely on the side of the supreme court.

By Sunday noon my phone was charged but I wasn't. The convention was over. A few stragglers remained, but our group more or less had the bar to ourselves. Our numbers were down a great deal, what with Jane dead, Hal in jail and Candace gone in search of an attorney for her father. I had a call into her though. Detective Washington had found out a few things Candace ought to know. Namely that Harold Burleson wasn't her birth father. The name on the original birth certificate was

John Lawson from Daytona Beach, Florida. It would be up to Candace, I thought, whether she decided she wanted to find another father. After the one she had for so long, the idea of any kind of father might be repugnant to her. She wasn't being charged with anything, although in reality she could have kept DeWitt Perry from being killed and me from being almost killed had she spoken up as soon as she suspected her father had killed Jane. And there was the problem of having attacked Lisbet Carson. I'd talked to Lisbet earlier that morning by phone in her hospital room, told her why Candace had hit her and put her in the trunk of her roommate's car, and promised her an exclusive if she didn't press charges. I told her the *Austin American Statesman* would probably buy the story from her. I don't think the thought of pressing charges ever entered her head after that.

Candace swore she didn't *know* what her father had done with either Jane or DeWitt Perry, she only suspected. And if it hadn't been for Candace, Lisbet Carson might have had a similar fate, not to mention yours truly. After Hal closed the door behind us in the boiler room, Candace had found the service elevator and made her way to Jerome and Willis's room, waking them and telling them what was going on. So, in essence, Candace had saved not only Lisbet Carson's life, but mine as well.

Listening to me for once, Detective Washington was also going to look into the death of Candace's mother, Wanda Macy Burleson. Some things that Hal said made me wonder how the poor woman had died.

We were quiet this Sunday afternoon, all lost in our own thoughts, when who should appear but the apparition in brown, namely the Beast herself, Angela Barber.

'I need to talk to all of you,' she said without preamble. 'Except you,' she said, looking directly at my husband. 'You may leave.'

Willis laughed.

'No, he's not leaving,' I said. 'Anything you have to say to any of us you can say to my husband as well.'

Angela snorted. It wasn't a pretty sight. 'Whatever!' she said. 'Just listen, all of you. I don't want one word about Hal Burleson leaking out! I will *not* have this convention's reputation sullied by that man! No offense, Jerome, but I've always said men don't belong in the romance genre, and I think I've been proven right.'

'Offense taken,' Jerome said.

Angela ignored him. 'As far as the media is concerned, I've told the reporters that Hal was unbalanced and had a *personal* problem with Jane. And that's how the story will remain! Do we understand each other?'

'I'm so sorry, Angela, but the *Star* called me this morning and I didn't know; I told them the truth,' Mary said.

'The *National Inquirer* called me,' I said, which wasn't true, but I could make a phone call later that evening. I shrugged. 'The truth,' I said.

'Did anyone else talk to *People*?' Lydia asked. 'I didn't mean to tell them *everything*, but that reporter was so sneaky!'

'I only talk to legitimate papers,' Jerome said. 'The *Post*, Washington, of course, not New York. Oh, and *The Times*, New York, not London, and my hometown paper called, the *L.A. Tribune*?' He shrugged. 'What was I supposed to say, my dear? I had no idea we were supposed to lie to the press!'

There was a full minute while Angela stared at us, each in turn. Then, without a word, she turned on her sensible brown shoes and left the bar. It started with a titter, a long smile, a knowing look. It ended with the simples, with every one of us laughing until tears were falling. It had been a very long weekend.

My phone rang and I picked it up, still laughing. 'Hello?' I said.

Elena Luna, my next-door neighbor, the one who's a detective with the Codderville Police Department, said, 'First, let me just say everybody's OK.'

I forgot to pack in my mad rush to the car.

Black Cat Ridge, Texas
Graham, Sunday

Graham woke up around noon, grateful that Grandma hadn't made them go to church. Usually that's what they did – the Methodist church in Black Cat Ridge when Mom and Dad were home; the Baptist church in Codderville when Grandma Vera was in charge. The Baptist church meant getting up an hour earlier because of the drive and the fact that they started fifteen minutes earlier than the Methodist church. But after the night before, they all got to sleep in.

Graham stretched, rubbed his face, and noted to himself that he was probably going to be grounded for the rest of his life. Then he thought about Lotta and next Saturday night. Maybe if he begged, did extra chores, paid back his sister the cash, and was incredibly charming for the rest of the week, he could get out Saturday night.

Not that much would ever happen with Lotta, he thought. Not with all those brothers and cousins and what have you. A guy could get killed trying to get to first base with a girl like that. If she didn't kill him, her kin would be lined up to do the deed. He grinned thinking about her.

Then he thought of the guy, the one who took Liz. The one who got away. He pushed it out of his head. More fun to think about Lotta.

Epilogue

I dug around in the attic until I found the old photo albums. The ones the kids had always looked at, the ones in the family room, showed baby pictures, single shots of all three children as they grew up, but no family shots until after the death of the Lesters, after Elizabeth had joined our family. I picked up the ones from the attic, ours and the Lesters, and took them downstairs.

Willis had the kids in the family room and the TV was blessedly off. They all sat on the couch, all four of them. I knelt in front of the coffee table and opened the first album, the one belonging to Terry Lester. Turning it for the kids to see, I said, 'This is Terry when she brought you home from the hospital, Elizabeth. Oh, and here's your dad holding Aldon, who's holding you. That's Monique next to him. She was twelve then. Aldon was six. Oh, and here's Aldon playing ball in the backyard with your dad.'

I picked up the old one of mine and opened it. 'Here's Terry holding you, Megan, when you were just a baby. See, there's Bessie – sorry, but you *were* Bessie then,' I said, tousling her hair. 'I'm holding you.' I looked at both girls. 'Terry and I were so happy we both had girls around the same time,' I said. 'We planned on raising you to be best friends.'

Megan put her arm around Elizabeth's shoulder and Liz leaned her head on Megan's shoulder. 'That's OK, Mom. We're better than best friends.'

'Yeah,' Elizabeth said. 'We're sisters.'

Graham made a retching sound. 'Gag me!' he said, and both girls jumped him, which I felt was the only appropriate thing to do.

Codderville, Texas

He stared at the computer that used to be his friend. No more emails. She'd even taken him off his number one spot on her Myspace. But he could still watch. Still see what she had to say and read her blogs, even get into her messages.

It wasn't really enough. He'd had her for a moment. She'd been his. She was so beautiful, his little sister. And he'd take care of her, just like he'd always planned. She'd come to understand and forgive him if he had to get rough. Sometimes life just called for a sturdy hand. He'd been too lenient with her, untaping her hands and feet, letting her think he was easy. Well, no more Mr Nice Guy. Next time she'd understand that big brother was boss! She'd get that message loud and clear.

He could have taken care of the others, right then and there. Those two kids. But there was that other one – the unknown quantity. Who was he? How did he fit in?

He'd have to come up with another plan, one that would take care of them all, the pretend brother and sister, the pretend parents. Leaving just Bessie. She was the survivor. She would always be the survivor. Just like him.

And they would survive together. He sat back in his chair. He needed a new plan.